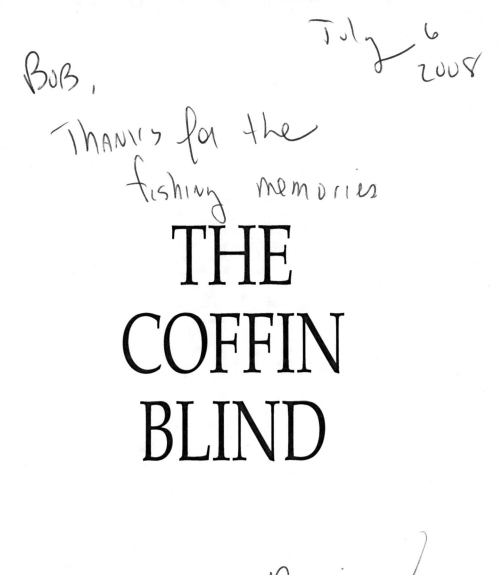

Bob,

Thanks for the fishing memories

July 6 2008

# THE
# COFFIN
# BLIND

*Mark Robbins*

Mark Robbins

www.pronghornpress.org

*To Kate for her encouragement,*
*support and creative ideas*
*and to Tom and Hillary*
*for sharing the outdoors with me.*

*If you have men who will exclude any of God's creatures from the shelter of compassion and pity, you will have men who will deal likewise with their fellow men.*

— St. Francis of Assisi
(1181-1226)

*Heaven is under our feet*
*as well as over our heads.*

— Henry David Thoreau

# 1

*This nightmare haunts me;*
*This nightmare defines me...*

I'm a teenager again, and first ice has lured me onto the lake. Unlike my face, the surface is smooth and unblemished. I chop a window into the silent world of fishes. Crystalline fragments tinkle on the surface. Rainbow fractures arc beneath my feet.

I punch through the plane that divides the gaseous world from the aqueous, and water gurgles into the void. I skim the hole, spread a tarp, and lay on my belly. My reflection, acne and all, stares back. Another glaring aberration: my right eye is icy blue, and my left, brown. And that's no dream.

Ice melts across my forehead as I peer into the "parlor of the fishes." I draw the tarp over my head and concentrate. Through speckles of plankton, the hammer-rigid form of a pickerel hovers over a weed bed, its flickering fins and pumping gills the only movement in this dormant realm. My minnow descends, struggling against the weight of the hook. The pickerel fins closer, poised to strike. Suddenly, the predator darts away. An otter, perhaps?

No.

The body of a boy slides into view, naked and waxen, with blue lips and genitalia. His eyes are closed, and his hair undulates in the sleepy current. Hollow cheeks remind me of an explorer entombed in a glacier. Bloodless lacerations mar his face.

The eyelids flicker, then open. Eyeballs roll back like white marbles. The ice child reaches upward, but the current sweeps him out of view, back into the gloom.

A shredded white altar boy vestment drifts past, scarlet cross embroidered on the stole glistening like droplets of blood.

Suddenly, he's there again, inches from my face, cataract eyes fixed in an unwavering stare. A stiff hand reaches up and caresses my face. Ice water dribbles beneath my collar. I want to flee, but the vision transfixes me. I study the face and colorize the image.

All at once, I recognize my brother.

His cold fingers encircle my neck. They creak and constrict. Suddenly, I'm choking. Shrill ringing pierces my ears. A shaft of utter cold radiates through my marrow.

His lips part and a raspy voice trickles out. *"Hear us, Brant."*

I pry myself from his death grip, throw off the tarp, and see black in the glaring sunlight. A distance away, I squint back. The hole splashes and seethes.

*Hear us!*

I block my ears, but his voice grows stronger.

*And if you won't save us*, he hisses, *do it for yourself.*

2

My biggest problem may be nightmares, but my second biggest's my mouth. You know that adage about a fish that keeps its mouth shut never gets caught? The same applies to humans. That's why at age thirty-five, I'm still a *Deputy* U.S. Federal Marshal. If I had a filter between my brain and my mouth, I'd be head marshal by now. If I had one between my anus and mouth, I'd be governor. Instead, I transport the dregs of society from jail to court, and from court back to jail in a futile effort to isolate them from the rest of our gentle world.

I have my faults, but also some virtues. I'm six-three and fairly built. My husky-blue eye may frighten children, but I've got 20/10 vision and could shoot the pecker off the chipmunk (assuming that chipmunks have peckers, a fact I haven't yet verified).

Chief Abu Garcia knows I'm a predator. That's why he sends me on assignments that would give rookies a major case of ass-pucker.

Anyway, one steamy August at three a.m., Wednesday morning as it were, I found myself on the grounds of the Norfolk County Jail, floodlights glaring and razor wire gleaming. I was about to transport a very big fish from this very little pond to a very nasty maximum-security tank in Florence, Colorado. The big fish (or carp, I should say), was mob boss Fiorello "the Piledriver" Pascucci. One week ago, he blew up a D.A.'s Lexus and decorated the John Hancock with the man's DNA.

I'm a brave guy, but some things scare the hell out of me. Getting blown up is one of them.

Prison Warden Victor Thorndike, decked out in shirt-and-tie, observed the transfer. Look up *hard-ass* in the dictionary, and Thorndike will stare back at you. Look up *lard-ass* and you'll find Pascucci.

Pascucci was a hairy-necked, confrontational fireplug of a guy, the type who'd flaunt his big gold snaggle tooth, yet would bash your teeth in if you stared too long. Armpit perspiration dampened his orange monkey suit as the guards prodded him ahead.

"What the focaccia?!" he stammered. "Where the hell are you dragging me?"

"To Logan," Thorndike replied, "courtesy of the taxpayer."

"A transfer wasn't part of the deal."

"Neither was torching the D.A."

One of the guards began to hum *Rocky Mountain High* by John Denver. It didn't sound half bad. Such talent. I nearly paged Paula Abdul.

Pascucci's face knotted. "Florence?"

"You'll have plenty of time to cool off in that tank, Fiorello. Three lifetimes, in fact." The Warden turned to me. "Get this miserable rodent out of here, would you, Deputy?"

So I did. Pascucci shuffled toward the van, his shackles clinking on the pavement. I prodded him into the back seat. Sweat beaded on his freckly scalp. The driver, a veteran Statie, edged onto the highway. We were headed to Logan Airport via the Callahan Tunnel, an archaic burrow hundreds of feet below Boston Harbor, then into the Tip O'Neill Tunnel, the so-called "Big Dig." In case you haven't heard, Boston Irish politicians and Turnpike authorities often have leaky tunnels named after them.

Anything underground makes me feel like a gerbil inside a Habitrail. Besides, Massachusetts tunnels tend to collapse on motorists.

The van reeked of body odor and Febreze. I began to get carsick, sweating like a pig beneath my Kevlar body armor. I kept one hand on my pepper spray and the other on my elephant-sized .357. I've used the gun before, but never the pepper spray. I'd rather subdue a prisoner with the butt of my pistol than asphyxiate myself on toxic gas. After all, this is Boston, not Baghdad. Please don't mention that to the Chief.

A cruiser led the way, and another trailed us down the lonesome highway; a stealthy transfer.

"What a travesty," Pascucci kept whining under his breath.

I kept my trap shut, but soon, old Fiorello began to squint at my ID.

"You're Brant Sherman?"

I nodded.

"The baseball player?"

Another nod.

"What the hell happened?"

I didn't answer.

"C'mon Sherman, give your fans a break."

"Fine. I tore my rotator cuff."

Pascucci smirked. "That's what they all say."

I almost strangled the bastard, but he was right. I *was* a good ball player. More than good. All State in high school, Rookie of the Year at Northeastern. I had the second highest batting average in the Cape Cod League, rare for a New Englander, a continent away from balmy NCAA Division One baseball factories.

Our own Red Sox had drafted me, and I wound up on the Portland AA squad. They promoted me to Pawtucket halfway through my second season where I hit like a maniac.

Behind the plate, I made even mediocre pitchers look good. If a runner leaned the wrong way, I'd gun him down. My throw-downs were like leading a duck. The only difference: five-and-a-quarter ounces of sweaty Rawlings instead of two ounces of chilled lead. You should have seen the look on the runners' faces when I picked them off. I'd pop-turn, fire, and reduce a triple to a humiliating ride on the pine.

The papers described my catching form as unorthodox because I'd dart after balls like a "crazed woodpecker." The locals ate it up. For a few months, a small but raucous fan club dubbed "The Peckerheads" — or "Pekka-heads," as they say in Dorchester — wore tee shirts with my picture on it, complete with my two-colored eyes. But that was fifteen years ago.

I *did* tear my rotator cuff, but it was only a partial tear. After that, I'd spiraled into a slump that wouldn't quit. There's a fine line between superstars and hasbeens, and I crossed that line. The team even hired the visionary hitting coach Walt Hriniak, of Yastzremski, Evans, and Boggs fame to snap me out of my slump. Nothing worked.

But I knew damned well what had caused the slide: too much thinking. Yogi Berra said players who think can't hit. I think I thought too much...

Pascucci interrupted my trance. "You know, Sherman, it's a sin to steal a man's freedom, and even worse to steal his dignity."

With great effort, I kept my yapper shut and kept staring out the window.

Ever notice how people with halitosis or drunks who smell like a brewery invade your private space? Pascucci leaned closer, and his breath almost made me puke.

"I'm still an influential man," he whispered. "It would serve you well to loosen my cuffs."

Strained silence.

"I've got carpal tunnel syndrome. Loosen the damned cuffs or I'll sue."

Imagining a flock of attorneys descending on a sea of injustice, I eased the shackles a couple notches. That's when Pascucci noticed my badge.

"Are you a sheriff?"

"No."

"What are you then?"

"A deputy marshal."

"*I shot the sheriff, but I did not shoot the deputy.* Ever hear the song?"

"*Hang 'em High,*" I replied. "Ever see the movie?"

It seemed inconceivable that the same country that gave us Michelangelo, DaVinci, and Rocky Balboa, produced the likes of Fiorello Pascucci...

Five miles later, he started jabbering again. "I'm a family man, Sherman, a townie, the salt of the earth. I even tip twenty-percent at Chinese restaurants."

I chuckled, and then regretted my mistake. If ducks ignored calls, they wouldn't get blown out of the sky. Federal marshals were no different.

"Please Deputy, I don't need cuffs. Let me depart with my dignity."

For an assassin, this guy was sure hung up on dignity.

"I can't uncuff you."

"A man can do *anything* he desires."

"Sorry."

Pascucci studied my face. "Damn," he said, "your eyes *are* weird. I ran over a Malamute with eyes like yours, Sherman; it used to crap on my lawn."

"I castrated a pug with a face like yours, Fiorello. It used to hump my leg."

I felt like decking him. *Never* rank on my eyes.

"You're a wiseass, Sherman," he continued, "but a smart one. Seems a shame, a big-leaguer risking his life for chump change. Glory days may have passed you by, but you ought to give me a call sometime."

Unlike the tactful and understated Don Corleone, this mob boss was brimming with braggadocio. Powerful men never boast. I began to question the true stature of Fiorello Pascucci.

Due to road construction and mandatory police checkpoints, our route to Logan Airport was indirect. The motorcade exited the Mass. Pike and spilled onto Storrow Drive where I caught a glimpse of Fenway Park, its famous flashing Citgo sign, and Boston University's Nickerson Field. To my left, the BU Boathouse, the stepladder profile of the Hyatt Regency, and MIT reflected on the glassy surface of the Charles River. In the distance, the spire of the old John Hancock glowed blue, indicative of clear, high-pressure weather. These landmarks often comforted me during lonely stake-outs on the streets of Boston.

As we passed the final checkpoint at the Massachusetts Eye and Ear Infirmary, Pascucci stopped talking. His silence made me edgy. Talkative prisoners were harmless; quiet prisoners were the ones to fear.

My ears began to ring the way they always did before something was about to go down. Suspension cables of the Zakim-Bunker Hill Bridge glowed electric blue in the still of night. We exited past the old Boston Garden and a brick building with a huge Celtic's shamrock painted on it, then headed into the "Big Dig."

Just before we descended into the tunnel, I caught a glimpse of the Italian North End where hare and salt cod used to hang in store windows. Lanterns illuminated cobblestone streets and peeling advertisements on brick buildings.

Pascucci also noticed what flashed by. "Heaven on earth," he lamented. "Best food, sweetest wine, loveliest women. *That's* where I belong."

I almost cracked a joke about how you can identify the bride at a North End wedding—she's the one with the braided armpits—just to tick him off. But I didn't because I admired the Italian North End, its people, and *ristorantes*. In fact, Pascucci was about the only *paesano* I didn't like.

Sadly, aristocratic Sicilian crime families have given way to so-called *gavones*, gang-bangers of every persuasion; far less thoughtful and artistic in their violent deeds. Horse heads enveloped in bloody bed sheets and offers you can't refuse have deteriorated into getting shot in the ass with low-velocity .45s. Not too creative, if you ask me.

I suppose transporting the last Italian crime boss out of Boston was an honor; but I was far too queasy to celebrate. The massive tunnel offered no comforting landmarks. Rows of fluorescent lights cast an eerie glow on monotonous tiled walls. As our motorcade progressed through the substratum of Boston Harbor, the ringing in my ears grew louder. Sweat began to bead on my forehead like the droplets of the Atlantic Ocean oozing through seams of the Big Dig.

Just as I spotted the proverbial "light at the end of the tunnel," two hefty pickups with tinted windows, halogen lights, and trailer hitches pulled into the lanes in front of us. Pascucci craned his neck. The trucks braked and fishtailed. Tires screeched. We skidded and slammed into one of the pickups. The other reversed into us. I whiplashed. The cruisers rear-ended our van and spun out. The impact sprung Pascucci's seat belt and threw him onto the floor where he wriggled on his back like an upended turtle. I whipped out my .357 and shoved him back down.

Both pickups screamed out of the tunnel, leaving the rest of us smoldering. All of a sudden, a Mack truck, bulldog figurehead gleaming, blasted toward us from the far end of the tunnel. Pascucci flashed a sinister grin.

Our driver's head rested on the steering wheel. High beams loomed as the mother of all trucks roared closer. I flung

Pascucci out the door and dove after him. The truck smashed into the van in a front-end explosion of glass and twisting metal. Sparking axles gouged the road. The truck backed off forty yards and idled. Officers in the cruisers were moaning.

I took cover behind the wreckage while Pascucci slithered along the guard rail. Two men in masks bounded out of the truck. One brandished an assault rifle with a banana clip and the other, a semi-automatic pistol.

The Piledriver shuffled into the middle of the road and began to wave his arms. "Get me out of here, boys!" The thug with the pistol ran toward him.

I focused my sights dead center on his chest and yelled, "Freeze!" just as the tunnel erupted in automatic gunfire.

The impact on the van threw me to the ground. I scuttled behind the wreckage, and bade my ass a fond farewell. The fusillade pounded the van in a deafening staccato, more palpable than audible. A minute later, skittering twangs trailed off. Now my ears *were* ringing.

Headlights from the mouth of the tunnel illuminated us through the fuming debris. Pascucci hobbled alongside his rescuer, nearly at the truck. I no sooner raised my revolver, when another barrage began to pummel the van. I took cover. Frantic radio voices crackled from within the cruisers.

So here I was, beneath the floor of Boston Harbor, fathoms below any bottom-feeder, with only a pistol for defense. The walls began to close in, the musty air and exhaust heavy in my lungs. I kept trembling like a bastard.

Shooting editor Clint Smith once said that a pistol is something you use to fight your way back to your gun. The thought wasn't reassuring. To the intellectual, I was *artillery-*

*challenged.* To the average meathead, I was *screwed.*

But there was no way I'd let myself die inside some stinking tunnel. Hemorrhaging to death a mile below sea level at the hands of these dirtbags would be humiliating. I could be crazy at times, but I had no death wish. None whatsoever. I liked my body. Do not fold, bend, spindle, or mutilate.

Wishing for standard-issue automatic instead of my six-shooter, I groped my carrier for spare ammo and cinched my Kevlar vest tighter. Shots continued to pelt the vehicles. I rested the .357 against my neck. Its cool metal suffused me with an icy-calm.

Sure enough, the shots paused. The machine gunner climbed into the cab to reload. Pascucci and his escort stepped from behind the wreckage. The escort flung his pistol up, but I was faster. At the muzzle blast, the gunman's hand erupted, and his pistol spun in a slow motion diver's arc, clattering on the pavement. He tore off his mask, revealing an unshaven face. The thug stared with mixed horror and wonder at the pulp and splinters of bone that had once been his hand. He knelt and began to whimper, rocking as he cradled the sad extremity like a baby.

The scene was touching, but I had no time to commiserate. The machine-gunner's fresh banana clip glinted through the cracked windshield. He rested the weapon on the dashboard, settled his head low on the stock, and took aim. Something about the flash of the barrel set me off.

My blue eye focused on a glimpse of flesh forty yards off. At the shot, the thug's right hand flew from the stock. I fired until the rest of the windshield exploded. The gunner rolled out of the passenger door and sprawled onto the pavement, blood streaming from his eyes. In spite of his hamburger face, he managed to whip out a pistol. An Uzi *and* a pistol? Talk about stacking the odds. It wouldn't have surprised me if the sumbitch had a SCUD missile up his bunghole. I aimed at his shoulder and disarticulated it with a single blast. He flopped back onto the road while Pascucci cowered. Like I said: I can shoot.

Searchlights flooded the tunnel, and sirens wailed closer through the undersea corridor. The truck driver screeched into reverse and I fired again. More glass shattered. The truck fishtailed backward into the wall. Radiator coolant bled green in the eerie fluorescence.

I speed-loaded six more rounds, this time Hi-Shock hollow-point magnums (when you care enough to send the very best), and slapped the action closed. My empties tinkled on the asphalt. The wreckage smoldered. I ran to the closest cruiser and flicked off the ignition. The trooper lay inside, his face chalky and contorted, and his legs splayed like a smashed puppet.

"My hips," he groaned, "they broke my freakin' hips."

"Help's on the way. I have to get Pascucci."

"You take out all four, Sherman?"

"Only three."

"There's one more. Watch it."

I nodded then bolted toward a markedly pissed-off Pascucci. His voice grated. "I could have made you somebody, Sherman."

I cuffed the Piledriver to a guard rail. So much for dignity.


Alarm beacons lit up the tunnel. Back at the van, I pried the driver's door open. The trooper was conscious now, short of breath, holding his ribs, forehead macerated by glass. Suddenly, his eyes widened. I whirled around just in time to see the fourth gunman pop from the wreckage—a jack-in-the box of the ugliest variety.

Flames burst from a shotgun muzzle. Whump! Gut-punched, I bellowed, caved around the impact, and rolled onto the ground. The shotgunner pumped another slug into his chamber. I barely made it onto my knees, but my retina and front sight had already locked on his chest. His trigger finger tightened, but I squeezed first and kept squeezing. Hollow-points busted through muscle, rib, and lung. The gunner flopped ass-over-teakettle onto the road, a six for artistic impression.

Then I collapsed, gasping, the wind knocked out of me. Something deep inside had burst. I groped beneath my body armor for guts, grateful that none had spilled out.

Broken mobsters writhed on the floor of the Big Dig, where even the crescendo of sirens couldn't drown out their wailing. That's all I recall before the stench of burnt rubber, gasoline, and gunpowder overwhelmed me.

# 3

I hate blood and gore, especially when it's my own. None too pleased, I found myself in Boston and Women's Trauma Unit on the gantry of a CT scanner, IVs pouring into my arms and oxygen desiccating my nostrils. My EKG trace galloped across a monitor. My left side felt like ground chuck, and I had a horrible earache. Pain reminded me that I was lucky to be alive.

Imagine my surprise as I backed out of the CT scanner and met eyes with a female doctor. In fact, they were pretty green eyes. She stood over me, and I stared back like a second grader who'd just peed his pants. When she introduced herself, I perked up because over the years, my personal connections had been limited to a dozen upper cuts, six roundhouse kicks, and half that number of meaningless dates.

"Abigail Reed," she said, "emergency doctor in charge."

"Brant Sherman," I said, "gunshot victim."

Her handshake was a no-nonsense one. Dr. Reed was the perky type of woman who didn't blow you away with her looks, but the more you stared, the more you realized she was cute. Very cute. Her jet-black ponytail contrasted with blue scrubs. She was athletic and intense, with a hard unpampered body. I noticed no wedding ring or tan line indicating she wore one.

I figured that checking out a woman within an hour of having been shot meant that at least one of my organ systems was intact. I smoothed my Johnny and gestured to the monitors.

"I'm not used to all this."

"You're not the only one," she replied. "I counted twenty news cameras outside the ER. What was it—some kind of a war?"

"Just a little August madness."

"Which eye did you shoot them with?"

"Huh?"

"You heard me."

"The blue one, if you must know."

"You're aware that only one in 2.4 million humans have your type of divergent iris pigmentation?"

"Painfully."

"I need to check your scan," she said, heading toward the monitors.

Dr. Reed was abrupt, but I swear she liked me.

In a control room, cross-sections of my torso reflected off the radiologist's glasses. He kept pointing to something, and

Dr. Reed nodded. I'd have fudged my shorts if I'd been wearing any. The automatic blood pressure cuff inflated, and nearly amputated my arm. I wanted out, and fast.

Dr. Reed returned. "The scan reveals a splenic laceration with a surrounding hematoma, a left lung contusion, and multiple broken ribs."

"Meaning?"

"That you're fortunate you didn't bleed to death, Deputy. The body armor saved you from penetrating bullet wounds, but you've sustained severe body bruises that require close monitoring."

"I have to get out of here."

"That's not my plan."

"I appreciate your concern Doc, but I can't stay."

"What's the problem?"

"I hate hospitals. And besides, Cosette's alone."

My answer flustered Dr. Reed. "Then we'll notify her that you've been admitted."

"She doesn't answer phones."

"Why not?"

"She's a Chesapeake Bay retriever."

"You'd compromise your health over a dog? I call that devotion, Deputy."

"Call it fear, Doctor. Her bladder's the size of a beach ball."

"Cosette, huh?"

"Right."

"So you're a *Les Miz* fan?"

I nodded.

"I suppose you'd have been one of those martyrs on

the barricade?"

"Only if I had my .357 to level the playing field."

She raised her eyebrows."I'd better page psychiatry."

"Don't bother, Dr. Reed. I'm too self-preserving to die for a cause."

"If your spleen ruptures, you will," she said, scanning my chart.

In this medical environment, I began to wonder what tangle of nerves, what body humor, what organ malfunction kept disconnecting my mouth from my brain.

Abigail Reed spoke up. "You live on Brattle Street. I live on Fayerweather. I jog the Charles and Fresh Pond every morning after my shift." She fidgeted for a moment. "I could walk your dog for you if you feel it's appropriate."

"Sounds more than appropriate to me," I replied, not particularly keen on bleeding to death. "Thanks."

"So who are you named after, Brant?"

"They named me after a goose."

"Excuse me?"

"A brant is an arctic sea goose," I continued. "My father was an outdoor writer and a game warden. I was born on Earth Day. He gave me a duck call for a pacifier. So when may I address you by your first name?"

"After you're discharged, Deputy, and I'm no longer affiliated with this place."

"When will that be?"

"Twenty-nine days, two hours and seventeen minutes. Not that I'm counting."

"Where are you headed?"

"Hawthorne Hospital in Concord. I'm the new ER director."

"I was born in that hospital."

"That's where I'm planning to be *reborn*," she said.

"I hope Cosette's no bother."

"None whatsoever; I love dogs."

"I appreciate it. My Dad's too ill to manage her."

"Any other family?"

"I once had a brother..." I said, my voice trailing off.

"I'm sorry."

All of a sudden, my chest began to flutter, and irregular blips flashed across the monitor. For the first time, I'd witnessed the true anatomy of a heart palpitation, incited by a good looking doctor, a bad memory, or a little of both.

Abigail Reed began to wheel my gurney down the long corridor. "PVCs. I need to get you onto telemetry."

At the ICU, Dr. Reed's beeper jangled, and she disappeared, just like that.


During the wee hours, investigators infiltrated the Unit and asked a million questions about my evening of gore and gunfire. My side began to throb, and my perforated eardrum ached. I finally booted the investigators out and tried to sleep.

Later, I heard the six a.m "eye opener" news broadcast above the beeping monitors. Just then, I noticed Head Marshal Abu Garcia at the nursing station. He flashed his gold star badge and entered. The Chief sported a blocky crew cut and a thick black mustache. Garcia was built like the proverbial brick shithouse.

"Great to see you in one piece," he said.

"Are you my second opinion, sir?"

"As a matter of fact, I am, Sherman: you're ugly, too."

I almost laughed.

"They tell me you'll survive."

"Thanks to the miracle of trauma plates and sit ups."

"That was quite a shooting clinic tonight. The first positive event ever to take place in that twenty billion dollar tunnel. The Governor's planning a commendation ceremony for you."

"I'd rather a tax break."

"It's amazing, Brant; not even a shotgun can stifle you."

"Thank you, Chief. By the way, what's happening with Pascucci's boys?"

"You blasted the hell out of them, that's what."

"They died?"

"Just the shotgunner. The others are minus a few parts, and the Piledriver's bought himself three months in solitary."

"That'll be rough on the knucklehead. He told me he's a people person."

"Guess who else you shot."

I shrugged.

"That guy in the truck with the machine gun, the one whose eyes are now full of windshield glass, is Eddie Rapala."

"Eddie 'The Rifleman' Rapala?"

Garcia nodded. "We've been after him for three years. He's earned himself a scholarship at the School for the Blind."

"I hate to inform you, Chief, but Perkins doesn't accept hit men."

I glanced at the TV just in time to see myself wheeled into the ER. The Chief turned up the volume. It seemed weird to hear my name on television, and even weirder to know that I'd just killed my first human being.

"Looks like you're in for a long fifteen minutes," Garcia said, settling into a chair. "So tell me, how'd you pull it off?"

"I dunno, Chief. I aimed at what I could see, and hit what I aimed at. Sort of like Bradshaw's Immaculate Reception."

"No doubt about it, you're an idiot savant when it comes to shooting."

"It hasn't done much for my social life."

The Chief sighed. "This night has been a wake up call for me, Brant. I'm done wasting you on transfers. Major Rocky Fallon of the state police phoned me last week. He's spearheading the Fenwick investigation."

"As in 'Dr. Charles Fenwick'?"

"Right. Fallon needs a point man, an inland version of a Navy Seal. He's chosen you."

"I'm out of commission."

"He's willing to wait."

"Offer him a blue-flamer."

"I can't risk it. Our orders come straight from the top."

"Why me?"

"You hold the record for collaring fugitives, twice the number of any other marshal. Besides, you grew up near the crime scenes. Are you familiar with the Colonial Inn?"

"Sure. That's where the Minutemen imbibe their 'Shots heard round the World.' "

"Let me tell you about the case that we've managed to keep out of the papers," the Chief continued. "A few weeks ago, Fish and Wildlife agents had a poacher named Cooney under surveillance for smuggling bear parts."

"Parts?"

"Gallbladders and penises. Asians use the gallbladders for liver disease."

"And the penises?"

"For aphrodisiacs."

"Like Viagra?"

"Right. Except a bear dies for every hard-on."

"For erections lasting more than four hours, Long Dong Wong should call his doctor or serious injury could result...."

"Cut it out, Brant. I'm serious. Just after closing time, a gunman forced Cooney to kneel in the parking lot behind the Inn to take Communion, but what he made him swallow was no wafer. Twenty minutes later, Cooney stumbled into the Barracks and barfed something onto the sergeant's desk."

"And you're going to tell me what it was?"

Garcia nodded. "A gallbladder, raw and green, specked with yellow, extracted from a diseased dog."

"That's a lovely story, Chief. It really chokes me up. With all due respect, why should I care?"

"Because the act was payback, just like what happened to Dr. Fenwick. A perp disguised as a phlebotomist injected Fenwick with AIDS and hepatitis-contaminated blood. The perp claimed it was retaliation for abuse of lab chimpanzees. We still don't know the blood source.

"An unidentified group that calls itself the Legion of Saint Francis has claimed responsibility. Researchers are afraid to work. The biotech and pharmaceutical industries are tanking. And there've been other threats. The State House is beginning to panic.

"We need a point man to track these maniacs. You've fished and hunted the Assabet Valley. You've inherited your

Dad's instinct. In short, Brant, the task force wants you."

"I'm no investigator."

"We'll team you up with Eldridge Weatherbee."

"The cold case guy?"

Garcia nodded. "The Bulldog's the best in the business, but arthritic and out of shape. He needs a pair of young legs to take his show afield."

The monitors kept beeping while my mind kept racing. My pulse pounded like the telltale heart because I wasn't thrilled about heading back to Concord. Besides, I avoid needle-carrying perps like the whack-job who injected Dr. Fenwick with contaminated blood. The more I thought about it, the more my side began to throb, and the more I felt like puking.

"So what do you say? Fenwick's case is national news."

"I dunno, sir. I've had more than my fill of doctors."

"Your salary would double," Garcia continued. "You'd escape this rat race and live closer to your dad. I have five days to produce a candidate, and I think I've found him. In the meantime, heal those ribs."

On the way out, the Chief whispered something to the head nurse who returned with a syringe. Instinctively, I guarded my keister, but instead, she injected something into my IV line.

"Deputy Sherman," she said, "you've got an order for morphine. Use it."

"I don't do drugs."

"Learn to," the nurse replied. "If you don't take deep breaths, your lung will collapse, and we'll have to acquaint you with the steel eel," she said, motioning to a three-foot long black scope on the wall. That's all it took. The morphine took the bite out of my side, and I fell asleep thinking about the Chief's offer.

*Through shrouds of slumber, I remember the event as if it were yesterday:*

I'm a teenager again. Timmy and I are kneeling along the unfrozen center Nashawtuc Lake, side-by-side shotguns poised to greet the ducks. I'm a seasoned hunter for a sixteen year old, yet for some reason, this afternoon I'm afraid. My ears begin to ring, softly at first, but steadily louder, more shrill, more acute. I think about calling the hunt, but danger was meant for waterfowl, not teenagers.

Northeast gales whisk ominous clouds past a setting sun, and squalls cast intermittent sheets of horizontal snow.

"These angel suits make awesome camouflage," I say to my brother. "Fold the collar to hide the crosses. Ducks are afraid of red."

"I hope the priests don't find out," Timmy replies in a preadolescent voice. His teeth chatter like mad. Timmy looks phantom-like in his white robe, snow swirling around him. Hollow pings of making ice resonate underfoot.

"How cold is it, Brant?"

"Below zero with the wind-chill. By morning, the whole lake will freeze."

"Bad news for the ducks."

"Don't worry, Tim, we'll spare them their misery."

Timmy runs his glove along the seams of his robe. "Stealing's a sin, right?"

"Not here, little brother," I answer. "This pond is our church, the ice is our pew, the wind is our pipe organ, and the sunset is our stained glass."

"Good, because I'm praying for a flock to land in our decoys."

"God's got more important stuff to worry about than

*shooting ducks," I explain.*

*"Then I'll pray to Hubert, Patron Saint of hunters."*

*"Never mind that, just pray your ass off for forgiveness once we're done killing."*

*Timmy aims at the bobbing decoys. "Which eye do you shoot with, Brant? The blue or the brown one?"*

*"The blue one."*

*"Dad says you're part wolf."*

*"Enough, Tim."*

*"Sorry."*

*Gusts keep the wooden decoys bobbing in the waning light. Anchored by weights resting on the edge of the ice, they swim parallel, jerked to attention by their tethers. We kneel, white hoods draped over our heads.*

*At first, the skies remain empty, and Tim begins to fidget. Fifteen minutes later, the sun dips lower, and apparitions materialize overhead. Wings whistle, shearing the frigid air. Flocks converge, and then descend.*

*"Look at 'em all!" Timmy whispers.*

*"Mallards and blacks. Big fat ones. Fresh from Hudson Bay."*

*I blow a hen mallard quack, my red raw hand cupped over the bell of the call like a mute. Questioning ducks scan back and forth, fixing their attention on the decoys and gabbling back. Wing beats murmur. The circles tighten.*

*I wriggle closer to the opening in the ice. The dark abrasion on the smooth integument of the lake ripples. The white ice gives way to black and then to water, a forbidding edge, a precipice attractive to boys and waterfowl. The nearest flock veers downwind.*

*"Scoot closer!" I whisper. "You'll never get a shot back there."*

*Timmy keeps staring at the open water, his button nose*

*a stinging shade of red.*

"Don't worry, Tim, it's safe."

But Timmy won't budge. Fear of ice is nothing to be ashamed of. Even grown men avoid lakes in wintertime, especially lakes with springs that refuse to freeze. But I know better, and coax him forward.

Looming larger, migrant mallards and red-legged Canadian black duck whir in descent. Necks craning, the birds call to the rigid impostors. A band glitters on an orange leg.

The flock pivots straight into the wind, feathering the gale, parachuting toward the open water.

I finger my safety. The ducks loom larger. At the last moment, they brake, preparing to light, bodies tipping up, exposing pale underbellies. Orange legs dangling, the mallards hang suspended over the decoys. I try to focus on one of the multitude.

"Take 'em!"

We lean into our shotgun stocks, slap triggers, and absorb recoil. The gale sucks away each barking report. My drake collapses, crimson droplets spattering the ice. Timmy's bird spirals into the center of the lake. The survivors backpedal, shrinking into the night.

Timmy jumps to his feet, waving his Parker overhead. "I got the banded mallard!"

The cripple paddles toward the far end of the spring hole. Magnum number fives erupt the water in a lacy spray. But the mallard dives and keeps swimming.

I won't let the Lake steal our quarry. I trot onto the hard ice and lift the dead drake by its legs. I bury my hands into the downy breast feathers and contemplate the icy perimeter. The wounded duck's head lolls, and its wings begin to flail.

"Think you can slide over there, Tim?"

*Timmy keeps staring at the seething water.*

*"Why not get the retriever?"*

*"We're losing light. What do you say?"*

*His eyes never deviate from the rippling surface.*

*Fresh flocks circle the cold dark sky, desperate for the open water.*

*"You don't want to lose a banded bird, do you?"*

*Timmy shrugs.*

*I coax the shotgun from his tight fists. It takes my brother five minutes to wriggle prone along the perimeter of the opening. He slows at frozen slush at the far edge, thirty yards off.*

*All of a sudden, my ears begin to ring again. I swear that somebody is watching us. I scan the shoreline, but see no one. Yet the feeling persists. My skin prickles, and it's not from the cold. My heartbeat quickens as if I'm the quarry.*

*"Hey Timmy," I shout, "forget the duck. Slide back over here."*

*But Timmy slithers ahead with newfound confidence. He turns his head so that his cheek rests on the ice. "It's okay, Brant, I'm not scared anymore."*

*A pressure crack thunders underfoot. Tim flinches. My brother is distant in the weakening light and in the gathering snow. My ears ring louder. Yellow eyes keep peering at me from somewhere. Cruel yellow eyes, the eyes of a predator. My heart pounds. Again, I stare across the windswept ice into the empty pine grove. I know someone is watching. I'm the guide. We need to get out of here.*

*"Forget the duck, Timmy. Come back!"*

*Mesmerized by the rippling surface, my brother squirms onward.*

*"Get your ass back here!"*

*Still, he pays no attention. He's listening to the voice of the ice, the voice that beckons boys toward the black edge.*

By now, the cripple has fallen limp, its green head bowed beneath the surface in acceptance of nature's final benediction. Wings outstretched, the bird hovers at the interface of air and water. Wind sweeps the drake closer toward the edge.

Timmy digs his right hand into an ice cranny and reaches for the bird with his left.

All at once the mantle of ice buckles. Timmy, not daring to move, clings to the edge, panting. "Help me!"

"I'll save you, Tim!"

"Hurry Brant, I'm losing it!" he screeches.

By the time I reach the spring hole, the peal of fracturing ice trips me mid-stride, throwing me onto my belly. I hover at the edge, nearly slipping in. A pressure crack booms.

The ice sags, and syrupy water flows across its surface, immersing Timmy. Then the ice buckles, and suddenly collapses. A piercing, high-pitched scream, a gurgle, and then silence.

In my terror, I imagine agitated water, spicules of ice, and bubbles swirling about my brother. Decoy lines entangle his arms like puppet strings. Timmy presses his face toward the light, but meets a ceiling of ice. He beats his fists against the impenetrable barrier. A school of yellow perch fin about the flailing underwater visitor. Absolute cold absorbs his body heat. Efforts diminishing, Timmy spirals into the depths.

I scream until I lose my voice. I kneel on my own patch of sagging ice, woolen pants and robe sopping up water. As it slowly begins to sink, I barely make it back to solid footing.

The lake calms. Sleet hisses into its trembling center, and encrusts the dead bird.

I snap my sixteen closed and fire volleys. The wind sucks away each pathetic report. The shoreline remains vacant. Through the *whispering snow, I swear I can hear someone laughing.*

*Stunned, I curse the ice, wondering why it collapsed under such little weight. But already, the snow has begun to fill in niches and efface clues.*

*A gust gathers my white vestment like a loose sail, its frozen seams whipping against me. I stare into the water. Nashawtuc lake has begun to heal its wound, a new membrane of ice closing in.*

*My stinging fingers confirm grim reality: Timmy was my brother, a little brother who had trusted me, and I had just watched him drown.*

*I drop my Parker onto the ice, stretch my arms overhead, and stare into the leaden sky. An orange ember of sun glows through a chink in the clouds. The spark sputters and dies, extinguished by the cold.*

*I cry my way home through Walden Woods as the nor'easter moans in the turbulence of night.*

"Call a code!" my nurse kept shouting.

I sat up, but searing pain threw me back onto the mattress. My chest kept fluttering, and the little green light on my monitor was a Parkinsonian ping-pong ball. At least ten slack-jawed interns crowded around me.

"He's conscious now," one of them said. "We'd better get a 12-lead before she gets here."

*She*, for certain, meant Dr. Reed.

"Deputy Sherman," my nurse asked, "do you have chest pain?"

"No. I had a bad dream, that's all," I said, embarrassed by my growing audience.

"Must have been one hell of a dream."

Abigail Reed burst onto the scene. "What in God's name is happening?"

"Your patient had a cardiac arrest," the nurse replied.

Dr. Reed waved the interns away and scanned my EKG. "Multifocal PVCs," she said. "Give him a hundred of Lidocaine, start him at two milligrams-a-minute, and get me a stat portable."

"It was just a nightmare," I repeated.

"Sure it was."

"A disturbed mind is a terrible thing to waste."

"So is a cardiovascular system."

Abigail Reed stared at the monitor, and occasionally at me. She felt my forehead. Her touch was as soothing, hands smooth as first ice.

"I must say, Deputy, this has been one interesting shift. Aren't you glad you decided to stay?"

After another hundred yards of EKG paper, my heartbeat settled down and the fluttering disappeared.

"No more ectopy," Dr. Reed announced, pleased with herself. "I thank your myocardium for its cooperation."

"My what?"

"Your heart. It's all about control. Now that you're stable, I'm off the hook."

"Your shift's over?"

"Finally. In another hour, I'll be bonding with Cosette down by the dirty River Charles. She may even forget you."

"Not likely, Doc," I said as the portable X-ray machine rumbled into the Unit. "That canine's my own flesh and blood."

# 4

Four weeks after my famous gunshot blast to the gut, recuperating at home began to bore me. It was an Indian summer morning, with static electricity crackling in the air. I was itching to make something happen and decided to visit my father at a hospice in Concord, twenty miles west of Boston. I hadn't seen the old man in awhile, and I missed him. Interestingly, that hospice was affiliated with Hawthorne Hospital, Dr. Reed's future workplace.

I backed the Jeep out of my driveway and nodded to an undercover marshal guarding my house. Through judicious intake of powdered protein, push-ups and sit-ups, I'd done some healing over the past two weeks. Who says you can't make steak out of hamburger?

I lived in a triple decker, still adorned with Christmas lights, nine months after the holiday (or three months early). Rusty Porsches and BMWs perched on blocks festooned the front yard, their dissected engines fragments of my landlord Julio's dismantled dreams. Julio once asked if the wrecks bothered me. I told him they added character to the stodgy People's Republic of Cambridge. Now, the property boasts over two dozen foreign cars in various states of "restoration," the subject of several town meetings.

Harvard trustfund liberals are open-minded, as long you agree with them. Dare to disagree, and they'll squash you beneath their Birkenstocks like a wad of goat cheese.

My twenty-year-old Wrangler stalled and backfired at the first intersection. If you are what you drive, I was a flatulent, crippled old man. Before I got shot, I considered shipping the Jeep to Hollywood for a *Pimp My Ride* restoration. Even Xzibit and his gear-head entourage turned me down.

Three weeks of not driving made me forget the frustration of greater Boston as I negotiated the rotaries of Alewife Brook Parkway. In case you haven't had the privilege of driving the great Commonwealth of Massachusetts, a rotary is an abortion of highway engineering in which traffic from five different directions converges in a random, chaotic, death-defying pattern. Yielding to another driver is as unthinkable as a bumper sticker announcing you've got herpes.

The State motto of New Hampshire is "Live Free or Die."

The State motto of Massachusetts is "It's All About *ME*."

Today, citizens were living up to the true meaning of their creed. It took me a half-hour to dodge the blue-haired grannies whose heads barely made it above the dashboards, their left hand turns wider than eighteen-wheelers, and grease monkeys in their elite turbocharged Chevy Cobalts and Geo Prisms adorned with spoilers and spinners.

Call me opinionated, but duck species exhibit predictable behaviors, and so do people.

Cosette kept panting, slobbering in Pavlovian proportions, drool oozing down the Jeep windows. No word of a lie, I began to consider the next red-eye to Alaska.

Just as I was about to lose it, rusted railyards gave way to subtle changes. Swallows dimpled the surface of Spy Pond, a site from which Colonials monitored the advance of the Regulars from Boston. Red-winged blackbirds dangling on cattails, Canada geese feeding on the median strips, and a hawk riding the drafts overhead proved that Nature still hung tough in suburbia.

As my trusty Jeep rattled up Belmont Hill, hotshots in Escalades, Navigators, and other shiny off-road vehicles that would never visit the wilderness whipped past me. I thought about purchasing a grenade launcher.

Soon, city yielded to suburbia, and suburbia to farmland. A few cleansing breaths eased my road rage. I swung down a side road, tipped my hat at the Paul Revere capture site, and passed Wright's tavern where colonials gathered during the Revolution. Sheep grazed in a meadow. Monarch butterflies and swallowtails, intoxicated by the scent of goldenrod and loosestrife, lazed in the air currents. It's amazing what you notice when you take your time, and even more amazing how we haul ass through life without pausing at the reststops, roadside monuments, and other places where our freedom was won.

About a half mile before Crosby's Corner, some

premature ejaculator in a yellow Hummer nearly rear-ended me. As I turned to flip him the bird, I noticed a mother opossum by the side of the road, dead as a smelt, with babies peering from her pouch. I would have stopped, but there was no breakdown lane.

That critter put me in a worse mood than the bad drivers because it reminded me of my brother.

Timmy once scooped a drowned woodchuck from the swimming pool. We had just watched a show about a kid revived after being submerged in icy water for over an hour. Timmy placed the woodchuck's bloated carcass on the cement. You'll never believe what he did next. You know those electrodes that you used to stick into the ground to gather worms? In case you don't, you'd soak the lawn, jam in copper rods, crank up the juice, and jolt hundreds of the wrigglers to the surface. Poetry in motion.

Democrats eventually outlawed wormers because some barefooted dolt electrocuted himself while standing in a puddle. Key legislation for sure.

Anyway, Timmy, a Frankenstein fiend, shoved one electrode down the woodchuck's gullet and the other into its anus. He announced that he'd spark the cadaver to life. When he plugged the device in, the groundhog twitched. You should have seen Timmy's face light up: God infusing life into Adam.

But that groundhog never saw its shadow again. Far from it. The carcass sparked, smoked, and then hissed. I unplugged the contraption to prevent Timmy from electrocuting himself. Kids are always trying to commit suicide, whether they mean to or not.

At a young age, I learned that the world's no stage, it's a trap—a snare, a pitfall, a steely trap with spring jaws poised to snap your unsuspecting neck. We're not players on this stage, but *prey*, no different from any other animal.

Anyway, poor Timmy held that woodchuck for an awfully long time. Soon he perked up and said, "I gave this old boy a jump-start to heaven."

To me, it was nothing more than a sizzle and fizzle, but I kept my mouth shut. Like I said, Timmy was a gentle child who thought the world was a gentle place.

Timmy perpetually rescued wild animals. He let all of his fish go and routinely "missed" five-yard shots at rabbits.

In my opinion, my brother was too sensitive. Timmy was a great kid, even for a little brother. No way would I let the Connibear traps of this world nail him. While my parents were busy getting divorced, I taught him about the outdoors. Fishing and hunting could soothe any hurt.

It didn't take much to transform a good kid into an emotional wreck. That much I learned from the novels and poetry that Dad made me read. Sensitivity was the Achilles heel of man. Numb people were happy people. Sensitive folks wound up pining away in fire-and-rain depression, hurling themselves off the Bourne Bridge in a Plath-like plunge, or shooting themselves in the mountains of Idaho.

(That last one baffles me. How do you assassinate yourself surrounded by cutthroat trout, sharp-tail grouse, and bighorn sheep? I can't bear to think of it.)

In case you're wondering why a federal marshal like me writes so good, it's because my father used to write an outdoor column for the *Boston Beacon*. After I got cut from Pawtucket, my father urged me to become a sports biographer, to write "what I knew." But the nanosecond I got my edgy freshman short story

*Confessions of the Nutcracker* back with a *D–* scrawled across the top and all passive verbs lacerated in red, I knew I'd never write for a living.

Professors hated passive verbs, but I loved them. *To be or not to be.* Action is fine, but only when there really *is* action.

Once in a while, an asshole winks, dimples, puckers, or glistens. But for the most part, *being* an asshole is what an asshole *does*. No Strunk will ever change that, unless it's Dr. Strunk, Professor Emeritus and Chairman of Colorectal Surgery.

Besides, who wants to write about the pathetic life of some immigrant who dog-paddles the Rio Grande clutching a baseball mitt in this teeth and goes on to win the Cy Young award, and gets bought for a hundred million bucks by the Yankees while the rest of his family gets tortured by some Dick of a dictator? Or a superstar who gambles or drinks himself into oblivion? Or a hero who withers away from Lou Gehrig's disease in the prime of his career? The story never changes: a struggle, triumph, fame, and death. No way would I write for a living. No way, nohow.

I never told my father how much I detested writing. Good writers always ended up committing suicide or pining away in McLean's. In order to write you have to be sensitive, to *feel*. Being sensitive means driving yourself mental. The more you delve into the world, the more it scares you. You'd have to be crazy *not* to go crazy. To enjoy life, at least to pretend to, one must stay "comfortably numb" (Pink Floyd, *The Wall*, disc 2, song 6).

Trust me, I wouldn't even be telling you this damned story if it didn't have to be told.

5

For some reason, I couldn't wait to visit my father. Even though Dad was the sick one, we'd always end up discussing my own tales of woe. I hated to burden him with my problems, but after our talks, I'd feel great, as if he were some brownstone Brookline shrink. I suppose there's no better confidant than a great dad, no matter what his state of health.

Emerson Hospice overlooked the Sudbury River on a rise local tribes had named "Clamshell Bluff." These days, the only natives pocketing clams were the administrators. I parked the Jeep in a shady spot and unrolled the window for Cosette.

The hospice hinted of antiseptic. Frail residents smiled at me, their necks and shoulders drooping as blades of grass beneath the weight of raindrops.

Dad's room overlooked the Sudbury River. It was the least a son could do for an outdoorsman spending the end of his life in the great indoors.

I watched my father from outside the room. He was snoring. Unaware of my presence, an attendant cased the room, pretending to clean. Her nimble fingers probed suitcases, drawers, and every nook and cranny that might harbor a tight roll of bills. No truffle would escape this boar.

The attendant's hands slid along the sheets, paused beneath the mattress, and produced a wallet.

A hand darted out and grabbed her wrist. The wallet tumbled onto the bed. Dad bolted upright and said in a hoarse voice, "She stuck in her thumb and pulled out a plum, and said what a bad girl am I."

The attendant stared wide-eyed at her wrist, manacled within the game warden's grasp. My father released the woman and flipped her five dollars.

Puzzled, she snatched the bill and darted out the door, almost colliding with me.

"Hello there, Brant," said my father, without turning his head. He labored to his feet. "Talk about being caught red-handed."

"You're still as sharp as ever, Dad."

There wasn't much left of the man except for his protuberant, fluid-filled abdomen. Summer squash yellow stained the whites of his eyes. Windswept bays and wintry forests had furrowed his face over the years. They were peaceful lines — not worry lines — channels of a tidal marsh in harmony with ebb and flow, with ice and sun, with dusk and dawn.

Dad patted me on the back, and then settled back onto the mattress.

"How're your ribs?"

"Better, thanks."

"It was clever of you."

"What?"

"Leaving no Pascuccis to retaliate."

"Thanks."

"How's Cosette?"

"Great. One of my doctors babysat her."

"A doctor, huh?"

"Yes. Dr. Abigail Reed, an emergency physician."

"Is she pretty?"

"Yes, as a matter-of-fact."

"So a nice-looking doctor took interest in my boy?"

"That's right, Dad. She'll be moving out here by summer's end."

"For once, things sound promising," Eugene Sherman said. "And speaking of promising, I got a call from Rocky Fallon. I heard he offered you a position."

"You heard right."

"Did you accept?"

"No."

"I'd love to see you happy before I leave this planet."

"I *am* happy. Happy as hell."

"No Brant, you're depressed. You view the world through *morose* -colored glasses. No wonder you're still single."

I kept staring out the window.

"What did you do when you were a boy?"

"Fished and hunted."

"What do you do now?"

"I hunt."

"I call it 'pest control.' Stop punishing yourself. The outdoors has always been full of risk. Little acts of nature determine the fate of birds and the destiny of men, and there's not a damned thing you could have done to save your brother."

"Unfortunately, Dad, I hold a less fatalistic view."

"That's a tough way to go through life, Brant. But let me ask you something: How do you feel after the other night?"

"Sore."

"That's not what I mean."

"Okay, it felt great to nail those chumps."

Dad nodded. "The blue eye observes with flawless acuity, the brown one sees the grim side of life. Chief Garcia noticed your gift and tapped into it."

"A painter named Vincent saw a lot of things and wound up hacking his ear off."

"Did you *feel* the danger in that tunnel?"

"My ears kept ringing, if that's what you mean."

My father nodded. "Use your perception, Brant, but use it outdoors. Nobody can take my game warden days away from me, no matter how sick I am now."

"With all due respect, Dad, outdoor jobs no longer exist. The Assabet Valley is now a glorified suburb. Kids have names that sound like dogs, and dogs have names that sound like kids."

"Even so, there's still a little wild left out here, son. Besides, you never know whom you'll run into."

I raised my eyebrows and began to think about Nashawtuc Lake. My father was trying to tell me something that I didn't really want to know.

"Give Rocky Fallon and Eldridge Weatherbee a chance. At least you won't be wasting away in court surrounded by felons—or worse, lawyers."

"You never managed to turn me into a writer, Dad. What makes you think I'll change?"

He smiled. "Because there's still a trace of poetry somewhere inside you."

An attendant delivered lunch. Dad removed the cover from his plate, revealing breaded fish shaped like Vermont, overcooked string beans, and mashed potatoes. He downed a cup of yellow pudding with a single gulp.

"You took it like a brookie on an alder fly," I said. "Or I should say a pike on a frog."

I watched my father. It was only a matter of time.

"I'm fading fast," he said, pushing his food aside. "I may not be able to hunt beside you anymore, but I'll always be with you. When you're in our duck blind, I'll be the wind stinging your cheeks. I'll be the little breeze on your neck when you're bass fishing at night, each rivulet you wade, and every forest you stalk.

"As I get closer to the end, I can feel my own parents watching over me, as I'll be watching over you. That's how it is with fathers and sons."

Aging hunters were known to ramble, but this time, I had the feeling I'd better listen.

"I heard that Bobblehead Bayliss willed his ashes stuffed into his son's decoys so that he could revisit the marsh each autumn," my father continued. "My request is less complicated."

"Shoot, Dad."

"Cremate me in my duck hunting gear, waders and all,

and I'll be looking down, smiling."

"You've got it."

In time, the game warden grew weary and I helped him get settled.

I began to stare out the window. Mist hung over the river's lazy bend, its surface a garland of water lilies. A muskrat left a wake along the far bank.

A bass burst through the languid surface. The violence of the strike and magnitude of the splash startled me. It had been awhile since I'd been fishing. Perhaps, too long. Concentric circles faded. That largemouth had sought its prey, and in a split second, committed.

If an old fish could seize an opportunity, I figured I should, too.

6

After two weeks of briefing, studying maps, computer programs, and videos with the State Police Criminal Investigation Unit, I moved into my new headquarters at Poplar Brook Wildlife Management Area. The log cabin's expansive storm windows overlooked the Sudbury River. Farther downstream, the Sudbury merged with the Assabet to form the Concord River, the site where the "shot heard round the world" gave birth to the American Revolution.

Swallows dimpled the river's calm surface. Despite the serenity, danger permeated the air. The marshy aroma re-awakened memories of duck hunting, the sport that screwed me up in the first place. At first, I considered driving away from it all, back to the city. But somewhere in the darkness, a vampire was lurking, and I held the stake meant for its cold heart.

The log cabin I'd moved into began to relax me. Clad in boxer shorts and a tee shirt, I tucked my .357 into a drawer, stretched out in bed and listened to the chirping crickets. The smooth river reflected the orange glow of a rising full moon, looming large and attainable over the cattails. Other than animal sounds, it was quiet. I marveled at the absence of cars, sirens, and human voices.

Curtains fluttered in a faint breeze. The air smelled clean and piney. The cabin had been a sportsman's club built in the 1940s. Faded deer heads flanking a fieldstone fireplace stared down at me. I imagined myself curled up with a woman on a braided rug in front of a crackling fire, insulated from a raging blizzard. Perhaps that girlfriend would be Abigail Reed. Perhaps not.

I hung faded family hunting and fishing photos, including a teenage version of myself straining under the weight of a five-pound smallmouth bass. The memorabilia complemented the muted watercolor of the cabin. For now, I was the Pope of Fisherman's Cathedral.

The summer sun had nearly set, and I sat down for a breather. Exhausted from chasing chipmunks and red squirrels, Cosette lay balled up on the floor.

"Quite the resort, huh girl?"

The dog canted her blocky noggin and furrowed her forehead. Just then, I heard the crunch of approaching tires.

I squinted out the window into the bright headlights of a state police cruiser. A stocky man in street clothes plodded up the driveway. I knew just who it was. I jumped into a pair of sweats and prepared to greet the Bulldog.

"Brant Sherman?" the visitor asked.

"That's me."

"Eldridge Weatherbee," he said, setting a cardboard box and his heavy briefcase down on the porch.

I shook his bear-paw hand. "Great to meet you, Lieutenant."

"Likewise. Nice job in Boston."

"Thanks. Excuse the mess."

Weatherbee peered inside. "Welcome back to Concord. I hate to barge in on you, but couldn't wait 'til morning."

I could tell that this big guy had a lot more stored inside of him than adipose. He was bubbling with information that he needed to share. He insisted that I call him by his first name.

Eldridge Weatherbee stood six feet tall with the rotund girth of a Soviet weightlifter, more solid than fat. His nose was pockmarked and his face ruddy. Pale blue eyes sparkled behind his glasses. Weatherbee's face was fixed in a perpetual smile. A thick gold wedding band, worn-smooth with time, indented his ring finger.

He inspected my mounted fish, outdoor photos and prints on the wall. "This place suits you, Deputy." He paused at my framed eighth grade composition over the fireplace and chuckled.

"*The Mating Habits of Spring Peepers?*"

I nodded. "Won me a scholarship to Conservation Camp."

"And I'm sure many admirers."

I motioned to a pair of chairs on the front porch. Moths danced around the lights to the background melody of crickets and frogs. We fished soft drinks from a cooler and settled into rocking chairs. Weatherbee leaned dangerously back in his with a torque that defied physics.

His root beer can hissed open. The lieutenant slurped the fizz and shook drops from his hand. "I took the liberty of having your commendation ceremony postponed. It's bad enough having your face plastered all over newspapers."

"I appreciate that."

Weatherbee reached into his coat pocket and produced two Skybars. "When I don't eat, my blood sugar plummets," he said.

I couldn't restrain a smile.

"Doctors advised me against junk food, but it's a nervous habit. Besides," he continued, "once I'm in the middle of an investigation, it can be awhile between meals." The lieutenant's girth more than compensated for such hard times.

Weatherbee unwrapped both candy bars and snapped them in the middle. He inspected them, and handed me two halves. "I'm a generous guy, Brant. What I have is yours, except the white-filled portion of my Skybars. I'm a connoisseur of everything from caviar to cannoli, but nothing compares to the gooey white stuff inside. Absolutely nothing," he said licking his lips. He popped the candy into his mouth and closed his eyes.

"*Salud*," he said.

I nodded, struggling with the less than ambrosial caramel half.

Officer Weatherbee swallowed and then spoke. "I'm sorry about your father. Good guys get sick, and assholes get healthier by the minute."

A fellow cynic. I was already beginning to like this guy.

Weatherbee patted Cosette and took a swig of root beer. "I have a bad feeling about this case, Brant."

My ears perked. Katydids buzzed and bullfrogs croaked in the distance. A night creature emitted a painful howl.

"We're dealing with major-league psychopaths," Weatherbee said. He snapped open his briefcase and motioned me closer. "These files are the histories of unsolved crime investigations, murders mostly." He motioned to photographs, some color, some black and white, with longhand scribbled along the margins. Weatherbee's demeanor suddenly became somber. I stopped chewing.

Little boys at birthday parties, a youngster in a Little League uniform, a high school student in her prom dress, a bride feeding her groom wedding cake, and a girl hugging her cocker spaniel stared from the pages.

Weatherbee began to tremble and his stare became glassy. "These victims are my family. Who speaks for them? Who pays for their funerals? Who covers the mortgage when a heartsick father is too depressed to work? Nobody, that's who. This is where I step in. I'll take a twenty year old cold case that nobody else gives a rat's ass about and trail the killer to the end."

"I can relate to that," I said.

"That's why we selected you. Anyway, I don't give a damn if these St. Francis perps are animal rights wackos or religious fanatics. I don't care if they're skinheads, pro-lifers, or ecoterrorists. I'm going to nail their sorry asses if it's the last thing I do. And it very well may be.

"These days, I'm full of arthritis, and I don't sleep. I believe I've got one more good case left in me. This one's worth my last effort.

"Like your hybrid eyes, you'll fit a hybrid role on the team: federal marshal, state police investigator, and game warden. Tomorrow, I'd like you to interrogate Dr. Charles Fenwick—a tough nut to crack. And in the afternoon, drop by Artemis Furs." Weatherbee hook-shot his candy bar wrapper around the rim and into the garbage can. "The business heiress, Paige Sagoff, is a certified knock-out."

I recognized the name.

The lieutenant continued. "She's the golden layer of the social upper crust, a sportswoman who shoots wild game and models Orvis attire."

"Interesting," I said, feeling adulterous thinking of someone other than Abigail Reed.

"Miss Sagoff can write volumes on how to roast a wild turkey and stuff it with truffles. Perhaps she knows something about animal rights activism in town."

"I'll be glad to ask."

The lieutenant nudged me. "This case is going to be one hell of a ride. Let's regroup tomorrow night at the Hapgood Diner."

I escorted Eldridge Weatherbee to the steps.

"Thanks for the Skybar, Lieutenant. I had no idea how fascinating eating candy could be."

"I can work twenty-four seven if I'm not hungry. The worst death for me would be starving. How about you?"

"I never really thought about it."

"Fire and *ice*, I guess," the lieutenant said.

I bristled at the word, and my ears began to ring.

"You okay?"

I snapped back to reality. "I'm fine."

"I hope so. Don't lose sleep over what we've discussed. Not yet, anyway. See you at the diner at six. Tell the hostess you're with me. She's named a booth in my honor."

The lieutenant pushed the cardboard box toward me.

"This is footage from the security monitors at Massachusetts Medical Center. They've been reviewed four hours either side of the attack but you may be able to turn up something in a broader window. Enjoy the show. Enhance anything pertinent. Then pay the good doctor a visit. He's expecting you tomorrow."

Weatherbee labored down the walkway to his cruiser and slid his overstuffed briefcase onto the passenger seat. He revved up the vehicle and waved. The forest swallowed up the cruiser's red tail lights as the lieutenant drove off.


I kept thinking about bubbles floating up beneath the ice and a desperate face pressed against its impervious undersurface. Heavy, dark water closing in. After awhile, an ice-calm, sleepy sensation overcame me.

Just then, the phone jolted me from my trance. I grabbed it on the first ring. Instant palpitations: Abigail Reed.

"How are you feeling?" she asked.

"I'm fine," I replied. "It's great to hear from you. In fact, this is the first phone call I've received in Concord."

"What have you been up to?"

"Moving into this log cabin."

"I hope you haven't tried any lumberjack stunts."

"Don't worry," I said. "My spleen and ribs are healing."

"How's the pup?"

"Fit and trim. For that accomplishment, Dr. Reed, I'd like to take you to dinner."

"Great," she said without hesitation, "I'll be in your neck of the woods this week."

"Where will you be living?"

"In a carriage house on Punkatassett Farm," she said. "I need a dose of tranquility."

"You picked the right time to move," I said. "The City of Cambridge now requires obedience certification to walk a dog."

"For the pet or the human?"

"Both, I guess."

"Who will enforce it?"

"Retired KGB."

"Well, there are no such rules where I'm headed," Abigail said. "My window overlooks a moonlit pasture."

"Speaking of the moon, have a look out the window."

"It looks like an apricot on steroids," she replied.

From Cambridge and from Concord, we stared at the moon for awhile before signing off. After that, I set up my DVD player and settled in for what proved to be one hell of a disturbing show.

# 7

Dr. Charles Fenwick, an associate professor of surgery at the tender age of thirty-eight, had discovered a potential cure for AIDS through controversial primate research. He and his staff had infected twelve chimpanzees with an aggressive form of an HIV retrovirus, an experiment that angered animal rights groups. Dr. Fenwick's clinical trial of the anti-viral drug Reverse Transcriptocide had been so successful in treating the disease, that *The New England Annals of Medicine* published his case report without revision. Overnight, research dollars poured in, and afflicted celebrities readied their checkbooks for the long-awaited chance of a cure.

That summer, headline news had featured Dr. Charles Fenwick in all his glory. That fame proved costly, as I was about to witness.

In this new age of bioterrorism, the Feds monitor all university and VA hospitals. I fast-forwarded through uneventful hours of the Massachusetts Medical Center parking lot footage that the lieutenant was kind enough to bestow upon me. Cosette was even more flatulent than usual, and as I got up to let her out for the fifteenth time, something caught my eye.

A BMW rocketed into Fenwick's reserved parking space on the second floor. It was six a.m. according to the time signature on the tape and there were only two other cars — which had been there all night — within the camera's view. I watched as Fenwick closed his sunroof and grabbed his briefcase. In my experience, nothing good ever happens in parking garages. The footage that followed confirmed it.

Professor Charles Fenwick wore a a suit and what looked like a Canali or some other high-end tie. I never bought fancy clothing, but *Queer Eye for the Straight Guy* had taught me enough to know that Dr. Fenwick did. He strode through the empty garage toward the stairwell and out of camera range.

I ejected the tape, checked my list and selected another from he stairwell camera that would likely catch Fenwick. I fast forwarded until the time signature matched the previous tape and he appeared again.

When he reached the stairwell, a thin woman ascended the stairs toward him. Long light-colored hair bounced with each step, hair so wild that it obscured her face. He paused, and so did I. The woman wore a dark halter top and a tight, high-riding skirt, her hips flaring beneath the straining fabric. The State Police hadn't run this footage yet, but it was a lot more interesting than what I'd seen so far.

From above, Fenwick stared. As the woman turned at the top of the staircase, I froze the image. Not a pretty sight. This heroin queen, obviously a prostitute, sported garish mascara. Bracelets dangled from pencil-thin wrists. Talk about livin' on reds, vitamin C, and cocaine...

A guy's libido hits rock-bottom before work, and I couldn't understand why a prostitute would hustle at such an early hour unless someone put her up to it.

They spoke for a moment. Fenwick looked nervous. As he began to flee, she darted in front of him. It didn't take an MD degree to tell that she had some sort of chronic illness, and I couldn't blame the surgeon for trying to escape.

I wondered why the Staties and Feds hadn't discovered this little exchange.

The hooker grabbed Fenwick's lapels and hung on tight. Fenwick shook himself free and flung her to the ground. Her knees were skinned and she kept holding her thigh, writhing, making no attempt to conceal her panties.

I could tell the doctor wanted to bail, but he glanced at the camera, knowing he was being monitored.

Tears had black-eyed Lola's mascara. The glassy eyes of a lifeless doll peered into Fenwick's soul.

Using his sport coat to cover his hands, the surgeon lifted the creature at arm's length. Tottering on high heels, she grabbed his shirtsleeve to regain her balance. He picked up his briefcase, stuffed the jacket in the trash can by the door, bolted down the stairs, and out of camera range. The woman hobbled back toward the parking lot and disappeared.

Fascinated, to say the least, I proceeded to a now famous Law Enforcement CD.

Dr. Fenwick observed his chimpanzees through a Plexiglas window in the primate enclosure. According to the news, he had implanted pumps directly into the chests of the sick apes in order to bombard the virus with a constant infusion of his Reverse Transcriptocide.

Inside the lab, the chimps bounced in their cages and clanged water dishes. All twelve of these apes had been infected, and all twelve were destined to be sacrificed. Their eyes sparkled, and mouths puckered like those of benign old men.

I wasn't keen on viewing the next sequence entitled *Doggie Lab*. For educational purposes, the surgical faculty recorded all trauma labs. This one taught me more than I wanted to know.

The medical students arrived in blue scrubs. All were anxious. Before them, twenty dogs were laid out supine, extremities bound, supple abdomens vulnerable to the razor-sharp scalpels held over them in tremulous hands. In life, these dogs would have never exposed their soft underbellies. In pre-death, they were powerless to resist. Their tongues flopped outside their mouths. Plastic breathing tubes connected to ventilator hoses which fogged and cleared with each rise and fall of the chest.

Dr. Fenwick burst into the room wearing Massachusetts General Hospital scrubs. He stared each medical student in the eye as he lectured. Most looked away. A few stared back.

He turned toward a harlequin dog, snapped on a pair of sterile gloves, and picked up his scalpel.

Over the next two hours, students made incisions and sutured them. They placed lines into vessels and tubes into chest cavities. Surgical residents practiced transecting bowel and sewing it back together. Tied knots. Cut suture. Too long. Too short. Professor Fenwick rapped their knuckles with a hemostat each time they faltered.

Gradually, the doctors-in-training dismantled the dogs. I'll spare you the rest.

At the end of the lab, garbage bags waited outside. The dogs had been reduced into smaller components of their complex whole. For that day, the adventure was over.

I must tell you, I hate sicko films about girls in European hostels being tortured and other such sadism. Movie directors should get the same treatment. Unfortunately, it was my job to watch this footage, which proved even more disturbing because these events really happened.

I entitled the next scene *Seeing Red*, another security camera segment of Professor Fenwick alone in his animal laboratory with his attacker:

I had learned that high-risk animal researchers like Fenwick underwent blood draws monthly in order to maintain staff privileges.

The laboratory tech was a big fellow wearing a surgical mask. Sparse reddish-brown beard and sideburns clashed with his hair, a bad brown toupee with an obvious gap between the hairpiece and scalp. What could be lurking beneath the toupee that could look any worse? The man seemed to avoid eye contact, and given his tacky appearance, I can't say I blamed him.

He swung a chair alongside Fenwick's desk and slipped on a pair of purple gloves.

Resigned to yet another employee health check, the doctor rolled up his sleeve and rested his arm on the desk.

The phlebotomist screwed a needle onto a syringe, cinched a tourniquet around Fenwick's arm, and cleansed the skin. Fenwick looked away, which I found strange for an invasive surgeon. In the background, a supine chimp suspended a bottle upside-down with its feet.

The phlebotomist snapped at a vein with his finger. Fenwick winced as the needle penetrated his skin. After rooting around, the tech loosened the tourniquet, withdrew the needle, and slapped on a piece of gauze.

The doctor glared at the tech. In time, Fenwick composed himself and straightened his arm on the desk.

The tech cinched the tourniquet and again took aim with a shorter needle, what I learned was called a "butterfly." Again, Fenwick looked away.

Blood began to flow into the syringe. Just then, with amazing sleight of hand, the tech switched it for another syringe—big, fat, and already full of blood. He shoved the plunger down, and injected the blood into the hapless doctor. The whole process took only a few seconds. I had to replay the sequence in slow motion five times in order to fully absorb the event, no pun intended.

The surgeon tried to pull away, but the stranger forced his arm against the desk. The surgeon thrashed, sending the tray with its vials and needles clattering to the ground, and glass shards skittering across the floor. The tech bolted to the door. Fenwick ripped the needle out. Blood oozed down his arm as he staggered to his feet.

The tech hesitated at the doorway. I couldn't lip read because of the surgical mask, but his words knocked the wind out of Fenwick. I figured that was when perp had told Fenwick that the blood was infected. The realization brought the good doctor to his knees.

Once the perp fled the lab, the surgeon triggered an alarm, staggered into the scrub room, and lanced his arm with a scalpel. He groped an emergency box on the wall and tore off its cover. Capsules spilled onto the floor. Fenwick scooped a handful into his mouth, downing the pills in a single gulp. He hugged himself, shuddering and staggering. Blood saturated his scrubs and smeared the sink and tiles.

In the background, the apes cocked their heads and stared. The alarm jolted even the sickest primates from their stupor. Excitement spread from cage to cage. Chimps and monkeys began to jump.

Charles Fenwick collapsed just as security slip-slided across the sticky puddles that had spilled from his body.

Wow.

I kept wondering why a man who had the world of medicine by the balls, a gorgeous wife, and two wholesome kids got stalked and mesmerized by a hooker, then injected with infected blood. And for what reason? Bad love gone worse? Professional jealousy? Vindictive med students? Angry lab monkeys? Call me crazy, but I figured it was more than bad biorhythms. According to my briefing, the good doctor wasn't too forthcoming with the Feds, and given the embarrassing interlude with the hooker, I can't say I blamed him. I sat on my sofa, numb for a while.

I didn't sleep much that night. Every time I began to doze off, I kept picturing the dog lab and those chimps rattling around in their cages. Why anyone would choose medicine as a career was beyond me. I kept trying to forget what I'd witnessed, but everything seems uglier at night. I told you it ain't good to be sensitive.

Early the next morning, at Massachusetts University Medical School, I waited for the elevator that would take me to the sub basement animal labs. A poster on the wall said: *First, Do No Harm: Boycott Animal Lab* beneath a photograph of a boy hugging a greyhound. Nearby, another poster depicting a student releasing a dog from its crate was titled *Go, Greyhound! And Leave Surviving to Us*. Interesting.

As I exited the elevator, an armed guard motioned me down a dim basement corridor. Hoarse barking erupted from within the laboratory kennels along the way.

"This is the old hospital," the guard said. "Visitors are few and far between down here."

Farther down the hall, the polished black marble floors became urine yellow linoleum, and the walls faded tile. Not exactly the Ritz.

As I turned toward the lab entrance, the guard gestured to a red sign posted over the doorway that said *Danger – Virulent Organisms*. I stopped in my tracks.

"Dr. Fenwick should be right out," he said.

The guard's footsteps trailed off. I gazed down the hall. My stomach began to churn and my hair began to prickle. Danger had visited this place. Remnants of terror hung in the air like whirlwinds of a dying hurricane.

I tiptoed to an enclosure marked "Primates" and stared in through a window. What I saw astonished me. Laid out on metal slabs were six shrouded corpses, each no more than three feet tall. At first glance, the cadavers resembled dwarfs, but upon closer inspection, I realized that they were chimpanzees. Wrinkly simian feet protruded from beneath the sheets, each great toe bearing a red tag. Limp arms hung toward the floor. The hands were cupped, furrowed palms upturned. The extremities looked alive and supple. I half-expected the little bodies to sit up, to tear off their sheets, to flex, to romp and to play. But the white shrouds remained as still as tents in a windless desert.

A woman cloaked in a white antimicrobial suit and helmet hunched over a corpse. She was sobbing. An African-American gentleman kept trying to console her, patting her back with oversized mitts.

Footsteps startled me. It was Dr. Fenwick. Unlike the charismatic bundle of energy I'd seen on videotape, the surgeon was now gaunt and sallow in his scrubs. Crow's feet radiated from the corners of his eyes.

I introduced myself. The doctor snapped his surgical gloves into a barrel and extended his hand. "Charles Fenwick. Glad you could make it."

For some reason, I hesitated.

"Relax, Deputy, you can't contract AIDS from a handshake."

I apologized profusely, then asked. "What's going on in there?"

"This is a dark day for us," Fenwick explained. "This is the first time we've sacrificed chimps." The surgeon looked away. "But I had no choice. None at all."

"Who are those two?" I asked.

"The young lady is my research assistant, Margaret Clouser, a veterinarian. Those chimps were like children to her."

"And the gentleman?"

"That's Hampton Seabrook, the chief anesthetist and manager of the animal laboratories. Margaret and Hampton are the most selfless human beings on this earth, which is more than I can say for myself." Fenwick noticed my pistol. "Or you, for that matter. You shoot people for a living, right?"

"Only when necessary."

"An artist expresses himself with a brush, I express myself with a scalpel, and you with a gun. In the scheme of things, it's all the same, I suppose." Fenwick sighed. "I've got the easy role around here. Hampton and Margaret are the ones who had to put the chimps down."

"It's strange to see the bodies laid out like that, so still and small," I whispered as if I'd wake up the dead monkeys.

"Bodies are all that they are now, I'm afraid. My treatment didn't cure them, it merely prolonged their life."

"I'm sorry."

"Not as sorry as I am."

I perceived Fenwick's meaning and looked away.

"It's okay, Sherman, at this point, I'm beyond self-pity." For awhile we peered into the lab. "Yet, there is a ray of hope," Fenwick continued. "See that cage on the end?"

Inside, an emaciated chimp hugged himself in the corner, the same chimp that I'd seen drinking its bottle on the monitor footage.

"That's Cheetah," Fenwick said, "sole survivor, the toughest of his peers. I'm trying like hell to save him: twenty cc's of Transciptocide Cocktail, three times a day through an implanted pump."

That poor monk was in one hell of a funk—a funky monkey, so to speak. "I'm sure he'll pull through," I lied.

"Like they say, hope springs eternal."

Dr. Fenwick was sweating.

"I'm beat," he said. "Mind if we continue this conversation in my office?"

The elevator swept us to the top floor, the eighth. An oriental rug, mahogany furniture, a leather sofa, a pair of Imari vases, and several impressive oil paintings decorated Fenwick's office. Soft classical music emanated from hidden speakers.

Outside, the bright sun shone over the reservoir. Geese paddled along the water's edge. A red-tailed hawk spiraled in an updraft created by wind banking off the Research Center.

"Quite a view."

Fenwick nodded. "I see that you gravitate toward the outdoors, Deputy. I've spent most of my life cooped up in hospitals."

"That's why you're famous."

"Don't kid yourself. If you crack this case, you'll be more prominent than any researcher."

"You've got an impressive place to think, Doc."

"Funny, I've just begun to appreciate it myself. I've been spending a lot of time peering from high windows. Anyway, have a seat."

Degrees and awards wallpapered the room, including a Harvard Medical School diploma, a Massachusetts medical license, a certificate from the National Board of Medical Examiners, and a Chief Resident award from Massachusetts General Hospital.

I glanced at a black and white photograph of Charles Fenwick and his medical school class on the steps of Harvard Medical School. Fenwick was the only clean cut member of his class during the age of skanky sideburns and Afros. A more recent picture featured Dr. Fenwick atop an alpine ski slope with his pretty blonde wife and blonder children.

Fenwick reached beneath the collar of his scrubs, manipulating a lump under his skin. That bulge, I'd learned, was an infusion pump connected to a catheter that ran into a vein beneath his collarbone. He slumped into his leather office chair and spun toward me. "So you're here to talk?"

"That's right."

"Your form of iris pigmentation is exceedingly rare."

"And you doctors won't let me forget it."

"Interesting. Did your schoolmates ridicule you?"

"Enough. I'm the one asking the questions."

"Touchy, touchy." Fenwick crossed his ankles and rested his heels on a mouse pad. "Do your thing, Deputy. Nobody else has bothered to follow up with me. I suppose there are more pressing tales of gore and mayhem in the headlines these days."

"Okay Doc. The Feds have already scoured this place and come up empty-handed. But I reviewed some footage from the security monitors."

"What footage?"

"Parking garage surveillance. With you on it."

He straightened. "So? What did you find?"

"Who was the woman, Dr. Fenwick?"

He grimaced. "You saw *that*?"

"Blow by blow, so to speak. So who was she?"

"You tell me. You're the investigator."

"Prostitutes don't frequent medical centers, especially at six a.m. Was she sent to stalk you? You nearly took the bait. Basically Doc, sometimes the little head tells the big head what to do."

"Excuse me?"

I glanced at the picture of Fenwick's wife. "Everybody checks women out, even married guys. It's no crime. I suspect you were attracted to her, that is, until you saw how nasty she was up close."

"Very good, Sherman, you're the top of your class. I'll tell you what happened if you agree to keep it confidential. A misunderstanding could damage what little semblance of a family life I have left."

I nodded. "Your secrets are safe with me, Doc."

"She said her name was Lola. She came on to me. I had no idea why."

"But now you do?"

Fenwick stared at the floor. "She was the blood donor."

"Someone paid her to accost you in the parking garage so you'd see how ill she was, which made the impact of the infusion of her blood all the more shocking."

"No argument there. She was hideous. Lipstick smudged her yellow teeth. Her nails were purple talons. She had sunken black eyes, like those of a corpse, and concentration-camp-translucent skin. She had thrush on her tongue and herpes sores on her mouth. That hideous beast lives in my nightmares."

"What did the phlebotomist say to you?"

"He said, 'That's Lola's serum coursing through your blue-blooded all American veins.' It was like getting kicked in the abdomen."

"Where's Lola now?"

Fenwick shrugged.

"Don't worry, I'll find her."

"Any other questions, Deputy?"

"Plenty. For starters, why were you having blood drawn?"

"Blood work is required for those of us who work with infected primates. Right after the dog lab, Occupational Medicine reported that I was overdue and would lose OR privileges if I didn't comply. I agreed to have the blood drawn that day."

"In your own research area?"

"It sounded better than waiting in Employee Health."

"Next question: Is it normal for the phlebotomist to be wearing a mask?"

"He claimed that he was recovering from strep throat. His explanation seemed reasonable."

"Can you recall what he said?"

"All too well. I asked the tech why he re-injected my blood. He said it wasn't my blood. When I asked whose it was, he said, 'Lola. L-O-L-A, Lola. Lo, lo, lo, lo, Lola. Just like the song.' I've always detested the Kinks. He began to sing in a lunatic falsetto, screeching with the chimps, mocking me."

"Anything else?"

"He said that the chimps deserved a good hoot. I can't get the noise out of my head, that raucous cacophony, ear-splitting like acid rock. He kept warbling all the way down the corridor."

Dr. Fenwick settled back in his seat. "He was bizarre, but educated. I doubt phlebotomy was his true occupation, but he knew about Elastoplast dressings and butterfly syringes. The man was large, more doughy than muscular. At first, he acted meek, but became abusive within seconds. He said, 'We wanted to watch you suffer.' "

"*I* or *we*?"

"He definitely said 'we,' as if he were part of a group. And he spoke in rhymes and alliteration, like a schizophrenic."

"We've checked the psychiatric hospitals."

"Check them again, but don't get your hopes up. Even if you catch this freak, he'll probably get off on an insanity defense."

"What can you tell me about his appearance?"

"The red hair and sideburns were bad fakes. His skin was pockmarked—a chubby guy with nodular acne. Also, he was wearing Nitrile gloves, so consider suspects with a history of a latex allergy or dermatitis."

I scribbled in my notebook.

Just then, Dr. Fenwick began to shiver. "Excuse me," he said, "I've been getting these fevers..."

In time, Fenwick shook off the chill, and I handed him a bottle of vitamin water from his refrigerator. He took a swig, and steadied himself. "Sorry about that," he said. "How about me asking a few questions?"

"Shoot."

"You work out, don't you?"

"Yes."

"How often?"

"A lot."

"Why?"

"To keep in shape for my job."

"Give me a break, Sherman. Most of America's finest don't look anything like you. What do you do?"

"Soloflex. Fifteen minutes, twice a week."

Fenwick tried to suppress a smile. "Really now, Deputy, what makes you torture yourself when a little voice inside your head tells you that it's too cold to run outside?"

"Okay, I want to look good."

"Now that's closer to the truth. Pushing your body makes you feel immortal. Exercise empowers you. Your body can defeat any disease when you're in shape. No bullet can bring you down. Nothing makes a guy feel more powerful than a workout. Nothing. Not money, not sex, not authority. At least it was that way for me."

Fenwick coughed into a handkerchief and continued. "Well, I'm not so sure that I subscribe to that theory any more. In just eight months, I've lost every ounce of muscle I've gained since high school. The process has accelerated because I've also contracted an aggressive form of hepatitis C. Some things you just can't power through."

He motioned to the photograph of his wife. "Candace was the best and the brightest, a Boston Chapter Junior League President. I met her at a Radcliffe social. In order to win her, I had to fight off at least a dozen other guys. We got married within a year."

Dr. Fenwick took a swig of water. "I was the only resident at Mass. General not divorced when I graduated. Candace and I grew closer under the pressure. The only disadvantage of every other night on-call, we'd joke, was that you missed half the great cases. The old codgers invited us to all of their faculty parties, probably to stare at Candace.

"But those days are over," Fenwick said, his voice cracking. "I've little doubt she'll remarry."

He regained his composure and raised his bottle in a mock toast. "To life," he said. "I hate to rant and rave, but whenever I notice somebody as fit as I used to be just a few months ago, it makes me jealous. Pretty selfish, don't you think?"

"Not at all, Doc."

"You seem like a good guy, Sherman. A little cocky, but okay for a cop. I don't suppose that you came to hear a soliloquy about my health, did you?"

"Not really."

"Then why *did* you come?"

"Investigators always revisit the first victim."

"I am *not* a victim. If I could get hold of the bastard who did this to me..."

"But you can't. That's why I'm here. You're a surgeon and I'm a hunter. Leave the hunting to me."

"The task force has already scoured this place. What do you have to offer?"

"Motivation. I've had my own share of tragedy. Let's talk again soon. No guarantees. Maybe something will surface, maybe it won't."

"Fair enough, Deputy, fair enough. By the way, what took them so long to send you?"

"To be honest, I don't know. I usually hunt fugitives."

Fenwick rolled his eyes. "That's reassuring."


For the next half hour, we reviewed a layout of the laboratory and details about the assault. Without warning, Dr. Fenwick broke into another sweat. He hugged himself in an afghan. He closed his eyes. The rigors dissipated as quickly as they'd appeared.

"I'm not sure how much time I have left," Fenwick said. "If you're planning to catch my attacker, you'd better hurry."

"I will."

"And one more thing..."

"What?"

"Kill the son of a bitch. It may defy the Hippocratic Oath, but I want him to die."

For awhile, we sipped our vitamin water in the green glow of a banker's lamp.

Fenwick cleared his throat. "One night, I had a weird thought: I began to wonder if this life has been some sort of test, a Board Examination that I'm failing. Have you ever had an epiphany like that?"

"Not really."

"You're a hunter. Don't you ever feel guilty about killing?"

"I don't apologize for it."

"Yet you are ambivalent?"

"Once in awhile."

"Well, lately, I've become ambivalent, too. What if everything that I've taught was wrong? What about the thousands of dogs I've dismantled over the years and the apes I've sacrificed?"

"You've taught doctors how to operate and nearly cured AIDS. Helping people was your goal."

"I was helping *myself*. Strange that my own suffering's made me realize it... Anyway, catching 'Nature Boy' will secure your place on a Wheaties box."

"When you're feeling better, Dr. Fenwick, why not head to my Department for a complementary workout?"

"That's a lofty goal, but doubtful for me."

Dr. Fenwick strode to the window and motioned to a silver Mercedes with its flashers on. "My limo has arrived."

"Limo?"

"Actually, it's my wife. I have optic neuritis and can't drive anymore." Fenwick said. "Candace and I listen to a different baroque masterpiece every week when she takes me to brunch. This week, it's *Bach's Brandenburg Concerto No. 4 in G major.* Care to join us?"

"Thanks, but I'm stuck somewhere between *Guster* and the *J. Geil's Band.*"

"In any case, the only benefit of this tragedy is that I've been spending time with my wife," Dr. Fenwick said, easing into his coat. "Here's a bit of advice, Brant, something I've learned the hard way: Having one woman who cares about you is what really matters. Never forget it."

"I won't, Doc."

Charles Fenwick III, MD, flicked off his office light and closed the door.

I headed back to the animal lab.


I'm no detective, but I spent an hour at the crime scene, pretending that I was the perp, envisioning how I'd get access. Suddenly, I heard whispering from a dark corridor of the sub basement where the anesthesia tech, Hampton Seabrook, sat cross-legged on the floor cradling a trembling greyhound. Saliva dripped from the greyhound's flaring tongue. Mr. Seabrook whispered into the dog's ear in a mellow voice bearing a trace of a southern accent.

"Don't worry, Molly," he murmured, "it'll be all right."

The dog was a tawny female with dainty paws. Greyhounds were sight hounds whose ancestors had been raised by the Pharaohs to chase down gazelle in the Egyptian deserts. But in this modern world, "win, place, or show" were all that mattered, and Molly's racing days were over. Hampton Seabrook rubbed her muzzle, and she managed a feeble wag.

When I tiptoed closer, Mr. Seabrook heard my footsteps above the whooshing ventilators in the lab next-door.

I introduced myself.

"Sorry to be sprawled out on the floor like this, Deputy."

"No problem," I replied.

"I figure what goes around, comes around. What we do to animals, we do to ourselves. I'd adopt this old girl if I could, but I'm already the proud owner of the Killarney Wonder and the Tipperary Tempest." He smiled. "My wife would shut me off if I bring home another one."

"Does it bother you, dissecting so many dogs, Mr. Seabrook?"

"Sure it does. Life doesn't make sense to me, and never did since my tour of Vietnam. We raise these dogs to run their hearts out for our pleasure. When they're too sore to continue, we dismantle them. Not exactly a fitting retirement for professional athletes. But one thing I do know: Dr. Fenwick and I have trained over a hundred surgeons, and that's a worthy mission."

"I noticed signs by the elevator protesting the labs."

Mr. Seabrook nodded. "Same story every year. Med students these days can be bold. Dr. Fenwick announced that any student who boycotts this lab will get a degree over his dead body."

I raised my eyebrows.

"Believe me, none of these students hated him enough to kill him."

"What makes you so sure?"

"Experience. These kids have been too preoccupied securing residencies to plot a crime like that."

"Do any flunkies fit the profile?"

"In this program, there *are* no flunkies. All are top college graduates."

"What can you tell me about Lola?"

Hampton Seabrook stopped patting the dog. "You know about her?"

I nodded. "You don't have to cover for Dr. Fenwick."

"I won't kick a man when he's down."

"Don't worry, Mr. Seabrook, this is between us."

"You sure?"

"Yes."

"Okay then. She's been admitted to Mass State with neurologic complications of AIDS."

I thanked Hampton Seabrook and left him with the greyhound nestled in his arms.


I drove to the Metropolitan State Hospital in a summer swelter and negotiated the steep driveway to the crest of a hill. The sad old hospital at the top was a heap of pockmarked brick and rusty fire escapes. My Jeep matched its style.

I made my way past a lineup of patients in wheelchairs parked in the shade of an oak tree. One amputee smoked a cigarette through a tracheostomy while others rocked back and forth in an autistic ritual.

The humid air inside the hospital hinted of urine. I asked a ward clerk for Lola's room, which was located at the end of a long corridor. Isolation precaution signs were plastered across the doorway. I noticed no medical chart.

Inside, a custodian was mopping the floor with bleach. Lola's bed had been stripped, and there was nothing else in the room except a knotted green trash bag. I asked about Lola, and the custodian pointed out the window. At first, I figured Lola was enjoying the day, but I didn't see her on the grounds. The custodian kept pointing. Then, I noticed the cluster of distant gravestones.

A nondescript dirt mound and a tiny granite headstone marked Lola's freshly-filled plot, soon to be effaced by crabgrass and ragweed. Like the other outcasts in this desolate graveyard, all traces of the woman would disappear, her only legacy, a wasting disease passed on to Harvard's Golden Boy.

I kept picturing a sweaty chaplain mumbling generic prayers with no mourners in attendance, and scruffy workers lowering a casket into a muddy hole surrounded by lime-green Astroturf. I imagined clods of clay thumping against a coffin nearly empty, save for an emaciated body sucked dry by diseases that Dr. Charles Fenwick shared.

The sight depressed the hell out of me, and I couldn't get out of there fast enough. As I blasted down the highway, my phone rang, and it was Fenwick. "Did you find Lola?" he asked.

"I found her all right."

"What did she have to say?"

"Not much."

"What do you mean?"

"She's dead."

"Are you sure?"

"Pretty sure, Doc, they buried her."

"I didn't expect her to expire so quickly."

I fumbled for something to say. "Don't worry, Dr. Fenwick, I'll catch the perp."

"Sounds like you'd better hurry."


On the way home, something drew me to the Buddy Dog No-kill Animal Shelter. I suppose I needed to see a few live dogs with hopeful futures. As a boy, I'd visit the pound each week, hoping I'd luck into a lost field trial Brittany, English pointer, or setter.

Perhaps one of the volunteers at the Buddy Dog Shelter, a bastion of animal rights, had a lead. My tires rumbled across an unpaved driveway. This non-profit agency had no money to waste on asphalt. A statue of a German shepherd protecting a kitten stood outside. I flashed my ID at the receptionist and asked for the manager.

The manager of the shelter, Diana Loomis, was a famed animal rights activist, quick-witted and sharp-of-tongue. Diana's defense of ducks had been so moving that for fleeting moments, I considered trading in my fowling piece for an eight iron. Diana Loomis wrote articles on protecting animals; my father wrote articles on catching and eating them. One thing for certain: Diana Loomis was *the* guru of animal rights.

The pound was overcrowded. Dogs danced in endless nose-after-tail circles within their kennels. Mongrels stood on hind legs, poking their wet noses though the chain link fence. Tongues licked my hand with desperate affection.

I retreated to an adjoining building which housed stray cats. An imposing tomcat stared out from one of the cages. The bushy creature, more raccoon-like than feline, hissed and arched its back. I flicked a wood shaving outside the cage. The tom snatched the shaving from between the bars and gnawed it into saliva-soaked sawdust.

Just then, the door swung open and a pair of Wellies squished closer, revealing Diana Loomis, older than I remembered, but still attractive for her age.

"I see that you've met Big Papi," she said.

"You mean the Green Monster?"

"He's available for adoption."

"Big Papi's too much cat for me, ma'am."

"So what brings you back to town, Brant?"

"I'm assisting on a state police investigation."

"Something related to the news, no doubt."

I nodded, encouraged that we were still on a first name basis.

Diana Loomis was a slim, classy, middle-aged woman who'd once had the hots for my dad. Silver highlights in her long black hair complemented her smooth complexion. A sterling animal charm bracelet jingled on her wrist.

"I'd love to catch up," she said, "but I'm off to a fundraiser."

"This won't take long, Diana. I'm looking for a lead in the Fenwick case. You've heard about it, right?"

"Hasn't everyone?" she answered. "Given my background, I'm a likely suspect, but I have no connection to that crime. You're not the first investigator to ask."

"You *are* on the board of every animal rights group in the country."

"And proud of it."

"Have you noticed anybody acting over-zealous lately?"

That question ruffled her. " 'Over-zealous'? As long as

animals are abused, we'll never cease to cry out."

"I'm not talking about crying out, I'm talking about lashing out."

"Look, if I had my choice, I'd neuter all trappers, but the fact is we're nonviolent."

"Are you sure you haven't noticed anything?"

"Nothing to speak of. I must say, after watching you pat those dogs a few minutes ago, I'm amazed that you still support the slaughter of wildlife."

"Hunting's not slaughter."

"It's murder, plain and simple."

"There's a lot more to waterfowling than death, Diana: decoys, blinds, retrievers..."

"I'm afraid the poor ducks don't share such a romantic view of your tradition. They're just trying to survive. No matter how quaint the backdrop, hunting's nothing more than killing. Sportsmen are the fanatics, not us."

"So what's the bottom line? Is it right that Dr. Fenwick should die? He was trying to alleviate suffering."

"Only human suffering."

"So you condone the assaults?"

"Of course not. With all these hungry mouths to feed I can't afford controversy."

"I'm not here to debate, Diana. What worries me is that there are maniacs stalking people right now. You should be as frightened as anybody else."

"The events *have* been rather extreme," she said. "I come on strong, but you need to understand my side of the story. In any case, I'll keep my eyes open."

"I'd be obliged."

"Perhaps one of these days you can redirect your Sherman charm and love of nature. Animals might benefit from your talent."

On my way out, I paused at the cage of the massive tomcat who yawned and stretched. I ventured my fingers between the bars. The cat leaned into me, and I scratched his back.

"He likes you," Diana said, unlocking the cage. "You're in elite company." She extracted Big Papi. "This big fella deserves a home," she said. "And you, my friend, have a way with animals." She offered me the feline.

I balked.

"If you can survive a mob hit, Deputy, you can handle this kitty."

I gathered the beast in my arms. As heavy as a dumbbell, he settled in and purred.

"Once you get past the hissing, he's just a big lug. Why not adopt him? Nobody else will."

"I don't know, Diana. I've already got a Chesapeake Bay retriever."

"Think about it. This could be the start of a great friendship."

"Big Papi wouldn't be the first over-sized pet in the Sherman family," I replied.

# 8

I changed into khaki pants and a fitted white Polo shirt, and then headed to Artemis Furs in Concord Center that hot afternoon. The tinkling of a bell on the door heralded my entrance. I flipped my shirt tail over the holster and flashed my badge at the manager, a petite fellow in his fifties, a tad light in the loafers, sporting a wine-red ascot and a diamond-studded pinkie ring. He ushered me away from the customers browsing through racks of raccoon, fox, ermine, and mink.

"I'd like to speak with the owners, please. I'm with the state police."

The manager stroked his pencil-thin mustache and chewed his lower lip. "I'm Gibbs Wainright. I run the store, but I'm not the owner," he said, making no attempt to shake hands. "You're the chap from Boston, right?"

"That's right. I'm here on a special assignment."

"You deal with the Mafia, don't you?"

"Don't worry, you're in no trouble."

Wainright relaxed. "Mr. and Mrs. Sagoff are on holiday in Greece," he said. "Their daughter Paige is in charge. I'll give her a call."

Mr. Wainright picked up the phone and cupped his hand over the receiver. No doubt the Pascucci event had impressed him. Whoever was on the other line had plenty to say about it, too.

Wainright hung up. "Miss Sagoff will speak with you at the estate. Twelve twenty-four Monument Street. It's the farm on the left exactly one and a quarter miles from the flagpole in the Center. Follow the cobblestone driveway to the end, and then turn right onto the dirt road. You'll find her on the shooting range."

"The shooting range?"

"Miss Sagoff is an accomplished shot. I'll never understand the appeal of firing at fake rabbits and birds, but follow your ears."

Monument Street was a throwback to the Revolutionary War, where stock market money had restored stately federals and colonials. The Old North Bridge peeked at me through the trees as I drove past. I caught a glimpse of the Minuteman statue presiding over "the rude bridge that arched the flood" and the grave of the first British soldiers felled in the Revolution.

A rickety bridge forded the Concord River, where the water was sluggish and smothered in duckweed. Poison ivy insinuated through stone walls. Horses in the pastures shook their manes and flicked their tails. On a gentle hill loomed the Buttrick Manse where Minutemen gathered before confronting British soldiers April 19, 1775.

Concord's colorful history was its blessing, but also its curse. The town attracted an endless onslaught of tourists and tree-huggers. As my sad old Jeep rumbled toward the estate, a convoy of yellow-shirted Lance Armstrongs kept weaving in front of me. Unable to pass, I backfired the exhaust which boomed like flintlock, scaring them out of their Spandex. The bikers careened into a gully as I blew past.

Farther down Monument Street, horse pastures extended downhill toward the river. Dad and I used to hunt ruffed grouse on these properties when the only fences were crumbling stone walls and the cover, woodcock-friendly poplar. What little forest remained was now conservation land overgrown with mature hardwood.

I passed Punkatassett Hill and turned into the long driveway leading to 1224 Monument Street, its expansive grounds concealed from the road. Curious that once the wealthy apprehend their piece of paradise, they sequester it from the rest of the world.

I steered up a cobblestone road, passed a Georgian mansion with imposing columns and continued onto a dirt road punctuated by barns and carriage houses with newly-shingled cedar roofs. Foxhounds barked in distant kennels. Glossy thoroughbreds fed from overflowing troughs. Bumblebees still reveled in late season goldenrod and Queen Anne's lace. Swallows banked across the pastures and dipped over farm ponds where rising trout dimpled the surface. Muffled reports of a shotgun echoed through the forest. I unrolled the window and craned my neck.

A tall, slim woman in shooting apparel held an over-and-under shotgun in ready position. Long blonde hair was gathered in a ponytail beneath a long-billed cap. Riding pants and black leather boots showcased her figure.

She leaned into the stock and shouted, "Pull." Barrels gleamed in the sunlight. A pair of orange clay birds from opposite directions crossed, and in two shots, vaporized.

Wow.

Shooting sportswomen were rare in greater Boston. She and an instructor rotated to a new station. Noticing the Jeep, Paige Sagoff removed her shooting glasses.

I parked the vehicle and introduced myself. The blonde handed the shotgun to her instructor. Paige Sagoff's beauty was disarming. She wore little makeup. Her features were symmetric: straight white teeth, blue eyes, textured eyebrows. Her only visible flaw was a port wine stain behind her left ear.

"Welcome to Artemis Farm."

"Thank you, Miss Sagoff."

"Call me Paige," she said. We shook hands for longer-than-normal. "Glad you could join us. I always enjoy meeting celebrities."

I kept staring at the most incredible shotgun-toting thirty-year-old on earth.

Paige motioned to her instructor. "This is my shooting coach, Malcolm Pearson, 'Kip' for short. Kip used to guide safaris—he's got a record Cape buffalo to his credit. He's also on the British National Skeet Team, and he's been a godsend for my shooting."

"Your methods seem to be working," I said.

Pearson grinned, revealing tobacco-stained teeth. "That's kind of you," he said with a British accent, "although I can't accept much credit. Miss Paige is a natural."

"Thanks, Kip," she said. "I've heard that *you're* quite the shot, Deputy."

"That was self-defense."

"In your profession, you try to prevent things from happening," she said. "In mine, we create games to *make* things happen. Care to try a round?"

"No thank you."

"Kip and I would be honored."

"I have to ask you a few questions," I said. "Besides, I haven't shot clays in years."

"I insist, Deputy."

I watched Paige without really listening to what she was saying.

"The article said that you were a wing shooter before you became a marshal."

I nodded. "My father and I used to hunt upland birds across the road."

"When you shoot, do you see brown or blue?"

I cringed. "Mind if we change the subject?"

"Sorry, but you have incredible eyes."

"Yours aren't bad either, ma'am."

Paige smiled, stepped forward, and grabbed my arm. Gleaming as the goldenrod and tansies in the meadow, her highlights reflected sunlight.

"Come, Deputy, we've got a lot to talk about. Shoot this round, and I'll reveal all."

There was no refusing the offer. Paige released my arm and brushed past. She was tall, nearly six feet.

"Arm the Deputy, Kip."

Kip Pearson opened Paige's gun case, revealing a stunning array of vintage side-by-sides and over-and-unders — Parkers, Purdys, original Spanish Berettas — each with an engraved barrel and a toned stock. Pearson handed me a Perazzi.

"Try this rascal."

I ran my hands along the Circassian walnut stock and admired detailed engravings of grouse on the receiver. This over-and-under would cost my year's salary.

I snapped the action closed, mounted the gun, led a purple martin, and to my surprise, painlessly swung through.

Paige smiled. "It's refreshing to meet somebody who appreciates firearms. This town is overpopulated by wine connoisseurs, but shooters are a vanishing breed."

"I've reloaded these sporting clay loads myself," Pearson added. "And filled each round with the perfect dram equivalent of powder, the finest shot and buffer to match your choke. It took years of field research to get it right."

"Sounds like the sort of research that I'd enjoy."

Pearson noticed my revolver. "That's a Korth/Beeman?"

"Yes, it is."

"I once used a Korth to finish off a rhino. Anchored him right in his tracks. Would you like me to secure it for you?"

"Thanks anyway. It's an appendage."

"Very well, then. Allow me to explain the first station. It's a confidence-builder; two straight away shots. I call it 'The Rising Pheasants.' Take your positions. And no cheating, Paige. Promise?"

Paige rolled her eyes. "Yes Kip, I promise."

He winked and tossed me a pair of shooting glasses.

"Paige has a way of frightening gentlemen, especially when she's carrying a gun."

"Give me a break, Kippy, I've got more respect for Brant than that." Paige clasped my arm and led me toward the firing line.

"Let's see a pair," she said.

Two birds sailed away seconds apart, one high and the other low. I imprinted their trajectories in my visual memory and stepped up to the line.

"Ready, Brant?"

"Ready."

I dropped a pair of 7 1/2's into the chamber, thunked the action closed, and called for the targets.

The first clay bird exploded in an orange spider web. I picked up the second as it sped away, fracturing it in thirds. Thankfully, my ribs barely hurt.

"Very nice, Brant."

Paige stepped to the line. Gold bracelets clunked against the gunstock. Her nails were French-manicured. She loaded, snapped the action closed, and leaned forward.

"Pull!"

Paige swung from bird to bird. Each target disappeared in a puff.

Kip escorted us to shooting stations along a woodland path. Each station was enclosed by lattice entwined with morning glories and clematis. We took turns powdering targets that emerged from behind stone walls, between trees, and from atop hills. Running Rabbit battue discs, erratic mini targets called the Crazy Covey, and vertical pairs called Towering Teal offered challenging shots. Nobody missed. The sweet smell of spent gunpowder hung in the air.

I snuck a glance at Pearson's Rolex. It was one-thirty. I needed to wind up this extravaganza.

"Thanks for the shoot," I said. "It's been great."

A bead of perspiration trickled along Paige's hairline, and dribbled along her port wine stain. "Not so fast, Brant. The next two stations are the hardest. This one's called The Whirring Woodcock."

"No offense, Paige, but I get the feeling that you always get what you want."

"There's nothing wrong with that," she said, motioning me closer. "And right now, you're going to play this game with me."

I raised my eyebrows. "Game?"

"Before we're done, this may turn out to be a very interesting game. Now watch these targets."

I steadied myself. Two yellow birds parachuted twenty-five yards away, and I managed to break both. Paige dusted each of her clays.

The final station was a duck blind suspended over the pond on pilings. According to the diagram, two targets would cross at thirty-eight yards. Kip handed Paige and me heavier loads. The pond reflected fluttering leaves. The breeze blew Paige's hair. I tried not to gawk.

Her voice interrupted the moment. "Ready?"

"Ready," I said, shouldering the Perazzi. "Pull."

The clay's undersurface reflected off the water. It was a long shot. I led the target and split it in two. I lagged behind the second and missed.

Paige flung off her shooting glasses. "Who do you think you're fooling? You muffed that target on purpose!" She shook me by the shoulder.

"Really Paige, you're taking this too seriously."

She hit me in the chest with two more shells. "Don't patronize me. Load up. And this time, try."

I shrugged.

Kip yelled from the trap house, "Everything all right up there, kiddo?"

"Yes Kip. Deputy Sherman had a lapse in concentration. Be a dear, and give him another pair."

"If you insist."

"I do."

I did as I was told, and destroyed the next two targets.

Paige adjusted her shooting glasses, steadied herself, and leaned over the railing. As the first clay sailed across the water, she swung through, and in spite of the distance, vaporized it. The second traversed from right to left. A breeze lifted the bird, and she chipped it.

"Dead bird," I said. "It deflected with the shot."

"That was as good as a miss. I'll master this shot even if it takes me a case of ammunition, Kip."

"I'm sure you will, Paige."

"This life of leisure is wearing me out, Brant. Fundraisers have been killing my shooting."

"But you shot a perfect score."

"Not perfect enough."

Pearson collected the guns and hulls as we climbed out of the blind.

"Time for lunch," Paige said. "Kip, would you get the horses?"

"Sure, you two run along."

We started toward the estate.

"I've had a great time," I said, "but I have to go."

"You need to eat. I'll have a valet pick up your vehicle."

The lieutenant knew what he was talking about. This investigation *was* much more than I had imagined.

We strolled beneath the canopy of elms that shaded the road. Paige moved as if she were gliding across the meadows. We ambled along the road, glancing at one another from time to time. I considered asking Paige out, but I didn't dare. After all, this was an investigation. Besides, Paige orbited a different universe from mine.

Inside the mansion, I freshened up in a marble powder room. I joined Paige in a dining room adorned with wine-red wallpaper and silk damask curtains running the length of its tall windows. A grandfather clock pendulum swung to and fro, to and fro. Muzzleloaders hung above the fireplace mantle. Brass lamps illuminated oil paintings of setters pointing grouse in the uplands.

A maid—or maybe the cook—complete with uniform, served mesclun salad with greens that looked like dandelions. Nasturtiums garnished the top. My stomach kept churning, not only from hunger. I sipped mineral water with a twist of lime and summoning my best etiquette, nibbled the salad.

"So Brant, what do you want to ask me?"

"I'm assisting the state police investigating the Fenwick crime. I was wondering if any activists have been threatening your fur business."

"We've had a few encounters. Nothing newsworthy, but annoying just the same."

"Encounters?"

"A scruffy bunch of Greenpeace vegetarians sprayed our white fox inventory with red dye last holiday season. The episode upset my parents, and sales plunged." Paige smirked. "When the Tofu-heads couldn't post bail, the jailer served them stale Big Macs."

"Have you had any problems recently?"

"Not really. Artemis Furs subsidized the new police station. The officers watch out for us." Paige waved her fork like an index finger. "I make no apologies when it comes to my family's business."

I placed my card on the shining cherry table top and pushed it toward her. "If anything else happens, let me know."

"You'll hear from me anyway."

I nearly choked on a bolus of chevre cheese. During the trout almondine and jardiniere of vegetables, my mind raced. My eyes settled on field trial trophies and bird dog collars on the mantle.

"Your dad was the game warden, wasn't he?" she asked.

"Yes. And yours?"

"Father started his fur business in Austria before he came to this country. He's headed to Scotland for a pheasant shoot. I'm meeting him to hunt driven perdiz in the Pyrenees."

I decided not to mention my rat shooting "safaris" at the Saugus town dump.

"I should invite you to one of our pheasant hunts. Have you ever been to a tower shoot?"

"No. Dad and I had to settle for chasing game in the

rough. And I mean rough. Swamps and briar patches, mostly."

"Don't sell yourself short," Paige said. "The life of privilege becomes monotonous. At least you have excitement in your work."

I touched my side. "Maybe too much."

"You live in town, don't you?"

"Actually, I just moved back to Concord."

"Alone?"

"Huh?"

"I asked you if you moved back to Concord alone."

Her directness caught me off guard. "Sort of," I replied.

"I thought you might be involved with somebody," she said. This *was* becoming interesting.

"I have a Chesapeake Bay Retriever named Cosette." *God,* I thought, *I'm such a jerk. I used the same line on Abigail Reed.*

Paige smiled. "You've got a very lucky dog."


We spent the next hour eating kiwi ice on the patio swing as hummingbirds imbibed from a cascade of orange trumpet flowers. Just then, my mud-spattered Jeep rumbled into the driveway. A valet raised his eyebrows at the Fish and Wildlife logo I'd stuck on the door. The poor fellow wiped his hands on a handkerchief and plucked fur balls from his topcoat.

I had lingered too long. To and fro flirtations challenged all professional boundaries. I shook Paige's hand. She drew nearer, soft hair brushing against my cheek.

"Too bad that I'm leaving the country," she whispered.

"Headed to Spain to hunt *perdiz*, right?"

"You're a listener, Brant. After that, father and I will be

riding in Portugal and Provençe. We'll be gone for six weeks, but I'll call you when I return."

I felt like making out with her right on the spot, but this was Paige's home and I was on an investigation. She released my hand and stepped back. We watched one another for an awkward length of time. I freed myself from Paige's gravitational pull, and headed for the Jeep.


As I drove off, I realized that I'd spent two hours with Paige Sagoff without uttering a single bathroom phrase or ethnic slur.

Sometimes I even amaze myself...

9

After visiting Paige Sagoff, I kept reminding myself that show-quality dogs with perfect markings never made field trial champions. The same rule applied to women.

It bothered me that I yearned for Paige simply because of her looks. The euphoria that gorgeous women produce confuses the hell out of me. Funny how a guy seems to have everything in common with a pretty girl, yet show him the same type of girl with average looks, and all of a sudden, they're incompatible.

Pretty women get all the perks just because they have smooth skin, lush hair, and straight noses. No doubt about it, Plain Janes are the underdogs in this society.

In high school, my closest friends were "not-so-pretty"

girls. I sought them out at parties and dances because they were genuine. They were always saying that your hair looked nice or that they liked your outfit. Besides, average looking women *listened*.

One time, this football Neanderthal made a crack about my "harem of ugly girlfriends," and I knocked him into next week. He was lucky I didn't kill him. There's no such thing as an ugly girl. If you really look at a girl, you can always find a redeeming feature. Besides, all children are nearly perfect before the cuts, bruises, acne, chickenpox, poison ivy, and sunburns of this world scar them. Even funny looking kids are cute. You just have to look a little bit harder.

My best friend was Mary Beth Cahill, about a foot taller than me and not the least bit pretty. Her face was plainer than plain, but she knew everything about me. Once, we even spoke about my brother. Spending time with Mary Beth helped me more than talking to psychiatrists. In a weird way, we really liked each other. I would have married that girl if she'd been attractive. Damned hypocritical to say the least.

By senior year, I was so confused that I skipped the prom. Funny thing, high school beauties get dumpy by age thirty-five, and their tattoos sag, while plain girls blossom and bear great-looking kids. Guys who married the Mary Beth Cahill's of this world bought themselves lives of contentment. Those who married the knockouts bought themselves years of misery. And those of us who did neither bought ourselves years of loneliness.

At six o'clock that evening, with visions of blonde hair still swirling in my mind, I drove to the Hapgood Diner. I parked the old Wrangler in a shaded space where I could keep an eye on Cosette, not that she'd be easy to steal.

The dining room was bustling. Ample posteriors occupied every swivel seat at the counter. Seasoned sixty year old waitresses wearing peach-colored uniforms kept shouting orders and flinging brimming plates of meatloaf, fish and chips, and sirloin onto the tables. Sweat plastered curls to foreheads as they labored in the backdraft of an oven.

I gestured to the hostess, a leathery woman who didn't bother to acknowledge me.

"Looking for a table?" she asked, without lifting her eyes from the cash register.

"Yes, ma'am."

"It'll be awhile," she said, paying out change to a customer. "A long while."

"I'm here to meet Lieutenant Eldridge Weatherbee."

The woman looked up. "Come again?"

"I'm with Lieutenant Weatherbee."

She stepped out from behind the register. "Why didn't you say so, doll-face?"

Weatherbee was already waving from a knotty-pine front corner booth. The lieutenant gathered up notes strewn across the table, and shoveled them into his briefcase.

I glanced at tarnished bowling trophies on the shelves, the jukeboxe, a mounted sailfish, and Coca-Cola signs. "I've never eaten here before."

"That's because your family didn't realize it was quaint," the lieutenant replied.

A waitress slammed down a pair of drafts, the heads spilling onto the Formica table, and we ordered.

"So, how'd you do today?"

"Fairly well. I spoke with Dr. Fenwick. He was tough at first. I learned that the source of his transfusion was a prostitute named Lola who had advanced AIDS and hepatitis. The Legion bribed her to solicit Fenwick and to donate a unit of blood."

"How'd you figure that out?"

"Video surveillance. I was looking at the garage tapes and caught Fenwick sort of bumping into her earlier that morning. He was embarrassed, and that's why he didn't volunteer much to the Feds."

"Interesting. Where is this Lola?"

"At the state hospital."

"What did she have to say?"

"Nothing. I was too late."

"We'll exhume the body. Did Fenwick tell you anything new about the perp?"

"Nothing you don't already know. But there's one thing that got me: the minute he described the man, it reminded me of something."

"What?"

"I'm not sure. Just something familiar."

Weatherbee sat forward in his seat. "Try to figure it out, son. If you can't, I'll get the boys from Quantico to speak with you."

The lieutenant was referring to profilers from the FBI Behavioral Support Team. But I wasn't up for psychoanalysis by Dr. Freud or Dr. Phil or anybody in between. No way, no how.

The conversation shifted to Buddy Dog Animal Shelter,

which didn't impress Weatherbee. The waitresses, aware that their favorite patron was talking business, kept their distance.

"Sounds like a decent first day," the lieutenant said. "Anything else you want to share?"

"I checked out Artemis Furs. I questioned the Sagoff's daughter at the estate."

Weatherbee raised his eyebrows. "What did you think?"

"She didn't have much to offer."

"Not much to offer? You think I just fell off the turnip truck? You're single, and she's a knockout."

"I didn't know my interaction with Paige Sagoff was relevant."

"Everything's relevant."

"Okay. I shot sporting clays with her and we ate lunch. It wasn't a big deal."

"Shooting on an estate and dining with a model sounds like a big deal to me, son."

"Fine. It *was* interesting. We ate trout almondine, salad that looked like flowers, and Kiwi sorbet. You'd have been disappointed — there were no Skybars."

"I'll ask you again: what did you think?"

"About the food?"

"No, about Ms. Sagoff."

"She's assertive and gorgeous and one hell of a shot. She'll call if anything happens."

"And you're hoping that something does."

"With all due respect, Lieutenant, why are you so concerned about my social life?"

"Because highbrow women exhaust investigators."

"You're kidding, right?"

Weatherbee spread cheese dip on a melba toast. "I'm not kidding. Over the years, I've witnessed promising young fellas like you obsess over girls they couldn't get. The suckers wound up stocking shelves at Save-Mart." The lieutenant devoured the cracker and chased it with a swallow of his draft. "Find yourself a stable social life."

"Somebody like Paige Sagoff wouldn't fit that role?"

"No, she wouldn't. Your face has been plastered all over the newspapers. Right now, you're a commodity for a socialite. When the dust settles, women like that leave you with nothing."

"I'm a big boy. I can take it."

"Believe me, Brant, find yourself a dependable woman, and you'll be a happier man in the long run. Take it from a guy who's been married forty years."

"I consider myself warned."

The meals arrived. Weatherbee wiped his glasses and dug into the pot roast. "When I'm embroiled in a case, I could eat the flowers off the table."

I glanced up from my twin lobsters and noticed a familiar face at the entrance: Abigail Reed.

"Excuse me, Eldridge."

I made a beeline toward her, and said hello.

"Hi, Brant. I was on my way back to Boston and noticed Cosette in the Jeep."

Either tentative or afraid to crack my ribs, Abby gave me a gentle hug.

"Glad you stopped in," I said. "I'm having dinner with Lieutenant Weatherbee. You should meet him."

"I don't want to impose," she replied in typical female fashion.

I took her by the hand and led her to the table. Eldridge wiped his mouth and stood up, his napkin dangling from his belt. I introduced them.

"Please join us, Dr. Reed," Weatherbee said.

"Oh, I couldn't."

"I insist."

Abby glanced at her watch. "I have an hour before my shift," she said. "I suppose I could share a bite."

Our waitress returned to the table and added a place setting. "What'll it be, miss?" she asked.

"Diet cola, please, and a salad."

"Dressing?"

"Light Italian on the side."

"We have French, *normal* Italian, Russian, Bleu Cheese, and the house."

"What's the house?"

"Roquefort. Extra creamy."

"Italian on the side, please."

Weatherbee frowned. "It's a sin not to order something more substantial, Doc, especially when the department's footing the bill."

"Okay," she said, scanning the menu. "I'll have tuna on whole wheat with lettuce and tomato. Hold the mayo, please."

The waitress rolled her eyes. "Everything here has mayo or butter, and lots of it."

Weatherbee said, "Folks these days don't appreciate good cholesterol, Ceal."

"If you ask me, customers would be better off eating what they want rather than having a stroke worrying about it. But you got it, sweetie." The waitress winked at Abby. "I'd walk off a cliff for this handsome devil." She patted Weatherbee's shoulder and refilled our water glasses then disappeared into the kitchen.

Weatherbee stabbed a pad of butter and wedged it into a steaming roll. "I'm sorry, Doctor, but in the Hapgood Diner, you don't measure trans fat in grams — you measure it in *pounds*."

Abby gawked at my heaping platter. "Interesting color combination: green pea soup and red lobster."

"Merry Christmas," I said.

"I'm glad to see that your injuries haven't stunted your appetite."

"Abby was the doctor who treated me when I got shot, Eldridge."

"No wonder you survived. So what brings you to Concord, Dr. Reed?"

"I'm the new ER director at Hawthorne Hospital. I met with the Credentials Committee today."

"Abby babysat Cosette while I was out of commission," I added.

"Damn," Weatherbee said, "my HMO doesn't do that for me." He thought for a moment. "I could use a clinical expert like you, Doctor. If there are further incidents, you and your staff will be the first to assess the victims."

"I saw your documentary on solving cold cases," she said. "You won an honor..."

"The Bulldog Award. It surpassed my Dill's Atlantic Giant Pumpkin blue ribbon at the Topsfield Fair."

Just then, the waitress appeared with Abby's plate. A whole can of white tuna fish shaped like a hockey puck crowned a mountain of lettuce, sliced tomatoes, and dry wheat toast. Weatherbee wrinkled his nose at the offering.

"Your meal looks disgustingly healthful, Doctor Reed."

"I try to keep my fat intake down," she said. "It's stress that I have trouble controlling."

"We all have an Achilles' heel."

"Not Brant," said Abby. "Other than unusual eyes, he has it all."

"Funny, we'd just been discussing that," Weatherbee said as he plunged two wads of butter into his baked potato. "If we crack this case, Brant will be the All American Hero, and I'll retire to my garden as my saner colleagues have."

Abigail slid closer to me. I cracked the lobsters and pried open steamers as discretely as I could. No doubt about it, shellfish were lousy date fare. Abby entertained Eldridge with medical stories. I felt more relaxed than I'd been with Paige Sagoff. In time, we finished our meals. The lieutenant and I ordered coffee, but Abby declined.

"Can doctors call in sick?" I asked.

"Not this doctor. But let's get together later in the week."

"If Brant gets tied up, give me a call, Dr. Reed," Weatherbee said. "Before you leave, I'd appreciate your opinion of the Fenwick crime."

"You would?"

Weatherbee nodded, and Abigail Reed took center stage.

"The motive seems obvious, Lieutenant. Whoever carried out the deed has been abused in his childhood. He despises those who inflict pain on animals. Time has intensified the hatred. That's why he left Dr. Fenwick a bloody mess."

"Do you think the perpetrator was a medical student or coworker?"

"No way. Hatred — not academic dysfunction — set this guy off."

Eldridge beamed. "That's what our profilers told us. If you're interested in helping me out, FAX me your resume and a copy of your medical license." He handed her his card.

She thanked him and said goodbye. Meanwhile I kept trying to neutralize the smell of lobster on my hands with after-dinner wipes. I dried my hands and escorted Abby to the door.

"The lieutenant is impressed with you," I told her.

"I'm not crowding you, am I?"

"Not at all." She stopped at the doorway and said, "Call me, okay?" then kissed me on the cheek, and headed for her car.

When I returned to the booth, Weatherbee flashed an ear-to-ear grin. "Now *there's* the woman for you."

"What makes you so certain?"

"Intuition. Abigail Reed is crazy about you. She's witty and good-looking, the perfect life-partner. End of story."

"That's a ringing endorsement."

"She's a caring person. You're a nice guy, even though you shoot people once in awhile. Make the right choice."

"What makes you think Paige Sagoff isn't the right choice?"

"Because sometimes, my friend, what you want and what you need are two different things."


Later that night, the concoction of legumes, mollusks, and crustaceans swirled in my stomach. I pounded out a set of light bench presses on the front porch with a backdrop of stars, moonlight, and chirping crickets. I welcomed the ache of lactic acid revisiting my muscles.

I should have been thinking about the perp, the disturbing images of Dr. Fenwick, Lola, and those greyhounds, but instead, I kept thinking about women.

Between sets, I thought about Abigail Reed, her face plain yet attractive in the moonlight. Suddenly, the image of Paige Sagoff rushed into my mind. Green eyes became blue. Black hair became blonde and blonde hair black, merging into an ambiguous composite. I closed my eyes, settled back down, and pumped out ten more repetitions. When I opened my eyes, the images separated.

The stars overhead were clearer than my understanding of women. And far clearer than the profile of the crazy bastard I was seeking.

# 10

Concord, Massachusetts: Home of the Labradoodle, the cockapoo, and the obese golden retriever.

I poked around the town with no particular place to go — as Chuck Berry once said.

No runs, no hits, and no errors. The honeymoon lasted one week.

According to Thursday's local police log, Reidel Swamp Wildlife Management Area in the pastoral suburb of Carlisle had been troubled by stalkers. I figured the culprits were just garden-variety perverts — so plentiful these days. Nevertheless, Eldridge Weatherbee advised me to take a peep at the situation, so to speak.

That humid Friday morning, a bank of cumulonimbus clouds loomed on the horizon.

Yogi Berra once said that one can observe a lot by watching. I planned do my watching near the main lot. The fall semester had just begun and today the area hosted several field trips. My Nancy Drew sense steered me toward a busload of Harvard students roaming the meadows on a bug safari.

From atop a grassy knoll, Harvard professors observed their students. I introduced myself, and the two invited me to join them. These academics were eccentric as hell, but lovable old farts. I figured they didn't watch TV, because neither recognized me from the Pascucci incident. The quirky pair, giddy at the prospect of spending a day outside the classroom, put on a show for my benefit.

Professor Abraham Lebowitz slapped a mosquito on his neck and remarked to his colleague, "Quite a buggy day, wouldn't you say, Beegley?"

"You bet your bippy," answered Harvard Professor Emeritus Beegley Spivack. "An enchanting day for collecting."

"Someday, my friend, you entomologists will come to your senses and study advanced life forms."

Professor Spivack squinted from behind thick, horn-rimmed lenses. "You can have your herpetology, Abraham. I could never bring myself to respect any vertebrate with a cloaca."

Spivack was a slender graying man, sporting a khaki shirt with a maroon bow tie and matching khaki pants. His flat-topped crewcut had gathered enough length to create a whirlpool-like spiral at the back. His hairdo resembled the hackle on a trout fishing fly, and with pride he told me that he'd been dubbed "Old Hacklehead." (No pun intended for those of you who tie).

Dr. Lebowitz, a rotund gentleman in his sixties, wore a white shirt, a safari hat, and hip boots. The men swung open the tailgate of an ancient "woody wagon" and stacked their nets, collecting jars, and journals on the ground.

Lebowitz eyed my revolver. "The tools of our trade are a bit different from yours, Deputy."

"Not as different as you think, Professor," I said. "You hunt bugs, and I hunt bad guys."

The two old fellas had a laugh over that one.

"Have you gentlemen noticed any stalkers on this property?" I asked.

Spivack smiled. "I caught Dr. Lebowitz gawking at skinny-dipping coeds, but that's the extent of it."

"I'm sorry I asked."

"By the way, Deputy Sherman, what did you study in college?"

"Criminal Justice, but I've bagged a butterfly or two in my day. My family spent lots of time outdoors, and my dad wrote an outdoor column."

"Wonderful. Once you're done investigating, grab a net and try your luck with us."

"We get paid to play outdoors," Lebowitz added. "As they say, 'Someone's got to do it.' "

The old duffers spread a checkerboard tablecloth on the tailgate. Dr. Lebowitz popped the cork from a bottle of sparkling cider and poured it into long-stemmed wine glasses. The professors offered me a drink, but I declined. They raised their glasses.

"To the insects," said Spivack.

"To reptiles and amphibians," added Lebowitz, savoring the bouquet.

"And especially to us—two old coots who never got rich, but made academia work for them." Spivack motioned to the students. "Great kids this semester, Abraham. No pre-meds."

"I'll drink to that."

I knew these old guys were hamming it up for my benefit, and I have to admit, they made me laugh. Meanwhile, their students unfurled their butterfly nets and pillowcase moth traps.

"Standing room only for your Bag 'em and Tag 'Em course again, Beegley," Lebowitz remarked.

"Let's get things straight: I teach *Introduction to Entomology*."

"That's not what the pre-meds call it."

"They've invented many names for what I do."

"And for who you are. What did they call you last winter?"

"I believe they termed me 'Beegley the ball-buster.' Yes, that was it: Ballbuster. *Balbusterius malignans*. Those buffoons couldn't even get their Latin right."

The two hot shits poured more cider.

"Beegley, you kill me, you really do. Woe unto any premedical student who stumbles into your course."

The entomologist flashed a sinister grin. "My motto is 'Float like a butterfly; sting like a bee.'"

"I've heard that somewhere before," Lebowitz said.

I smiled. Another hard-ass professor, I thought, just like Dr. Fenwick.

Dr. Spivack nodded, and raised his voice for my benefit. "Early in the semester, pre-med overachievers study organic chemistry notes while I'm lecturing. I pretend not to notice. Then, when it's too late to withdraw, Old Hacklehead's Venus flytrap slams shut. All of a sudden, my mood changes. I demand that each student name obscure species in Latin, an impossible task for pre-meds overwhelmed by physics and organic chemistry. The clowns struggle to keep pace, but it's hopeless. So long Mercedes Benz. Bye-bye, Beverly Hills Plastic Surgery Associates. Time to pack your 2.1 grade point average and start swabbing the men's room in Dad's office."

Dr. Lebowitz choked on his cider and held his hand up. "Stop, please! I'll aspirate, for godsakes."

But the Professor Emeritus was on a roll. "On the final examination, students must name over a hundred insects, moving from station to station every forty-five seconds at the sound of a shrill buzzer. Time-urgency rattles even the most steadfast would-be doctor. The highest grade I've ever awarded a pre-med was a B minus. I later convinced the young lady to apply to veterinary school."

"Way to go, Old Sport."

"Last quarter, a herd of fuming pre-meds and their parents chased me across campus. They threatened to have me fired."

"What did you say?" I couldn't help asking.

"Life's unfair—and unfortunately for you, I've got tenure."

Dr. Lebowitz kept holding his sides. "What's that species they named after you again, Beegley?"

"*Solenopsis spivacensis.* The Iberian fire ant. It sure beats

*Balbusterius malignans."*

"A fire ant, huh?"

"Like I said: 'float like a butterfly; sting like a bee.' "

Spivack downed his cider in a single gulp. "Insects are blameless. It's people who bug me."

Soon afterward, the aged comedians bade each other farewell.

"Mind if I follow you into the bush?"

"I'd be honored, Deputy. Enjoy the show."

Lebowitz disappeared down a pathway leading to the turtle pond, while Spivack ambled toward the fields. Keeping my eyes and ears open, I followed.

Beegley Spivack's students hovered through ground fog, murmuring with excitement.

Flowers trembled with bees, elderberry and chokeberry plants slouched beneath the burden of their fruit, goldfinches and kingbirds flitted through the goldenrod, and cumulus clouds drifted across a cobalt sky. The professor headed toward the students, nets protruding from his armpits like appendages. Glistening leopard frogs leaped ahead of his loping strides.

I should have done more exploring, but this quirky professor piqued my interest, and I kept trailing him. Blackberry juice stained the students' faces. My criminal justice classes were never this much fun.

The professor dumped his gear onto the grass. "Today, the outdoors is your library." The students fell silent to a background of breeze and bees.

Spivack turned to a bushy-haired student whose face

was particularly magenta, his tee shirt "tie-dyed" with juice. "Eat up. Berries are a lot more healthful than dorm food."

The professor plucked a handful of blackberries and popped them into his mouth, puckering to keep the juice inside. "Revel in the splendor of the outdoors," he blubbered.

His theatrics mesmerized his students and me.

"Breathe in. Heighten your senses," he said.

Monarchs fluttered with lazy wing-beats. Intoxicated by the scent of flowers, even quick red admirals, painted ladies, azures, and coppers slowed their cadences. Suddenly, a large black and yellow butterfly fluttered past.

"A tiger swallowtail!" Spivack shouted, grabbing his net.

He began to chase the butterfly with the gawky stride of a stork. Spivack high-legged through the goldenrod, swishing his net. The yellow blur began to gain speed and altitude. But the swallowtail was no match for Old Hacklehead. At fifty yards, distance began to narrow. At seventy-five, the butterfly was just out of reach. At a hundred yards, with one lunge and a Herculean swing, the professor netted the swallowtail. The students cheered, and so did I.

Spivack waited for them to catch up. Panting, he displayed his prize.

"My purpose for catching this butterfly is twofold: one, to prove that I'm not such an old fart after all, and two, this big Lepidopteran is a superb specimen to mount. Collecting can be rigorous. I've recommended that we make it a varsity sport.

"Now, before we split up, let's review rules of the chase: First, never collect specimens that are mating, especially coupled dragonflies that are abundant now. I hope others afford you similar courtesy someday. Most importantly, we must discuss dispatching your specimens."

Spivack and his students trooped to a picnic table on which there was a cardboard box labeled *POISON!* The professor removed a mason jar labeled with a red, white, and blue-painted skull bisected by a lightning bolt.

"Cool," said a student. "Grateful Dead."

"My tribute to Jerry Garcia," Spivack replied. "Though I doubt that our specimens are very grateful." He shook one of the bottles. Granules sifted inside.

"This chemical is more toxic than your roommate's socks, so be careful. You are forbidden to keep these killing jars in your dorm rooms. The crystals on the bottom are calcium cyanide, a fumigant that smells like almonds. If you inhale, your parents will have wasted your tuition."

The professor slipped a jar into the net, trapped the butterfly inside, and secured the cover.

"Swallowtails are graceful, even in death," Spivack said. The butterfly's proboscis began to uncurl and its antennae began to twitch. Wingbeats attenuated.

The Professor's eyes widened. "I love the smell of cyanide in the morning!"

"God," I heard a student whisper, "Old Hacklehead is whacked!"

From his peripheral vision, Spivack observed the clean-cut fellow, muscles rippling beneath his varsity football tee shirt. To a geek like Spivack, I figured gym rats were even less desirable than pre-meds, but someone had to fill the tail-end of the bell-curve.

"Remember, class, we are all aerobes. The cyanide that killed our friend could do the same to us," Spivack said. He removed the asphyxiated butterfly with forceps. He pinned the insect to a piece of styrofoam and spread each wing beneath a cardboard band. "Symmetry," he said. "In nature, beauty is symmetry." He used a quill pen to scroll the label.

The collectors shook insects from pillowcase traps into the killing jars.

A nerdy student emerged from a hemlock grove with an insect in his net. "Dr. Spivack," he said, "see what I just caught!"

The professor squinted at a butterfly with chocolate brown wings edged with tan. The butterfly flapped, revealing blue spots.

"Lovely," said Spivack, "a mourning cloak with closed wings is as innocuous as a fleck of bark, but with wings unfurled, it takes one's breath away." Spivack reached into the net where the butterfly perched on his finger. "*Nymphalis antiopa*, the mourning cloak. Colonists named this noble butterfly after a death shroud. According to their superstition, the first person to spy one each spring would die."

"Do you believe that, Professor?" the student asked.

"On the contrary, Marvin. Mourning cloaks bring me luck."

"He's one incredible insect."

"Like the mourning cloak, *you* can amaze if you dare to unfurl your own wings."

Marvin smiled as he unscrewed the lid of his killing jar. Compliments from this professor were obviously hard to come by.

My two hour search that morning produced little more than a few roaches (of the *Cannabis*, not the *Arthropoda* variety).

A big cumulonimbus cloud filled the sky. Thunder rumbled in the distance. Humid air crackled with electricity. Poplar and aspen leaves exposed their light undersurfaces in a gathering breeze. I headed home.

Three hours later, I got a call from the lieutenant.

"Brant," he said, "we've got problems."

"What's going on?"

"Someone tried to suffocate an entomologist in Carlisle. Damn near killed him."

My heart leapt into my throat. "Where?"

"Reidel Swamp."

"Who?"

"Professor Beegley Spivack."

"You've got to be kidding! I just interviewed the guy."

"The Lord works in strange ways," Weatherbee said. "Pick me up at the station. And don't forget your bug spray."

I slammed a red-headed pin into the topo map in my cabin to mark the third crime scene. The realization made me tremble like a lifeguard who'd let a swimmer drown. I hauled ass to pick up the lieutenant. The Jeep lurched into the state police barracks. Weatherbee squeezed into the passenger seat. Storm clouds darkened the sky.

The lieutenant nudged his chin at a bug light behind the barracks where mosquitoes hissed and sputtered. "Ironic, isn't it?"

"How so?"

"We fry them, they infect us. Maybe encephalitis is payback."

"A fly is a duck is a deer is a human?" I said.

"Huh?"

"That's what the activists say."

Something large sparked and sizzled on the coils of the bug light. "Must've been a sparrow," Weatherbee said.

The vehicle sped down Barrett's Mill Road, past corn fields where a farmer was fogging his crops.

"My wife won't let me spray our yard," Weatherbee continued. "She says that pesticides accumulate in her 'breast receptors.' "

"Breast receptors?"

"Insecticide ends up in fatty tissue."

"Then I suppose breasts would qualify."

"The old lady bought me a bat hotel to control the mosquitoes. Unfortunately, the bats never moved in. But the starlings have. Now, I'm dealing with piles of guano *and* mosquitoes."

Weatherbee's humor failed to console me. By the time we reached the crime scene, I had a huge lump in my throat. I thought about pulling a U-turn and speeding back to Julio's triple decker in Cambridge, far from my birthplace, this hell-hole west of Boston that produced nothing but grief and guilt. But I kept driving.

State troopers waved us into the Conservation Area parking lot. Yellow tape demarcated the perimeter. A strengthening breeze rustled the vegetation. Rows of evidence bags rested on Spivak's woody-wagon tailgate. I inspected killing jars, lunch boxes, a half-eaten apple, twisted eyeglasses, a split-open plastic water jug, car keys, a wallet, and other depressing items. A photographer took close-ups of torn laundromat plastic, the plastic membrane the perp had used to suffocate poor Old Hacklehead. With gloved hands, the investigator kept trying to smooth flapping edges. Another investigator aspirated mucous with a syringe.

It floored me that a trivial membrane, even thinner than ice, could separate a victim's lungs from the oxygenated world. It wouldn't take long for the politicians to enforce "Laundry Bag Permits to Carry" to be included with pistols, mace, dynamite and other weapons of mass destruction.

The team had spray painted a body silhouette of the professor on the ground. Urine stained the dirt within the outline of his pelvis, including his baggy pants.

Unlike those CSI shows on TV, where some hotshot medical examiner disembowels a victim while eating a baloney sandwich, real murders disturb the hell out of me. Even more disturbing, I'd just been talking to the victim. Why was Beegley Spivack attacked so soon after I questioned him? Was there a connection? I kept trying to convince myself that the crime was random, but somehow I felt like a treacherous decoy that had lured a duck to its fatal landing. I turned away from the evidence.

A member of the state police forensics team dusted the vehicle for fingerprints. A camera flashed intermittently over her shoulder. The blunt-cut brunette looked up and smiled. She had the white straight teeth that orthodontia and fluoride produce.

"How goes the battle, Sergeant?"

"Rolling prints in this wind is tough, Lieutenant. And there's no DNA under the professor's fingernails."

"You'll find something," said Weatherbee. "Hang in there."

Weatherbee motioned me aside. "Susan Pfleuger is the most meticulous member of my team," he said. "If she'd been working in Los Angeles a decade ago, a famous running back would be spending his time behind bars these days instead of on golf courses."

Investigators interviewed the students. Some wept as troopers escorted them into state police shuttle vans.

The impending storm had grounded the police helicopters. German shepherds and their handlers coursed the meadow while cadets searched in a grid pattern. Others swept the area with metal detectors. The lieutenant left the scene, then trotted back.

"That was Abigail Reed," he said to me. "Talk about a crummy first ER shift. She told me that it wasn't just cyanide that got Spivack. A leather belt fractured his windpipe. His CT scan shows brain damage from lack of oxygen, not exactly appropriate for a Harvard Professor Emeritus."

Another lump welled up in my throat as we crept toward a rusty Volkswagen Rabbit with its rear window splotched with multicolored Harvard parking stickers. Professor Lebowitz, still in hip boots, sat on the hood shivering.

Weatherbee spoke up. "Dr. Lebowitz?"

"Yes."

"I'm Lieutenant Eldridge Weatherbee of the State Police Criminal Investigation Unit, and you've already met my partner. Can you shed any light on this?"

Lebowitz motioned to an empty cider bottle sealed in an evidence bag on the tailgate. "Ask Deputy Sherman. This morning, Beegley and I toasted to our good fortune. Three hours later, I found my best friend cyanotic with a plastic bag over his head." Lebowitz stared away, his lower lip quivering.

I felt sorry for Lebowitz, and even sorrier for myself.

"Was everybody together?" Weatherbee asked.

"These kids stuck to me like glue. Most of them avoided Beegley. The poor fellow's been through a lot in his life, including stillbirth of a son."

"Stillbirth?"

Lebowitz nodded. "After forty years of teaching, Beegley Spivack has developed a hard carapace. Students rumored that he and his ichthyologist wife had concealed their child, a monster with a malformed brain, in a dark corner of their cellar where 'Little Lloyd' bobbed in an aquarium of formaldehyde. Students can be cruel."

The lieutenant nodded. "I understand. Does anybody hate Dr. Spivack enough to suffocate him?"

"I doubt it, sir. You could try to compile a list of students who got C or less in *Introduction to Entomology* over the years," Lebowitz continued, "but that's one huge data set."

"Was anybody else with your Harvard group?"

"No, and we'll never be back."

Ahead of the storm, agents cast tire prints in the parking lot. Thunder rolled. Heat lightning merged with camera flashes.

"What's the latest on Beegley?" Lebowitz asked.

"He responds only to painful stimuli," Weatherbee answered.

"Just as I feared; Beegley's a brain-stem preparation."

"A what?"

"A brain-stem preparation. A pithed frog can live indefinitely if it gets the right nutrients." Lebowitz shook his head sadly. "People like that spend the rest of their lives on tube feedings, contorted and seizing in urine-soaked beds." Lebowitz raised his voice. "I'm a bleeding-heart liberal, but anybody who could do such a thing to Beegley Spivack doesn't deserve a place in this world."

I spoke up. "I assure you, Professor, when I catch this creep, I'll spank him hard."

"I hope so, Deputy. For Beegley's sake."

We walked away.

"Bad grades or professional jealousy aren't the motives in this one, Brant. It's about wasting humans who torture for a living."

The Grateful Dead skull killing jar glared from the tailgate.

"This is about animals," Weatherbee continued, "even lowly bugs."

The lieutenant began to sketch the crime scene. "Someone stalked the man. Check out the thicket near the entrance."

I jogged to the overgrown area, too tangled to grid-search. Feral ornamental grass had been freshly-broken, and stalks pointed against the prevailing wind. Someone had smeared spittlebug froth on the vegetation. I had missed every clue.

My heart began to pound, and my ears began to ring, as if someone were watching. Sedge grass gave way to blackberry bushes which tore at my pants. Wind rustled poplar leaves overhead. The skies grew darker. Weatherbee was right. A perp had observed the woody-wagon from this hollow. I skirted the tangles and advanced toward the entrance.

I pushed farther into the dense cover. Bark and thorns had been stripped from a blackberry bush. Blackberry thorns could tear the flesh of any fool mindless enough to blunder through a thicket. I crawled deeper into the tangle. A cardinal skirted out of the cover and perched above me, red and glistening as a drop of blood. Its metallic chirping resonated through the gloom.

A mosquito bit my neck. I swatted it, wiped my hands on a fern, and forged ahead. Ah, the adversity of summer—poison ivy, stinging nettles, hungry mosquitoes, ticks, leeches, and blackflies—all poised to assault humans.

Clumps of briar and sweet fern concealed the rotting foundation of an old barn. I startled a mockingbird from its nest in a lilac bush. Mockingbirds often collect forensic evidence: hair, foil, and other materials. I edged closer. Sure enough, a glimmer within the nest caught my eye—a blood droplet on a strip of plastic. For once, I was grateful for long thorns. I focused my pen light on the specimen and radioed Weatherbee and forensics.

Sergeant Susan Pfleuger photographed the specimen. She then slipped on gloves, lifted the plastic strip with forceps, and coaxed the droplet into a test tube.

Weatherbee shouted from the road. "Finish up in there. The sky is about to let loose."

The wind strengthened and moisture spit on the team. I expanded my perimeter and stumbled onto a pathway. Tire tracks led toward a gap in a stone wall fifty yards away, traversing a grove of red pines.

I had always admired red pines, the cathedral of red squirrels and ruffed grouse. The telephone pole-straight conifers grew in parallel rows. Their bark reminded me of jigsaw puzzle pieces.

But this grove was asymmetric. Tire tracks had agitated the pine needles. Lady slippers had been crushed. I noticed bark on the ground and a fleck of white paint on a tree trunk. By now, I was at least eighty yards away from the other investigators.

My stomach began to churn, and I began to sweat all over again. Cold eyes seemed to peer from the shadows, and there were peals of thunder. I gripped the handle of my trusty .357, and calmed myself.

*The woods will speak to those who take time to listen,* my father used to say. *The answer is always in the woods – you merely have to find it.*

I directed the team toward the newly-discovered pathway. Soon, photographs flashed, videotape ran, and investigators scoured the forest in a rebirth of enthusiasm, gleaning evidence ahead of the storm.

Later, Eldridge and I rode home through torrential rain. Lightning struck a nearby tree. Birches listed in the wind. Sheared leaves jammed the windshield wipers.

"It's going to be a late night," Weatherbee said. "Pfleuger found us some carpet fibers to analyze. I'm planning to ask your friend Abigail Reed to help me out with the blood analysis. I hope this gory introduction to the emergency department hasn't unsettled her."

"She's used to it."

"I wouldn't take that for granted, buddy. You ought to call her."

I nodded.

The rain subsided in Concord. I accelerated down Lowell Road.

"You redeemed yourself by finding that blood specimen," the lieutenant said. "Sometimes, Brant, it's better to be lucky than good. You're a little of both."

"If I were good *or* lucky, I would have caught the maggot before he smothered the professor."

Just then wrappers rustled, and I caught the scent of chocolate.

"Trouble is that your malnourished, Brant," said Weatherbee. "Remember Popeye?"

"Sure I do. Why?"

The lieutenant flexed his arm. "Because Skybars are my spinach."

After I dropped the lieutenant off, the timing of Spivack's attack began to bother me again. Why did the professor get mugged the very day I interviewed him? I recalled the creepy sensation of eyes staring at me from the depths of the forest. Had the stalker been watching me? Was he amongst us?

I kept hoping that the blood DNA would match a subject in the CODIS database because this event promised to gnaw at me for a long time.

I had to purge myself of guilt and the two Skybars the lieutenant forced me to eat, so I jogged the dark back roads that night. Afterward, I listened to my phone messages.

The first was from my father. The second message was from a shaken Abigail Reed, warning me to be careful. But the third message nearly stopped my heart.

It was Paige Sagoff:

*"Hi Brant. I was disappointed that you didn't have more investigating to do at Artemis Farm. I'm at Logan now, delayed by the storm. By the time you hear this, I'll be on my way to Spain." A pause.*

"*I'm hosting a black-tie Hunter's Moon Ball at the estate on Saturday night October twenty-first, and it would be wonderful to see you there.*"

I stared into the receiver, grateful for the call, yet, at the same time, tormented.

Sleepless nights were getting old.

# 11

Three days after Professor Beegley Spivack's assault, Weatherbee awarded me a pleasant assignment: spending a day with Dr. Abigail Reed. The lieutenant valued my connection to his local medical resource. No doubt, he also wanted to keep my mind off Paige Sagoff.

I drove Abigail to a rolling hill overlooking Fairhaven Bay, a lake-like bulge in the Sudbury River. Cumulus clouds scurried across a blue sky. I led Abby to a knoll, lush with alfalfa and clover. Bumblebees and monarch butterflies lazed on the blossoms. An osprey eyed us from atop its perch as I unfolded a blanket.

"What a view!" Abigail Reed said.

I uncorked a bottle of wine, which opened with a bang. "Not a bad spot, is it? My father and I used to train retrievers here. We'd launch dummies propelled by .22 blanks."

"Do all of your conversations revolve around firearms?"

"Guns have always been part of my life."

"Guns almost ended it," she reminded me. "My parents didn't allow weapons in our house."

"Then they'd have been mighty uncomfortable in mine."

Abigail sipped the wine. Her hair was gathered back in a braid. Her green eyes sparkled. She wore no makeup. Faded jeans hugged her slim figure.

Abigail Reed was here, and Paige Sagoff, half a world away. At this moment, Paige might be romancing a matador or flamenco dancer in Barcelona. Who could guess the intentions of the elite? I turned toward Abby.

"Do you like the wine?"

Abby held the glass up and turned it in the sunlight. "It's got a discreet fruity fragrance with just the right harmony of tannin, esters, fruit, and alcohol."

"Whatever you say."

She laughed. "I took a wine-tasting class a few years ago, but actually, I don't know what I'm talking about."

"You had me convinced."

"Seriously, the wine's great. Where'd you find it?"

"Bolton."

"You mean Bourgogne, France?"

"No, I mean Bolton, Massachusetts. It's a blend of Concord grape and elderberry. The best of 2005."

"Everything about you is different."

I wasn't sure how to take that but decided it was a

pretty fair observation. "I'm not conventional, that's for sure," I said, folding my arm behind my head. "When I was a kid, I got beaned by a foul ball at Fenway. Dad said I was never right after that."

"I'll consider myself warned. Anyway, how'd you get Eldridge to give you a break?"

"Until they find me a fugitive to hunt, I've got time off. Eldridge encouraged me to spend it with you."

"That's flattering," she said. "But there's another reason. Weatherbee knows you need a diversion. I've witnessed more than my share of trauma, yet I keep picturing Professor Spivack wheezing and cyanotic every time I close my eyes. How do you handle it?"

"Poorly. I never sleep more than a few hours a night."

"You never relax?"

"Nope."

Abby took a long swallow of wine. "I used to spend my nights rehashing ER scenarios from the night before. That sort of stress takes its toll."

"No argument here."

"So what do you think about this case?"

"It pisses me off."

Abby motioned to the .357 anchoring the corner of the blanket. "How long have you been like this?"

"Like what?"

"Hypervigilant."

I shrugged.

"It wouldn't hurt to get a night's sleep once in awhile, would it?"

"You lose things when you're not watching," I said.

"Things?"

"And people."

"Let me ask you something. Was that nightmare in the ICU about your brother?"

"Yes."

"What happened to him?"

"He drowned." I considered changing the subject, but she was a listener. "When I was sixteen, I led my brother onto the ice duck hunting and he broke through. I couldn't save him."

Abby drew in her breath.

"One of us was meant to drown that day. I wish it had been me." A breeze whooshed through the pines. "They never recovered his body."

Abby sat up and hugged me. Her body was warm. "All teenagers make mistakes," she said.

"Not like that. I've been replaying the scene in my mind every night for the past twenty years, but with editing."

"Editing?"

"In the new version, it wasn't an accident. Somebody was watching from the shore, somebody who *made* it happen. There's a sabot slug in my shotgun, and I shoot the imaginary bastard."

"Do you find retribution therapeutic?"

"Very."

"To what end?"

"To watch the maggot suffer the way my brother did, and the way I still do. Sorry I'm not more spiritually-evolved, Abby, but at least you know what you're getting yourself into."

"Did the police investigate?"

"As best as they could in the middle of a snowstorm."

"And their conclusion?"

"Teenage negligence."

The breeze swept milkweed dander past as we stared at the lazy river.

"You can't just blast your problems away with the pull of a trigger."

"Sometimes you can."

"Why do you think your brother drowned?"

"Because I wasn't careful enough."

"You really believe that?"

I shrugged. "Maybe somebody loved ducks, and hated hunters."

"Like the Legion of St. Francis?"

I shook my head and stared at the ground. "There's only one person to blame, and it's me."

"You don't really believe that. You fear discovering the truth, yet you're driven by it. Something drew you back to Concord, something unresolved."

"What?"

"You've always suspected that there was more to your brother's death than a random accident of nature."

I straightened. "How do you know that?"

"During that nightmare in the ICU, a nurse heard you yelling at someone. I wonder if the imaginary assailant you fantasize shooting may not be imaginary at all."

"It was just a dream."

"Dreams reflect reality. Danger follows you, or you attract danger. The asphyxiation of Professor Spivack was far from random. After that little exploit in Boston, your face was plastered all over the newspapers. Concordians recognize you.

Make no mistake, small towns are worse than hospitals. People talk."

"Let me get this straight, Abby. You think that I'm instigating these events?"

She nodded. "You're a challenge for this legion, a challenge that will make every one of their crimes front page news."

Abby's comments made me squirm. "Sounds like you've given this a lot of thought," I said.

She smiled. "More than I care to admit. And while we're on the subject, why do you think Major Fallon and Lieutenant Weatherbee chose you for the task force?"

"Because I know this area, and I can shoot."

"You're not the only U.S. Marshal who can shoot."

"Okay Doctor, why *did* they choose me?"

"Because you're compelled to undo what happened twenty years ago. If you catch these terrorists, the state police will take credit and Eldridge can retire to his pumpkin patch, basking in the memory of his final sting."

"And what will it do for me?"

"I'm not sure, but it's something to do with your eyes."

"Huh?"

Abby nodded. "Through the blue eye, your world is clear and unequivocal, and it's okay to kill. But your world through the brown eye is an ambivalent one."

"That's a heavy theory."

"You'll never bring your brother back, Brant, no matter who you shoot." She paused, maybe realizing the conversation was swirling into dark water. "So what do you want out of life?" she asked with a smile.

"To live vicariously through a son who'll catch for the Red Sox and lead them to another World Series."

"And what else?"

"A simple existence," I said. "I want to chase grouse until I'm so tired that I'll sleep the night away without dreaming. I want someone to share life with. But it has to be a safe life. And right now, there's danger out there for me and anybody I'm close to."

"No wonder you're alone. Your world is empty, as cold as ice."

I bristled. Suddenly, hands reached up from the depths, fists beating on the unyielding undersurface.

Abby nudged me. "Come on Brant, snap out of it!"

I hurtled back into the world. "Sorry."

Abby was shaken. She wrapped the blanket around me. "What happens when you space-out like that?"

"There's buzzing in my ears. I see and hear things."

"You mean you hallucinate?"

"No, it's all real."

"You turned gray, Brant," she said. "That's not normal." She began to rub my shoulders, and her voice softened. "My poor troubled boy. What goes on inside that head of yours?"

I shrugged.

We sat silently for awhile, gazing at an osprey hovering in a wind current.

I decided to change the subject. "How much do you know about advanced pancreatic cancer, Abby?"

"A fair amount. Why?"

"Because my father has it."

"Where is he now?"

"In the hospice. My father's a neat guy. You should meet him while he's still alive."

"I'd like that," Abby said. "I could review his chart for you."

"Thanks."

We finished our wine and rolled back onto the blanket, staring at the clouds. An elderly couple and their golden retrievers hiked into view. They hesitated before disappearing into the woods. That's when I reached for Abby. We kissed for the first time, a hungry kiss, and the moment grew more passionate, more intense. I drew her closer.

"I can't believe you were delivered to me in an ambulance," she whispered.

I closed my eyes and tried to purge visions of blonde as I kissed her again.

# 12

For the next six weeks, I spent most of my time fishing, working out, and digesting my food. Abigail Reed and I never took our relationship to the next level, so to speak. Sure we shared a few intimate moments, but she was too wrapped up in her ER job to enjoy the experience, and I was getting bored with the lack of movement in the case.

Eldridge Weatherbee's call shattered the tranquility of one Saturday morning.

"Coffee break's over, Brant. I'm at the Rod and Gun Club."

"What happened?"

"The excrement has hit the ventilator, that's what. The Legion planted hooks in hamburgers at the Fall Fishing Derby, with thirteen kids impaled."

"Are you sure?"

"Of course I'm sure. These damned hooks look sharp

enough to skewer a mosquito. A fisherman called them a Japanese name."

"Gamakatsu?"

"Yes, that's it. Talk about body piercing."

I cradled the phone against my shoulder as I climbed into my jeans. "I still hold the record for the smallest trout ever caught at that Derby — a five-inch brookie." I said. "I'll be right down."

"No Brant, head to Walden Pond."

"Why Walden?"

"Activists have been protesting trout stocking there. If the loonies are worried about fish, Walden's where they might emerge."

*Emerge.* The term evoked images of mayflies or 'emergers' hatching on the smooth surface of the lake to be inhaled by cruising browns and rainbows. I'd spent many younger days flycasting Adams, Light Cahills, and Quill Gordons to trout feeding in the pellucid waters of Walden.

"Wear that environmental police jacket I gave you, and keep your eyes open."

Crying erupted in the background. "I have to cut you short," Weatherbee said. "I'm en route to the hospital."

A rush of panic swept through me. "Damn."

"What?"

"It's Abby's shift."

"Better give her a call."

I dialed the emergency room. Abigail spoke in short fight-or-flight sentences. She was now just an ER doctor bracing for a flood of traumatized children and hysterical parents.

"You're about to receive thirteen kids impaled by fishhooks, Abby."

"Make that fourteen, Brant. Thirteen *more* than this facility can handle. Have you ever tried to disgorge a fishhook from a child's tongue? It's an experience not to be missed, I assure you."

"Maybe *I'm* the one with the black cloud."

"Sure seems like it," she said. "These ER shifts have been twice as hectic as my shifts in Boston. Patients around here are privileged and demanding. The most disturbing cases relate to this Legion of St. Francis. This job's a nightmare."

"Believe me, Abby, you've made the right decision. You'll see."

"Listen Brant, I don't want to get into it right now, but you seem distracted. That's not helping, either."

Guilt rushed in like a tide. I glanced at a postcard from Valencia, a postcard crowded with longhand, a postcard I'd read at least twenty times.

"Please call me after your shift," I said.

Sirens and commotion in the background interrupted a long pause.

"Okay. Goodbye."

Women were perceptive as hell, no doubt about it.


Twenty minutes later, I parked on a hill overlooking Walden Pond. From a distance, the pond was green and glacier-like, ribboned by a sandy shoreline punctuated by changing red and orange maples. Sandy embankments fell sharply to the water along its far banks.

Walden attracted Thoreau pilgrims by the thousands. Visitors loved the place to death each year, but the tired pond struggled to recover vestiges of itself. Sweet fern and daisies encroached on Walden's trodden pathways.

All bodies of water, even worn-out ones, held a few secrets for those willing to seek them out. Nighthawks still boomeranged overhead on summer evenings. Geese and ducks still migrated overhead and took refuge in Walden's coves. Kingfishers still scolded from overhanging branches. The Fitchburg Railroad still whistled from Walden's far bank, unchanged since the time of Thoreau.

Tales of Walden's fathomless depths had always intrigued fishermen. Each summer, trout retreated into the cold and mysterious thermocline. Some hold-overs grew large, sporting the bright markings and hooked jaws of their ancestors. Each autumn, a few of these monsters would venture into the shallows.

Hatchery trucks had just stocked the pond. As usual, word had spread among the retired, the hooky players, the shirkers, and the unemployed. The fishermen dotted the shoreline, their rods propped by forked sticks. Bobbers, bells, flags, and fluorescent rod tips that signaled strikes were the hallmark of the bait fishermen. The anglers stood as fixtures on the shore, their hands buried in their coat pockets, and billows of cigarette smoke wafting from their mouths. Occasionally, they'd banter. But their eyes never deviated from their rod tips as they meditated on those slender filaments that connected their souls to the depths of the pond.

If you questioned these men, trout were what they were

seeking, yet as Thoreau once wrote, most fished without understanding what had lured them to Walden in the first place.

Every so often, a fisherman would rebait his hook within a squirming nightcrawler injected with air or a marshmallow that would float above the bottom in view of the trout. Others lovingly tipped their hooks with salmon eggs, meal worms, cheese, minnows, canned corn, or a smorgasbord of these delicacies. Jars of pink, fluorescent-orange, chartreuse, and rainbow-sparkle Powerbait also dotted the shoreline. Trout and fishermen found this product of corporate science irresistible. *These are the days of miracle and wonder...*

A fellow who couldn't afford to fill his wretched vehicle with gas or buy his wife an anniversary present wouldn't hesitate to load his reel with the most-expensive synthetic copolymer line.

A school of trout cruised the shallows and inhaled the offerings. Lines drew tight. The seasoned anglers, attuned to any movement, grabbed their rods. For the less-observant, bobbers bobbed, flags flew, and bells rang. Fishermen gritted teeth, and set the hooks. Rods throbbed with welcome resistance. But gut-hooked trout were little match for eight-pound-test and drags screwed tight. Flopping fish were hauled ashore and clipped to chain stringers.

This was the fate of trout: to be born and reared in a hatchery, to be trucked to paradise, only to be caught, beheaded, and consumed once they'd found it.

The fishermen congratulated each other and compared their catch. But their joy was short-lived. Leaf-peepers in their late twenties or early thirties sprinted toward the sportsmen. New hiking boots and Patagonia coats screamed, *City Folk!*

The nature lovers began to agonize over the flopping trout. One woman, oblivious to water rushing into her Bean boots, waded into the shallows to release the fish. The anglers manhandled her ashore. Beyond the snarl, a fly fisherman in a float tube kept casting.

An argument followed. I trotted down an embankment toward the beach.

"Release those fish!" a young woman shouted at a hulking, pimply-faced teenager. A pair of trout thrashed on the shore beside him. The teenager gritted his teeth in a solemn effort to rebait his hook with a green marshmallow, a pink salmon egg, and kernel of corn. Fish began to rise offshore. He cast toward a swirl, his two-ounce pyramid sinker hitting the water with a thwack!

"Let the fish go, you murderer!"

In spite of his imposing bulk, the fisherman hung his head. One of the activists nudged a brookie back into the water, but by now, sand coated the fish like Shake'n Bake. The trout wriggled, righted itself, and then turned belly-up.

By now, at least a dozen fishermen had joined ranks. This was an event worth watching.

"Go back to your commune, Biffy," shouted a fisherman in a Red Sox jacket.

"Ya, leave the kid alone," a *Yankees Suck* crusader added. "He's not hurting anybody."

"Not hurting anybody?" a protester said. "Trout feel pain. They mourn whenever their loved ones are reeled in."

A fisherman in an Army field coat smirked. "Mourn, do they?"

"You wouldn't sink a hook into your dog and watch it

suffocate, would you?"

"No, but I wouldn't mind watching you suffocate, Granola Boy."

Another fisherman blew cigarette smoke from his nostrils. "See this guy?" he said, pointing to the overgrown teenager. "His name's Derek. He's not right. If I were you, I'd hit the road."

"Are you threatening us?"

"No, I'm warning you. It's sort of like a movie rating. If you think he's scary now, he's even uglier when he gets mad."

"Why won't he let the fish go?"

The fisherman flashed a wry smile. "I'm sorry, ma'am, the boy just likes to watch 'em suffer."

"You're sick..."

"Maybe so. But I'll have a word with him."

The fisherman whispered into Derek's ear. The young man nodded, then waded into the shallows with his fillet knife and began to eviscerate a large trout, its gills still gaping. The onlookers groaned as a sticky concoction dribbled down his sleeves. Fins stiffened. Derek wiped his hands on his pants, removed the head, and smiled. "Look Freddy, the heart's still beating!"

The activists urged me forward. "Do something!"

I approached the fishermen. "Can't you guys tone it down? Things are getting ugly."

"We just heard what went down at the Sportsman's Club," the man in the field jacket said. "Now *that's* ugly."

"Look, be reasonable."

"Are you trying to tell us what to do with our fish?"

Sportsmen could be a pig-headed lot if you rubbed

them the wrong way, but most were sensible. I read the name tag on the army jacket and softened my voice. "I'm a fisherman, too, but with behavior like that, Mr. Pettengill, you won't make many friends."

"I'm not looking for friends, sir, just a little peace and quiet."

An older fisherman, gaunt and eighty-ish, peered through his thick lenses. "They're nothing more than well-dressed terrorists."

"Those chumps puncture our tires," added a ruddy fisherman whose shirt proclaimed that he *was* the man from Nantucket. "They roll boulders down the embankments. Last summer, a scuba diver snipped our lines. It's gotta end."

A young Goth in black jeans and platform shoes with five hundred pierces in her eyebrows, lips and nose kicked over Pettingill's tackle box. "Get hooked on compassion!" she yelled.

Pettengill steamed, his gin-blossomed nose turning pomegranate-red. "Compassion, huh? You look like you just French-kissed a stapler." He waved a broken-back minnow lure inches from her face, three sets of razor-sharp trebles glistening in the sunlight. "Try *this* on for size, sweetie."

Mr. Pettengill turned toward me. "Please sir, get these fruitcakes out of here."

"I'll have a word with them."

I approached the activists. Most were clean-cut and educated-looking.

"It's illegal to harass fishermen, folks."

"But they're breaking a higher law," their spokesman said. "I feel like a Holocaust spectator."

"How often do you venture out to Concord?" I asked.

"We're not talking to you."

The group began to amble away. I stepped ahead of them. "Not so fast. Show me your IDs."

"We want attorneys."

"I need to ask you a few questions."

"What if we refuse?"

"I could haul your butarskies down to the station."

"Fine. Ask away before we change our minds."

"Who are you?"

"Carter Morrow."

"Where are your people from?"

"South Boston, West Roxbury, Arlington, Beacon Hill, the North End. This is my girlfriend, Faith."

The Earth Mother with an impossibly long kinky ponytail forced a smile.

"Are you affiliated with any organizations?" I asked Morrow.

"We belong to *every* humane group," he said, wind tousling his curly hair.

"Where were you this morning?"

"In Boston having coffee and bagels. We drove straight here afterwards." Morrow rummaged through his pockets and waved a receipt. "See? This is from *Finagle a Bagel*. Whole wheat with low-fat veggie chive."

"Have any of you herbivores been to Carlisle lately?"

"I don't think so," Morrow said. The rest of the group indicated that they hadn't, either.

I believed them. These were activists, not terrorists.

"Are you familiar with the Concord Rod and Gun Club?"

Morrow nodded. "We call it 'The Rotten Gun Club'. Why?"

"Because somebody planted hooks in food at the kids' fishing derby today."

The news flustered Morrow. "Now wait a minute, sir. We got upset with those sadists, but that's no crime."

"We'd never hurt a living thing, least of all a child," echoed Faith.

"Do you know Diana Loomis?"

"Of course," Morrow said. "She's the Gandhi of animal rights, and by no means a terrorist."

Just then, I noticed one young man studying my face. "Hey guys," he said in a sarcastic tone, "know who this is? The cop who hammered the Piledriver. He's no game warden."

When the loudmouth noticed my U.S. Fish and Wildlife patch, he smirked. "You've got the eyes of a husky, and the forked tongue of a snake."

"Put a sock in it, dinkweed."

"I have my rights."

I grabbed him by the shirt, but he refused to shut his mouth.

"You're a public servant. A dumb gorilla. Get your damned hands off me, or I'll have your badge."

My face steamed. Somebody had to show this loser who was boss. I deposited him on the wet sand, took off my badge, and waved it in front of his face.

"You want my badge, douche bag? If you want my badge, come and get it." I picked him up, spun him overhead like a big-time wrestler, and tossed him into the drink.

"All right, all right, sir," Morrow said. "You've made your point."

Nervous, but cooperative, the others volunteered business cards. Most worked in software companies, taught, or ran small businesses.

I dismissed the group and headed toward the beach. Multicolored marshmallows and Powerbait bobbed on Walden's surface, a sight that resembled a bowl of Lucky Charms.

The fishermen had fanned out along the shoreline again, tending to their lines. I inspected their catch. Each angler was licensed and had kept no more than his legal limit.

I approached the grizzled old codger who lifted a stringer that held a thrashing eighteen-inch rainbow trout.

"Nice move on that PETA-phile," he said. "The boys and I deducted him five-tenths for his entry, but otherwise, it was a thing of beauty."

I smiled. "Looks like you've had quite a day, Mr. Pettengill."

"Just offshore, there's a hole that I've been fishing for the past twenty seasons. Caught this big boy on my Master-Bait."

"Tell me about this animal rights crowd. Have you noticed anybody unusual?"

"They're all pretty weird, if you ask me."

"Have you seen anybody with red hair or bad skin?"

"No."

"Any new fishermen?"

"No, just us regulars." Pettengill patted a sheathed knife on his belt. "But these days, you can't be careful enough."

Just then, the fly fisherman outfitted with neoprene waders and a float tube sloshed out of the water, and pointed to Thoreau's Cove.

"Excuse me, Officer. See that sloppy chap with the pirate patch? He's been poaching all morning."

I raised my eyebrows.

"Judging from the trips he's made back and forth to his car, the fellow must have stowed five times his legal limit."

"Thanks buddy. I'll check him out."

"No bother. It's our trout he's stealing."

The fisherman he'd fingered sported tangled graying hair, an eye patch, and a two-day-old beard. The fellow looked haggard, as if he'd worked all night. He huddled into his faded Army parka as I asked to see his fishing license.

His name was George Kazanjian, age fifty-four, from the blue-collar town of Maynard. He knew all the facts that authenticated his license.

"How's the fishing?"

"Pretty good," Kazanjian said, lifting his stringer. "I've caught this fifteen-inch rainbow and a brown."

I scanned the surroundings.

"Anything else?"

"No."

"You sure about that?"

"Yup."

I kept staring at him, and he began to fidget.

"Is there a problem, sir?"

"I think you've got a lot more trout stashed away than I see on this stringer. Let's take a little walk."

"Where?"

"To your car."

Kazanjian reeled in his line, and snapped his bait into the water. He stuck his hook into the rod butt, folded his stool, closed his tackle box, and began to lumber up a steep dirt pathway.

"All that's in the car are my wife and kids. They're

bored as hell."

"They ought to get out and enjoy the scenery."

"Fresh air aggravates my wife's asthma. The old lady and I had a little spat. I warn you, she's in an ugly mood."

"I'll take my chances."

Oblivious to her sons' fighting, an overweight woman sporting tired blonde hair with dark roots read a magazine in the passenger seat of a rusty white Buick. Chocolate smeared her sons' faces. Styrofoam coffee cups and fast food wrappers inundated the rear seat. On the back bumper was a *Kiss My Bass* sticker. The windows had begun to fog, and the kids kept rolling them up and down.

Kazanjian's wife glanced up, and the children stopped arguing. I smiled at them. For a moment, George Kazanjian relaxed, until I hit him with the whammy.

"Please open your trunk."

"Huh?"

"I said open your trunk."

The fisherman obeyed. The trunk light had burnt out. I saw no trout, but the scent was unmistakable. I rummaged through tools and blankets.

"I've got nothing to hide," the angler said.

I reached in and lifted a false-bottom. Underneath, two dozen brook, brown, and rainbow trout glistened in the sunshine.

"Nothing to hide? You're twenty-one fish over the limit. You could end up with jail time for this. Why'd you to kill so many fish?"

"I figured I'd take what the government doesn't give us." Deflated as his old radial tires, the fisherman leaned against the back of his car.

"Poaching is poaching," I said.

"Look, you caught me. Do what you have to, just don't rub my nose in it."

"May I see your driver's license?"

As he reached into his pocket for his wallet, a silver bracelet flashed in the sunlight.

"That's an MIA bracelet, right?"

"Yes it is."

Kazanjian rolled up his sleeve. Shrapnel wounds riddled his arms. "My buddy went down in Laos."

"Excuse me," I said, turning away. I peered at my own smooth forearms, then downhill at the pond where the rest of the fishermen stood as still as statues. Sun shimmered on Walden's rippling surface. The maples were brilliant shades of red and orange. The woods began to resonate with wisdom. Voices whispered in the pines. Chickadees and nuthatches became merciful judges. Today, only nature presided.

The poacher's runny-nosed children had resumed punching each other. Kazanjian leaned against the Buick, his body wrung out of real fear decades before.

"After careful consideration, Mr. Kazanjian, I've determined that those fish died of natural causes."

"Huh?"

"You heard me. The stockies in your trunk wouldn't have survived the freeze-up. Just make sure you eat those fish. Here's my card. I'll speak for you if you get stopped on the way home."

"Look Warden, I'm no sympathy case. I'm willing to take the rap."

"You're free to leave."

Kazanjian smiled. "You had every right to take me to the cleaners, but you didn't. I owe you."

"No, buddy, I owe *you*."

One of the boys poked his head out of the window. "Are we under arrest, Daddy?"

"No, little man, I just got a fishing lesson, that's all."

I waved to the family, and then started back down the hill. About half way to the pond, I felt a tap on my shoulder. It was the veteran again, winded by the jog.

"What is it, Mr. Kazanjian?"

"I was thinkin' — it's a shame."

"What's a shame?"

"The Legion of St. Francis messing with kids. Kinda makes you wonder who'll be next, doesn't it?"

"What possessed you to follow me?" I asked.

"Because I figured out who you are and why you're here. Sorry I didn't recognize you at first, Deputy. My wife studies journals like *People Magazine*, and she noticed your eyes. The Staties sent you out here to track down the Legion of St. Francis. We need to talk."

"I'm all ears, George."

"The Legion of St. Francis has been hassling sportsmen for years. We call their leader 'Nature Boy.' He knows how to stalk men, and then fade into the forest."

"Then why have you kept it a secret?"

"I dunno, but after Cooney swallowed that gallbladder, the fishing and hunting fraternity realized that Nature Boy was more than some drunk's hallucination." Kazanjian shielded a cigarette from the breeze and lit it. "Down at the Rod and Gun

Club, we have a bounty for whoever can nail the sucker."

"Leave him to the authorities."

"No offense, Deputy, but this Legion is beyond anything your Department can handle."

"Why?"

"These predators know the woods and the shadows. They disappear like ghosts. They know how to stalk men," Kazanjian said, puffing cigarette smoke into the breeze.

"Is this fact, or legend?"

"A little of both, but you know what I'm talking about."

"What makes you so sure?"

"Not to rip open an old wound, Deputy Sherman, but your brother died a little young, didn't he?"

I didn't reply.

"The boys at the Rod and Gun Club remember. And then there's microfiche..."

I pictured the faded headline, and tried to suppress my trembling.

"This Legion's been around much longer than the police care to admit," Kazanjian continued. "At first, people figured you were just a kid who failed his brother, then choked under big league pressure. But after awhile, a rumor began to circulate that somebody or something drowned him."

"Who?"

"Some kind of phantom, I guess."

"I don't believe in ghosts."

"Maybe you should, Deputy."

I began to shudder like a madman, and managed to clear my throat. "Look, George, I don't believe in folklore."

"Yes you do. You can't explain why, but you know what I'm talking about. By the time us townies were convinced, you were a washed up baseball star who'd faded from our lives. But that's old news. Now, we want to help you."

"Fine. How do you propose to catch Nature Boy?"

Kazanjian shrugged. "If I knew it all, I wouldn't be driving that wreck you saw in the parking lot."

"If you find something, George, call me. I ought to get going."

"You think I'm bullshitting you, Deputy Sherman, but I had a job in Intelligence when I was in Southeast Asia, and I owe you bigtime."

"There were no strings attached when I let you off."

"All the more reason I want to help. Me and my buddies notice everything. That's why we catch so many fish. It's instinct. You have it, too, like your father did."

I smiled. "I used to be jealous of fellows like you, George. They'd always limit-out. If you're onto something, call the hotline."

"The state police and the Feds won't nail these creeps. It'll be a ham-and-egger like me who follows his hunch. When my boys find something, you'll be the first to know. This generation of Staties is far too young to show us vets respect. But not you, Sherman. You're a good man."

"It would help my Department."

"Screw your Department; I want *you* to catch the perpetrator, and so do the other guys. Your dad used to treat us right, and we want him to have the last laugh. To hell with the reward."

"I'm surprised you remember my father."

"Oh, we remember. If you catch the bastards, you'll get promoted."

"That's not what I'm looking for."

"Maybe it'll bring you something that you *are* after. Anyway, I've gotta go. I've got a carload of attitude to deal with, and way too many fish to fry."

George Kazanjian lumbered back up the hill. This one-eyed veteran had lots of insight. Perhaps I'd run into him again someday, but more likely not. People come and go and make promises they can't keep. He meant no harm. Kazanjian was Armenian, and in spite of their mono-brows, all Armenians are good shits. Not that I'm one to generalize...

I cleansed my lungs with cool air. Wind rustled the pines overlooking Thoreau's cove, the place where a man once tried to live his life deliberately two centuries before.

Anybody else would have arrested the poacher, but this time, I'd marched to the beat of my own drummer.


The next day, I got a call from Eldridge Weatherbee.

"Brant, what possessed you to throw the lieutenant governor's nephew into Walden Pond?"

"He's one poor excuse of a nephew," I said. "And besides, he needed the bath."

"Well, I must have apologized to the lieutenant governor fifty times. The department sent her roses. In the future, try a little diplomacy."

"I'll do my best," I lied.

# 13

Life in Concord was about as exciting as an intentional walk.

September passed uneventfully into mid-October, with plenty of physical evidence, but no substantial leads.

Hunting fugitives is nothing like TV episodes during which inside of an hour, a murder, a climax and a stunning conclusion flashes before you. For most marshals, moments of pursuit were precious and few. I had the distinct feeling that such moments were even fewer in suburbia.

I hadn't seen much of Abigail Reed. Whenever we spoke, she acted as if I were to blame for the victims who had tweaked her sense of inner peace.

I decided to give her a call. "Hi stranger," I said. "How about dinner?"

Her tone was controlled and detached. "Not tonight."

"Are you working?"

"No. You and I need a little distance."

"*More* distance?"

"Look Brant, I care for you far more than I should, but you're looking for something else. I can sense it."

"What the hell are you talking about, Abby?"

"You keep your eyes open when we kiss."

"So?"

"Let's just say that this relationship wasn't what I signed up for. I was wrong to date a patient."

"How much time do you need?"

"I'll let you know."

There was a long pause. She wasn't going to say anything else.

"Okay then, whenever you're ready, give me a call."

"I will," she answered in a tone that didn't reassure me.

Given my interest in Paige, I didn't blame Abby. Women were intuitive. I figured that any nice-looking career woman who made it to her mid-thirties without marriage had been burned before. No way could I change that. Yet a hollow feeling overwhelmed me when I went to bed that night.

The next morning was opening day of pheasant hunting season in Massachusetts. Conservative presidential candidate Senator Perry Stillwell would soon arrive at Bolton Flats Wildlife Management Area, and that's just where Eldridge and I were headed on this frosty October morning.

All presidential politicians pretended to be macho sportsmen in recent years, even before a famous vice-president shot his quail hunting buddy in the face. In the 1980s President George Bush caught a bluefish in Kennebunkport and waved it in front of the cameras, blood and slime smearing his seersuckers. Bubba Clinton duck hunted in Arkansas before graduating to more physical pastimes. Michael Dukakis — looking more like Rocky the Squirrel than a warrior — marshaled an armored tank. Even stranger, John Kerry, ketchup-loving liberal, took to the midwest cornfields goose hunting for the cameras.

I was against this whole damned political charade as Senator Stillwell prepared to defend the Commonwealth against squadrons of stocked pheasant.

"What's the senator trying to prove?" I asked, steering down Lancaster Turnpike.

"He's hunting for votes, not birds," Weatherbee replied.

"Massachusetts is an anti-hunting state. Let him go to Maine where it's legal to shoot dogs and hikers."

"Stillwell wants to kill his dinner to prove that he's not just another bureaucrat, Brant. But don't fret; he's a Secret Service protectee and their agents are the size of linebackers."

"That means they'll sink deeper into the mud."

"Like it or not, you've been assigned to help them."

"Any chance that Stillwell won't show?"

"None whatsoever. He'll be flushing birds by the time the cameras start rolling."

A rose-tinted sunrise illuminated the horizon. Cosette craned her neck out the window, her wet tongue flapping in the breeze. Overripe apples clung to the bare branches in the orchards alongside the road.

Eldridge leaned back in the passenger seat and rubbed his belly. "Thanks for breakfast. Those cheese blintzes hit the spot."

"My pleasure."

"You should eat more."

"I don't eat before I hunt."

"Is that what you'll be doing?"

I shrugged, and Weatherbee changed the subject. "How are things with you and the lovely Abigail Reed?"

"Fair to poor."

"Why?"

"The violence has been getting to her."

"That's a shame. Are you sure that blonde hair isn't clouding your mind?"

"No way. I've mastered my emotions."

Weatherbee raised his eyebrows. "I'm sure you have."

The Jeep accelerated down the steep grade that led to Bolton Flats Wildlife Management Area. At the foot of the hill, cornfields, marshland, and scrub stretched out on either side of the road, cradled by the Still River to the east and the Nashua River to the west. Blaze-orange hunting vests stippled the edges of the fields, stark against the brown rushes and pin oaks.

"It looks like a giant Easter egg hunt," Weatherbee observed.

"Except those kiddies are toting automatic shotguns with five-shot magazines," I replied. "When pheasants run the gauntlet, the battalion will start banging away."

"Lovely."

"I used to trail Dad on his game warden rounds. It seems like yesterday that shot was pelting off our Filsons."

"No wonder you're accustomed to getting gunned-down."

"Bolton Flats is a melting-pot of hunters bearing shotguns and personality disorders of all persuasions," I continued. "For the first twenty minutes, Dad would observe the sky-busters blasting their testosterone surge at anything that moved. Then, he'd confiscate weapons and write citations."

"And you call this 'hunting'?"

I nodded. "Upland bird fever. Woodcock, grouse, or pheasant suspended over a set of well-oiled barrels, and the scent of gunpowder in the air."

"I'll take your word for it, pal."

We cruised past management area signs imprinted with partridge and northern pike logos. Mist hovered over the marshland. My ears popped as we descended into the valley.

An assortment of mud-spattered trucks jammed the parking lot. Setters, pointers, spaniels, retrievers, wirehair pointers, and a few unidentifiable brainless barking machines strained at their leads. Sportsmen craned their necks for a glimpse of the candidate. I steered into the lot. Troopers waved me ahead as news crews readied their gear.

"Will you look at this?" Weatherbee said. "Standing room only. I'm heading to Surveillance. Catch you later."

I parked in a field beyond the lot, pulled on a pair of hip boots, and opened the rear door for Cosette, who bounded into the field to relieve herself. Just then, I felt a tap on my shoulder. It was Major Rocky Fallon, a distinguished man in his sixties with a ruddy complexion. I'm not the type to get hung up on rank or titles, but I straightened a bit when I shook his hand. The morning sun accentuated his crow's feet.

"Like most Irishmen, Brant, my parents would roll over their graves if they knew that I'm sticking my neck out for a right-winger like Stillwell. But I need you to keep an eye on him."

I patted my .357. "I'm ready."

Fallon gestured to the Secret Servicemen wearing sunglasses, black suits and wires. "Those poor bastards look like something out of a movie, don't they?"

I nodded. "And they forgot their hip boots."

"You may have to pull yours up even higher once Stillwell starts talking. Meanwhile, let me introduce you to the field director."

Mr. Imler was a humorless CIA drone who recognized me from the Pascucci incident. Flanked by refrigerator-sized agents, he acknowledged me with a nod.

Protesters had begun to assemble in the parking lot. Police kept trying to channel them away from the podium.

Soon, black Lincoln Towncars rolled into the parking area, out of place among the jeeps, trucks, and blazers adorned with dog crates and gun racks. Secret Service agents parted the spectators.

Fallon sighed. "I'm hoping that the dog will lock up on a bird right away so Stillwell can enjoy his photo opportunity and leave without a fuss."

"It may be too late for that, sir."

Fallon patted me on the back and disappeared into the crowd. In the distance, Cosette wove through the cornstalks, sniffing birds. Oak leaves fluttered in a soft breeze. Crows circled overhead, then swooped, cawing in raucous discord. My stomach began to churn, and I called Cosette to heel.

Eldridge tapped me on the shoulder. "You ready?"

"All set. For what, I'm not sure."

"How's the Major holding up?"

"He's stressed."

"Rocky's a good man, but he can't win. We have no authority to protect Stillwell, yet if anything happens, he'll take the heat."

"Pheasants run like hell before they flush."

"Then try to stay with him."

I motioned to the Secret Service. "Won't I be stepping on their toes?"

"Let's find out."

Two agents in dark suits kept scanning the area. Weatherbee introduced himself and flashed his badge, but the agents just stared back. I didn't know much about the Secret Service, but one thing for sure: these fellows had the personality of a bicycle seat.

Ever notice how dogs always seem to embarrass you? Cosette didn't fail to disappoint, depositing a movement that would have rivaled Beethoven's Ninth in D major. She then began to wind her muddy torso between the agents' legs. I leashed the beast and apologized. Afterwards, I offered my help.

"The senator's wearing a wire," one agent said. "Just steer us in the right direction and stay out of our way. That goes for your dog, too."

"The flats are swampy," I replied. "You'll need waders."

The agent sneered at my hip boots and gestured toward a helicopter. "We've got it covered, Deputy."

Both men walked away.

A shiny black Suburban with tinted windows rolled into the parking lot. Secret Service agents cleaved an opening through the crowd. Protesters jeered when Stillwell emerged. A sign showed Stillwell displaying a trophy pronghorn antelope and brandishing a scoped rifle. The caption said: *A Kinder, Gentler America?*

We edged toward the candidate, who stretched his legs and opened an aluminum travel case containing a vintage Purdy. Someone in the crowd blurted, "Arms are for hugging!" The candidate smiled and slipped his hands into a pair of leather shooting gloves.

"Do you always hunt with doubles, Senator?" a reporter asked.

"Of course," he replied. "Side-by-sides are the instruments of gentlemen. Democrats use autoloaders. They squeeze off all five shots before they know what they're shooting at. They'll spend your tax money the same way."

Stillwell assembled his gun. "This old fowling piece was my daddy's and his daddy's."

"Senator, can you speculate why no Democrats are challenging you?"

"Because Democrats can't hit a bull in the butt with a banjo."

Laughter overpowered boos. A band of supporters chanted, "Per-ry! Per-ry! Per-ry!"

An anchorwoman asked, "Senator, don't you feel bad about killing animals?"

Stillwell pursed his lips and nodded. "That's a good question. Shooting pheasant and quail is a way of life, ma'am. In the great state of Nebraska, there's not a red-blooded boy in class on opening day of bird season."

"In the wake of the recent school shootings, is it right to instill this type of violence in our children?"

"Violence? I'd argue that if more parents spent time hunting with their kids, there'd be a lot less violence."

Stillwell's speech was well-rehearsed. "At least my children understand where their food comes from. They've grown up better for it. That's how we live in the heartland. When you raise animals or shoot them to survive, you care about them. Tell that to the folks who buy their meat laid out on white Styrofoam sealed in plastic wrap."

The lieutenant nudged me. "Ain't he slick?"

Protesters began to wave signs.

The hunters cheered, "Save a few for us, Perry!"

The candidate raised his voice, "A mallard in every pot, and two deer hanging in every garage."

Stillwell grinned, flashed a thumbs-up sign, and opened a custom dog crate revealing his sleek liver-and-white Elhew-bred pointer.

Jake leaped from the tailgate and sauntered toward Cosette, who strained at her leash. The pointer attempted to mount her, but she growled and flipped the dog onto his back, pinning him by the scruff of the neck. Jake submitted, nostrils flaring. Red-faced, I burst through the crowd, pried Cosette from the pointer, and hauled her to the Bronco.

Stillwell's dog huddled between his legs and trembled. "It's okay, boy," the senator said. "Let's hope that the voters around here are more receptive."

The crowd erupted in raucous laughter.

Weatherbee shook his head and whispered to me, "You sportsmen are one weird lot."

Jake drew in air, his nose quivering and jowls flapping. Secret Service men formed a protective semicircle around the candidate as he ambled toward the field. Cameramen followed.

Weatherbee said, "Here's where we part ways, Brant. Good luck."

I trailed Stillwell's bodyguards along a path where the gurgling of a brook and the rustling of cornstalks overwhelmed the jeers of protesters. The hunting party paused at a rickety wooden footbridge. A newsman narrated as he filmed.

One bodyguard held a radio. "The fields are clear," a voice crackled.

Another agent handed Stillwell twenty gauge loads.

The senator drew in a breath of fresh air and chambered the rounds. "Find me a bird, Jake!"

The hunting party creaked across the footbridge, but two large agents stepped in front of me. "That's far enough."

"I'm from Special Operations."

"We know who you are, Sherman. We're detaining you."

"Why?"

"Imler's orders."

I argued, but the agents wouldn't budge.

Secret Service men and the news crews crossed the bridge and continued through waist-high goldenrod. Their polished shoes kept sliding on frost heaves. The party disappeared around a bend leading toward the cornfields.

A radio voice announced, "We're heading into the field. Jake's already birdy. This shouldn't take long."

A pause.

"Stillwell's running. Get up there with him, people! Senator, slow down!"

"Where the hell are the birds, Sherman?" an agent asked.

"New England pheasants don't fly, they run."

"Marvelous."

The voice on the radio continued, "Be advised that the dog is ranging ahead of us with the senator in pursuit."

There was another pause, then a firm voice. "The senator is approaching an unauthorized area. Stop him before he reaches the scarecrow."

I bristled. Any scarecrow in this hard-hunted area would have been blown away weeks ago in target practice.

"I don't feel good about that scarecrow," I said to the agent.

"Then discuss it with your therapist, Sherman. In the meantime, back off."

So I did.

The radio announced, "The dog's birdy, but keeps relocating. Stillwell's twenty meters in front of the scarecrow."

My ears began to ring. I darted past the agents and pounded across the footbridge, bushwhacking through brush and tearing though spiderwebs until I tripped. A woolly bear caterpillar clung to sedge in front of my face. Scaly stalks of harvested brussels sprouts plants reared from the ground like serpents.

Through field glasses, I watched Stillwell and his bodyguards in the distance. A ring-necked pheasant was weaving through the stubble.

Muddy to their knees, the agents lagged behind Stillwell. Cameramen struggled to keep pace. Stillwell held his gun at ready position. Jake pointed at the running bird which refused to cooperate. Jake circled the bird, and relocated.

The scarecrow hung from a cross looming high above Stillwell. Straw protruded from torn seams of a red flannel shirt and green overalls. A rumpled hat shaded its brow. I focused on the head, a rotted jack-o-lantern, its face caving in upon itself.

The mouth blubbered like a toothless old man. Empty eye sockets peered at Stillwell. The figure's left arm was lashed upright, waving hello. Its gloved hand waved in the breeze. A glimmer caught my eye. I focused again. A tripwire.

"Stop! Stop!" I screamed, sprinting ahead.

The bodyguards looked back. Camera crews kept filming. A pheasant flushed out of range. Stillwell fired, and missed. He and Jake began to chase the bird. Caught in mid-stride, the pointer buckled. The scarecrow listed. Suddenly, Stillwell sprawled headlong. The scarecrow's arm snapped down, and I hit the ground.

A crimson explosion burst from the heart of the scarecrow, engulfing the field in a flash of light and a roar that echoed through the bottomland. Shrapnel whistled past, striking trees at the edge of the field. Flames plumed and consumed themselves. Smoke rose into the air, and debris rained down. The blast had leveled the hunting party and the reporters. Within seconds, the helicopter hovered over the catastrophe. A crater smoldered where the scarecrow once stood.

Agents stumbled into the field. I dashed toward the fallen. Camera crews kept filming. Stillwell's dog bounded away at breakneck speed, disappearing over a swale. Everybody but Senator Perry Stillwell staggered to his feet.

A bodyguard pressed his folded handkerchief over a gaping wound in Stillwell's neck. Air wheezed back and forth through a tissue flap fluttering over his windpipe. Wounds punctured his face and fluid oozed from his eyes.

"I can't see!" the candidate gurgled.

A Eurostar state police chopper landed, and flight surgeons dashed toward the senator. The medics pried Stillwell's hands from his eyes and taped eye shields in place.

I glassed the perimeter. Dozens of police vehicles had already converged on Lancaster Turnpike.

Weatherbee's voice blasted from the radio: "What the hell's going on?"

"Stillwell's been hit by a mine."

"Is he alive?"

"Barely."

"It's bedlam here in the parking lot! Scour the fields. Hurry."

"Ten-four."

The rest of the Flats seemed clear of humans and land mines. The Nashua River, which bordered the property, was vacant. Ringing in my ears dissipated. Danger had visited the Flats, hit with a vengeance, and passed.

The paramedics were busy back at Point Zero.

"Mobile to Trauma Team. Requesting medical control. We're en route with a fifty seven year old male victim of an explosion. Be advised this is *not* a drill. The victim has a blood pressure of 148/90 respiratory rate of 30 with stridor. He's sustained wounds from..."

"Number four lead buckshot," I interjected, prying the projectiles from a stump.

"Buckshot," the medic repeated. "His injuries include an open tracheal wound, second-degree burns, and penetrating ocular injuries with loss of vitreous fluid. We're running Ringer's wide open. Our ETA is twelve minutes."

The team wrapped Stillwell in a blanket and loaded him crosswise into the helicopter, his muddy boots protruding from the cabin. The chopper lifted and disappeared into the southwestern sky while other medics scurried to treat the less seriously wounded.

Sirens screamed closer. The agent who had detained me brushed past, but avoided eye-contact. He was disheveled and shaking.

I raised my voice. "Like I told you: never trust a scarecrow."

Weatherbee lumbered into the field. "Rocky's turning a scary shade of purple right now."

"It was a homemade device loaded with black powder," I said, "rigged like a land mine. There are shards of a metal canister all over the place. I gave the area a once-over, and it's clear."

"The analysis unit should be here any minute. How bad is Stillwell?"

"Blind, with his wind pipe ripped open. Other than that, he's fine."

The team went to work. The K-9 unit paced over two hundred and fifty acres without locating a suspect. Two hours later, FBI agents swarmed the crime scene.

The lieutenant and I trudged back to the parking lot. Crowds had lined up along the access roads. News helicopters buzzed overhead.

The lieutenant sighed. "I'm not sure who or what the hell we're chasing anymore. This case is weirder than a purple M&M."

Suddenly, I got dizzy and my ears began to ring. I closed my eyes, and saw Timmy's cyanotic lips and nail beds. Marble eyeballs peered upward through the ice.

"What's going on? You look crappy."

I shook it off. "I'm okay."

The disturbing memory faded.

"I swear it's low blood sugar," Weatherbee said. "Next time, try the blintzes."

I regained my equilibrium. "Your insight is amazing, Eldridge."

That night, the explosion played itself out on national television again and again. America couldn't get enough of it. Abigail Reed surprised me with a call. She seemed relieved that I hadn't been blown apart.

"I'd have heard if something happened to you, right?" she asked.

"You're still listed as my primary contact, Abby. You'd have been the first to find out. I can change that if you want."

"No. It's fine."

"I have to admit, this case *is* starting to get old."

"Unfortunately, you'll find plenty on the news to remind you about it."

I watched the explosion repeatedly bloom across my television screen.

"What kind of bomb was it?"

"Lead shot, gun powder, and a canister of compressed gas."

"What kind of gas does that?"

"We don't know."

"This may be way off-base, Brant, but in pharmacology, I learned that some anesthesia gases had been taken off the market because they were explosive."

"Tell me more."

"One agent called cyclopropane was so volatile that it

used to spark with electrocautery. Ask Materials about it."

"You have a knack for this stuff, Abby. You ought to spend more time with the team."

"No thanks. These days, I've been filling my mind with more positive imagery."

"When you're ready, will you give me a call?"

"Maybe when you least expect it," she said.

# 14

I took a long, hot shower at the end of the day. In time, the water washed away specters of torn trachea and punctured eyeballs. But an uneasy sensation began to well up, one I couldn't force down the drain. The crimes *had* escalated since I'd returned to Concord. Was somebody messing with me?

One thing for sure: the perpetrators had won again. But this time, it wasn't my fault; I'd warned the team about Stillwell's foolhardy hunting escapade. Major Fallon could point his finger at inept Washington bureaucrats.

It seemed inconceivable that such a staggering volume of data—finger and tire prints, vehicle registrations, animal rights memberships, over nine hundred social security numbers, electron surface microscopy of buckshot, carpet fibers from

Carlisle, and blood DNA typing—had been fed into computers without a match. This team kept mopping up carnage without doing much to prevent it.

Who were these leaders I'd agreed to assist? Was Major Rocky Fallon merely a scapegoat? Was Lieutenant Eldridge Weatherbee, the Bulldog, a selfless visionary, or an over-the-hill endomorph motivated more by his hunger than his ideals?

Now that Senator Stillwell had fallen, the FBI had smothered the case. Busloads of Feds were pouring onto the crime scene, shuffling through fallen leaves, investigating places they knew nothing about. The odds of collaring a terrorist myself were now slim.

Business had begun to boom in the area. At the epicenter of the crimes, Concord had become hallowed ground to those concerned with animal rights. Busloads of pilgrims were spilling onto the streets. Bistros kept selling out of veggie wraps. Carvers in the Decoy Shop and painters in the Walden Gallery worked overtime in an effort to satisfy the burgeoning market.

Tourists in Nature Boy sweatshirts clogged the back roads and trampled the shores of Walden Pond, gathering pebbles, mussel shells, fallen leaves, or any other memento they could sneak out. Park rangers cited a New Jersey couple for pilfering stones from three hundred-year-old walls at Merriam's Corner. Historic landmarks such as the Author's Ridge Cemetery, the Buttrick Manse, Emerson's Birthplace, the Alcott Orchard House, and the Concord Museum, for the first time in their existences had been forced to turn people away. There was nary a Halloween pumpkin, a gourd, nor an ear of Indian corn left at Verrill's or Palumbro's farmstands.

I finished showering and listened to my messages. The first was a call from Paige Sagoff. Instant palpitations.

"Hello Brant. I'm back," the message said. "Having you at the party would be a wonderful welcome-home present."

I gulped. Quite an invitation. Being rich obviously had its perks—you tour European estates for two months, and then get welcome-home presents.

I decided to forget the Legion of St. Francis for awhile. 'Twas time to test my fortune with the beauty from Monument Street. Why should I feel guilty about it? Abigail Reed had been the one who had asked for this hiatus in our relationship. I knew the lieutenant wouldn't be pleased; but what made him the world's expert on women?

I slept that night with great expectations for the weekend.


The full moon illuminated Monument Street that chilly Saturday night. I steered into the Sagoff estate. Silver, black, and white Mercedes, Beemers, and imported sport utility vehicles crammed the driveways. Stars glimmered against a cloudless sky. The terraces were vacant, but silhouettes bobbed behind frosted window panes.

I peered into a tuxedo-filled ballroom. A constellation of diamond necklaces glittered against a firmament of black gowns. I smoothed my hair and straightened my tie.

At the door, a butler took my coat. Guests waltzed to a quartet's music. I knew no waltzes—or polkas, tangos, or jitterbugs for that matter—and edged outside of the crowd. In the center of the room, a colossal ice sculptured horse strode across a pasture of white roses and calla lilies, light refracting through its transparent musculature.

The Hunter's Moon celebration was a black-tie-only affair. I remembered Thoreau's admonition: *Be suspect of any endeavor that requires you to wear different clothes.* Nevertheless, I was grateful that my resuscitated old tux still fit, with only a two or three moth holes to show for its years confined to the back of my closet. A monotonous sea of black and white rippled before me, revealing no blonde hair. Just then, I felt a tap on my shoulder. It was Mr. Wainright, manager of Artemis Furs. I'd have bet my life that he was a Liza Minnelli groupie.

"It's a pleasure to see you again, Deputy Sherman."

"Thanks, Mr. Wainright."

"Please, call me Gibbs."

"By all means."

"It's cold out tonight. It seems like yesterday that you and Paige were shooting in the heat of summer. I heard that your visit was a productive one."

"I suppose it was."

"Those activists certainly turned the election around in a hurry, didn't they, Deputy?"

I looked away.

"I'm sorry. That was a thoughtless comment," Wainwright said. "I suggest you forget your troubles this evening."

"I'll do my best."

"I must confess this Legion of St. Francis investigation has me riveted. Makes what I do for a living seem superficial."

"There's virtue in everything, Gibbs."

A server presented an hors d'oeuvres tray and described

the offerings: partridge in black grape sauce *a la vigneronne*, native green wing teal in port wine marinade, *canard sauvage* with pecan and oyster stuffing, poached goose breast with garlic creme sauce, and medallions of quail wrapped in bacon.

I helped myself. The appetizers had a delicate texture and a subtle gamey taste. Wainright and I continued to intercept the servers at every opportunity.

Wainright chased an appetizer with a swallow of his martini. "Kip Pearson says you're as good a shot as he's ever seen. Most rich fellows are patsies. Unlike Paige's other suitors, Kip and I like you."

"What makes you so sure that I'm a suitor?"

"We know. But don't be embarrassed. It would be tough for any man to resist Paige, don't you think?"

I shrugged.

"Don't worry, you're in good hands. Enjoy yourself and try to relax."

"Thanks. By the way, where is she?"

Wainright motioned to the dance floor. "Somewhere in there." We peered into the crowd. "Paige is hard to approach at gatherings like this. She knocks herself out for her guests. If they fail to rave about her parties, she takes it hard."

"Life is rough, I guess."

"Not as rough as dealing with a disappointed Paige Sagoff, so eat, drink, and pretend you're enjoying yourself."

"You're telling me to enable her?"

"Guilty as charged. Fantasy is the true currency of the wealthy, Deputy. It would behoove you to get used to the idea if you want to know the lady better. Follow me."

Wainright led me toward a cluster of middle-aged men

distinguished by designer glasses and smooth tans. The nucleus of the gathering was the achingly-beautiful Paige Sagoff. She wore a brilliant diamond necklace. A shimmering waterfall of white-blonde hair contrasted with a sleek emerald velvet gown. I kept trying to convince myself that she wasn't all that gorgeous. It didn't work. A couple of notches lower on the food chain would have suited me fine. Paige brightened when she noticed me, and broke free of her admirers.

Paige brushed a quick kiss just past my lips. I held my breath as her hair caressed my face. She took me by the hand and led me toward the guests.

"Ladies and gentlemen, I'd like to introduce you to my friend, Brant Sherman," Paige announced. The guests nodded politely.

She cleared her voice. "You may remember Brant from the news: *Deputy Marshal* Brant Sherman, the man who stood in the line-of-fire protecting Senator Perry Stillwell."

Now the guests were interested! Businessmen gulped the last of their drinks. The crowd hovered, drawing closer.

For the first time that evening, men stopped gawking at Paige. I fielded questions about the Stillwell bombing and what it was like to be hit by gunfire. At first, I didn't mind; those wealthy buffoons would never experience a gunshot wound unless self-inflicted as a result of a stock market crash.

For the next half hour, I recounted details of the Stillwell blast, which kept the audience spellbound. Even the quartet stopped playing.

When I paused for a drink, a crisp CEO charged forward with a business card in hand. "Please call me," she said. "You'd be a spectacular motivational speaker."

Another alpha-woman waved a copy of the *Boston Tribune* picturing me at the Stillwell scene. "Would you mind signing this for my son?" she said. "A personal note would be great. His name's Kennedy."

"First or last?"

"Kennedy's his first name. He wants to head the CIA when he grows up."

"I'm glad he's not setting his sights too high, ma'am."

The crowd began to suck me dry. I looked toward Paige and motioned to the door. I followed her to the refuge of the parlor. But the curious kept filtering in.

"We need a few moments alone, Paige. It's been awhile..."

"Oh, there's plenty of time for that. I've got important friends who want meet you. We can't disappoint them."

"I never intended to be the newest addition to *Who's Who in Law Enforcement*."

She dismissed me with a wave of her hand. "Don't be modest. I have to stick to my agenda."

"Agenda?"

Paige nudged me toward a jovial cluster of cigar smokers. I shook more hands. For tonight at least, these socialites were my back-slapping buddies. One thing that we didn't share was a seven-figure salary.

She continued to parade me before politicians, company presidents, lawyers, and dignitaries.

"Brant," Paige said, "I've got to make the rounds. My friends are enthralled by your stories. Keep it up. I'll be right back."

Before I could protest, she disappeared into the crowd. Gentlemen trailed her like puppies. The music resumed.

I was famished. Over the next two hours, I consumed the equivalent of a flock of ducks, a gaggle of geese, and a covey of quail. Conversations about mutual funds and places I'd never visit in my lifetime were beginning to bore me. Meanwhile, Paige engaged a bevy of pencil-necked geeks who kept supplying her with drinks and hors d'oeuvres.

After downing pomegranate and persimmon tarts, I realized that there would be no intimate dance with Paige Sagoff. A chortling and guffawing circle of elite besieged Paige all evening.

Faces like hers launch ships and make generations of men stupid, I thought. I started toward Paige, but hesitated. No doubt about it, she was a knockout, but I would not embarrass myself.

For the next hour, I forced myself to mingle, dodging questions about eye color, and discussing the economy with venture capitalists whose secretaries' bonuses were ten times my salary. I found myself staring out of the window at the Hunter's Moon. This party was even more isolating than deep forests or dark recesses of the 'hood. I headed toward the bar and ordered a Black Russian, which reacted with the fowl and tarts in my stomach. Soon, I found myself yawning.

Love affairs with celebrities always end in disaster. Even tabloids say so. And Paige was a quintessential celebrity.

Two hours later, Gibbs Wainright and Malcolm 'Kip' Pearson, the shooting guide, emerged, feeling good and still drinking. "Have you found Paige, yet, Deputy Sherman?"

"Oh, I found her...for about five minutes."

Pearson chuckled. "That's about four minutes longer than most. Consider yourself honored."

"Honored?"

"Paige is an elusive trophy," Kip Pearson said. "I doubt that you've had much trouble with women, but Miss Paige is in a class of her own. Be patient."

"There's much more to life than riding the emotional whims of a *prima donna*."

"Actually, Paige is quite fond of you."

"I'm sure she is."

"Steady on. Patience, my boy."

"I'm sorry, but I'm running low on it right now. Thanks for lobbying for me. Tell Paige she can call me if she finds the time."

I grabbed my overcoat and made a beeline for the Jeep. At the end of the driveway, I peered down Monument Street in the direction of Abigail Reed's carriage house. I pictured Abby, scurrying about the emergency room on her graveyard shift.

At the Sagoff estate, silhouettes mingled behind the frosted glass in the glow of the ballroom.

I thought about both women on my lonely drive home, and for a fleeting moment thought about looking up Mary Beth Cahill.

As two prophets, Eldridge Weatherbee and Mick Jagger, once implied: sometimes what you want and what you need are two different things.

# 15

*Three weeks later, mid-November:*

"Damn!" I yelled, recoiling as the rat trap in the attic snapped, narrowly missing my fingers. The trap flew into the air, spattering chunks of peanut butter and cheese onto my face.

It was five a.m., and the patter of little feet and gnawing overhead had kept me awake all night. Cosette had spent the evening growling at the ceiling.

As the temperature dropped, woodland critters sought the warmth of my cozy cabin. But benevolent visitors like chipmunks weren't nocturnal. Large droppings meant Norway rats. Big ugly Coumadin-resistant rats. Rats that squealed and bit. Rodents as aggressive and sneaky as criminals. There was danger in their jaws, sharp teeth and calculating eyes. In short, the slithering bastards gave me the creeps.

The attic tingled with rat energy. By the light of a single dim bulb, I finally managed to set the less-than-perfect mousetrap without amputating my digits. I slid the monstrosity toward a hole chewed in the insulation and crossed my fingers.

I descended the ladder back into the bright light of the cabin. Too restless to sleep, I took a predawn drive and parked on Heath's Bridge overlooking the Sudbury River. Over the past few weeks, I'd done a great deal of thinking on that bridge. Ducks began to fly from the backwaters, the same coves which we'd hunted years before. It was only eighteen degrees. Slow heavy river water had begun to make ice. A molten sunrise oozed onto the anvil of a horizon.

My family had fished and hunted this fringe of civilization when waders were rubber, not neoprene, when only pirates and women wore earrings, and when folks drove off-road vehicles off the road. Trapping paid for my first catcher's mitt and my dirt bike.

Babe Ruth once owned a farm on the Sudbury River two miles upstream. From his own heated duck blind, the "Colossus of Clout" bagged mallards in the off season.

Our trap lines yielded muskrat, raccoon, and an occasional mink, which we sold to Boston furriers. We'd catch the animals in a Connibear body-hold spring trap with rectangular jaws and a trigger in the center. A muskrat swimming along its trail would trip the trigger, and metal jaws would snap shut. Instant death.

One time, I discovered a chewed-off raccoon paw fixed in the jaws of a body trap. Over the years, I had managed to steel myself to killing, but the memory of that little extremity still bothered me.

Nobody around here trapped anymore. Or so I thought.

As the sun reflected off the glossy plane of the water, I watched dawn unfold. Suddenly, I noticed something floating upriver and grabbed my binoculars.

It was a hunter's sneak boat, a low profile sculling craft camouflaged with reeds. As the boat drifted closer, I noticed a man clad in waders, arm's length gloves, and a coonskin cap lying face down on the deck, cheek to cheek with dead raccoons and muskrats. I focused. His scruffy old face was a half-frozen shade of blue. As the craft drifted closer, I noticed something even more gruesome: the trapper's leg had been severed, a suspender serving as a makeshift tourniquet above his knee. The bones of his lower leg glistened in the morning light.

My pulse quadrupled as I activated the task force.


Hawthorne Hospital's ER was already bustling. A Bedford ambulance crew transported a patient on a backboard. In adjacent rooms, children with croupy coughs clung to their weary parents. An asthmatic was puffing from some sort of vaporizer. Meanwhile, the "walking well" with sore throats and splinters fidgeted in the waiting room.

Nurses hovered over another stretcher bearing a pale, sweaty patient with irregular blips on his heart monitor. It didn't take a cardiologist to diagnose this heart attack.

Sure enough, Abigail Reed darted into the cubicle.

"Give him one hundred and sixty milligrams of aspirin, a bolus of 5000 units of heparin, and I'll push the t-PA," she said.

She injected the drug. Within minutes, the man's color improved, and he gripped her hand in thanks. Too busy to notice me, Abby headed to the next patient.

A sobbing elderly woman flanked by her children exited the trauma room. Inside, the unconscious trapper was packed in blankets and rigged to monitors. I approached the lieutenant who was watching from a stool in the corner.

"What happened to the old man, Eldridge?"

"I'm not sure. What kind of water craft was he in?"

"A sneak boat. They look like floating caskets."

"For the ducks or the hunters?"

"Supposedly, for the ducks."

"Well, that's not how it turned out for this poor chap. His name's Warren Arbogast, an old riverman."

I stared at his bloated, unshaven face.

"The man's leg was amputated," Weatherbee continued. "Sliced clean through his tibia and uvula."

"You man 'fibula'?"

"Whatever. Step up to the stretcher."

I edged closer. The stump was wrapped in gauze. Blotches of maroon on the dressing faded to concentric shades of crimson, pink, and plasma-yellow. Hemostats clamped something deep within the muscle.

Weatherbee removed a wallet and hunting license from an evidence bag. The soggy license began to tear as he unfolded it. State and federal duck stamps had been affixed to the front. Ink from the trapper's signature had run. We fit the fragments together.

"Mr. Arbogast lives in Conantum, a half mile upstream. He was half-frozen by the time you discovered him," Weatherbee explained. "He was trapping on refuge land."

"Successfully, I may add."

"How do you explain the leg?"

"I'm not sure, but since great whites are scarce around here," I said, "we know where the finger points."

Weatherbee nodded. "Once he warms up, we may get an opportunity to question him."

I thumbed through sopping dollar bills, a Ducks Unlimited membership card, and a driver's license. I stared at the picture, and then at the victim.

"What do you suppose happened?" Weatherbee asked.

"Same thing Arbogast did to the muskrats."

Weatherbee nudged his chin at the mangled extremity. "I've never seen a trap do *that*."

Abigail Reed strode into the room.

"Hi, Abby."

"Looks like you fellows are up to your old tricks," she said in a curt tone. "Anyway, I have to check the wound."

Abby tied on a surgical mask and snapped on a pair of sterile gloves. "Gather round, guys."

The lieutenant and I did as we were told. Weatherbee motioned a state lab photographer forward as Dr. Reed uncoiled the gauze, exposing the stump. The skin resembled joke-store rubber. Muscle glistened. Angled hemostats clamped a transected artery reminiscent of penne macaroni. The leg was a neatly-sliced rib eye steak.

"What do you suppose took the leg off, Abby?" the lieutenant asked.

"A rasping blade."

"Are there any other injuries?"

"None to speak of."

"People don't sit back and let someone hack their leg off, do they?"

"True enough," Abigail said, "but a person might hold still if he had to amputate his own leg, right? The edges are as crisp as osteotomies, the cuts that orthopedic surgeons make. That makeshift tourniquet fashioned from wader suspenders saved his life. This was an intentional amputation. Frighteningly, unless a drug shows up in Mr. Arbogast's tox screen, he was lucid throughout the whole procedure. Since there's no sign of a struggle, he must have done the deed himself."

"Are you saying what I think you are?"

Abigail nodded. "Question him while you can."

Abigail got an overhead page. She covered the wound, snapped her gloves into a waste can, and grabbed the phone.

"My patient is ready for the OR," she said. "He's received four units of O negative, Kefzol, and tetanus prophylaxis. I've debrided the wound and clamped the popliteal artery just below his knee. Hurry, before we lose the rest of him."

Eldridge and I observed Abby from a distance. She moved with the confidence of someone in her own environment. In her scrubs, Abby's disciplined physique was harder than Paige Sagoff's. A wistful sensation overcame me. *This* was a real woman.

I edged closer. "Can Mr. Arbogast answer questions?"

"He's hypothermic, but you can try."

Just then, a nurse grabbed Abigail by the arm. "Febrile seizure in room three." Abby darted from the trauma room.

Weatherbee nudged me toward the victim. "Go ahead. I'll hang back here."

Arbogast's face was bloated and waxen. I stared. Suddenly, the face blurred and became the pale apparition of the child beneath the ice. Marble-white eyeballs glowered. I blinked. The room whirled, and there was ringing in my ears. I braced myself on the stretcher and held tight.

*If you're too afraid to save me, do it for yourself.*

Suddenly, I visualized the crime scene: the trapper shuffling through the marsh, approaching his set, when all at once, the water churned, and the jaws of a massive bear trap sank into his leg like an alligator. Vapor spewed from his mouth as the marsh whirled around him — a vertiginous tumult of starry indigo sky, dying sunset, cattails, fleeing ducks, and agitated water. As he buckled, I sensed cruel jaws biting deep into his leg and the sickening crunch of fracturing bone.

Then I pictured a bow saw in the trapper's hand as darkness began to swallow the marsh. I could feel the trapper's terror, his conflict, as he cinched the makeshift tourniquet around his thigh. The blade moved back and forth, tentatively at first, metal teeth rasping through his rubber waders parting the skin, warm calf muscles dividing like scrambled eggs, shredded tissue hot on his hand, sawteeth grating bone so that his marrow reverberated, until mercifully, the lower leg angulated and collapsed.

Warren Arbogast teetered into the dark water, and like a child pulling a loose tooth, ripped what little tissue connected him to the ponderous trap. He struggled through the shallows, icy edges cutting into his rib cage, until he collapsed over the gunwales of his sneakboat, cheek to cheek with sneering raccoons on the deck.

A stark silvery moon cast its judgment on Warren Arbogast. And so did a giggling lunatic watching from Heath's Bridge.

Weatherbee jarred me from my trance with a shake of my arm. "What's going on, buddy?"

I shook off the cold. Bright lights in the room reappeared, and the buzzing trailed off.

"The last thing we need around here is another patient," a nurse said. "Are you all right?"

"I'm fine," I said, regaining my equilibrium. I edged toward the stretcher. EKG monitors beeped and intravenous lines dripped in the background.

"Mr. Arbogast, can you hear us?" I whispered.

He didn't respond. I cupped my hand over the trapper's ear.

"Open your eyes, sir. You're in the hospital. The police are here."

A quarter moon of eyeball rose from beneath the horizon of a lid.

The puffy eyelids flickered.

"We're here to help. Do you understand?"

The eyes twitched again.

"Who did this to you?"

A faint voice trickled from his larynx. I gently lifted his oxygen mask.

"Who did it?"

Garbled words spilled forth. I perceived the sound and understood.

"Anti's," I repeated. "He said 'anti's.' "

"What's an anti?"

"Somebody opposed to hunting and trapping." I turned back toward the victim. "Did you see anybody, Mr. Arbogast? Anybody at all?"

The trapper indicated that he hadn't.

My eyes rested on the bloody stump.

Eldridge spoke up. "We need to review the videotape of last week's wildlife hearing and interview everybody who attended it. We need to interview their mothers and their fathers, their uncles and aunts, and third cousins twice-removed. I mean everybody."

"And we need to head out to the Sudbury River," I added. "There's a leg out there that may point us in the right direction."

"I can hardly wait," Weatherbee said.

We left the trauma room. I paused in the main emergency room where Abigail Reed was listening to the chest of a croupy child. As the boy breathed in and out, Abigail caught sight of me and smiled faintly.

Eldridge slapped me on the back as we stepped through the automatic doors into the crisp morning.


The lieutenant and I motored downstream in a bass boat powered by a hog of a 225 four-stroke Mercury. Posing as our figurehead in the bow, Cosette sniffed the air. I negotiated the river while Weatherbee hunched in his swivel seat, huddling in his state police windbreaker. His bulbous scarlet nose clashed with his orange life preserver.

"I hate water," he whined above the engine.

By the time we reached the river near Heath's Bridge, divers in dry suits had begun to search. Bobbing on the surface, they resembled playful seals. Buoys marked their pattern. Boston Whalers idled nearby. One boat kept crisscrossing the river, trolling a torpedo-shaped device called a Side-Scan Sonar Unit. A lazy wake trailed behind.

The team was fortunate; it was a bright, calm day. The temperature had reached an almost-bearable thirty degrees. Dozens of state police vehicles and news crews had assembled on Heath's Bridge Road. Hip-booted cadets searched the riverbanks.

A swirl erupted in front of the bass boat, and Cosette leaned toward it.

"What the hell was that?" Weatherbee asked.

"A tiger muskie," I replied.

Eldridge split a Skybar in half, and as usual, saved the white filling for himself. Suddenly, the dog began to snort, and her jowls quivered.

"Atta girl," I said. "Hunt 'em up."

I steered toward an opening that led to the marsh and raised my voice above the outboard. "I'd set my traps in there," I said, pointing to muskrat lodges. "The place has always been crawling with rats."

"Rats?"

"*Musk*rats. Trappers' main quarry."

"Anybody who'd voluntarily head into this swamp ought to have his head examined," said Weatherbee.

Just then, I noticed some cracked ice. Cosette's snout pointed in the same direction.

"What is it?"

"A trail. Let's check it out."

The boat's hull clattered against the skim ice. I killed the engine and pressed the automatic tilt button. Weeds garnished the lower unit. I poled the vessel another twenty yards until the vessel grounded.

"What now, Gilligan?" the lieutenant asked.

"We take to the water."

"No way."

"You're the Bullfrog, for crissakes."

"It's 'Bulldog.' And Bulldogs don't swim."

I presented the lieutenant with a pair of chest waders. "You don't have to swim."

"I've got a bum knee. You go. Getting muddy is why we hired you."

"Okay then. You stay on *terra firma*."

I stepped into my old camo waders and wriggled my toes. The waders still fit, reminiscent of pass-shooting ducks in the flooded backwater. I pointed into the shallows. "See those branches? They mark the trapper's sets."

"Just find the damned leg so we can get the hell out of here."

I lowered myself into the waist-deep water. Chewed cattail tubers and husks floated about me. Muskrat lodges rose above the marsh. Using an oar as a wading staff, I groped along the mucky bottom, towing the boat by the painter.

"When the bow runs up on the ice, rock your weight forward so the hull cracks through," I said to Weatherbee.

"That shouldn't be a problem."

"I'm serious. I want the vessel nearby in case I get stuck."

As I shuffled forward, I encountered branches driven into the mud. Marauding "do-gooders" used to locate traps and heave them into the depths. Trappers had to be cunning, especially poachers. Branches with whittle marks just above the water line were Arbogast's subtle indicators.

Crunching forward through the skim ice with a wading stick, I shuffled along a drop-off, toward an alder branch, and gaffed the trap's chain. Water churned as I lifted. The weight of a muskrat resisted. The river gave birth to a stillborn carcass clutched by steely forceps. The animal's lips had rolled back in a permanent grimace. I squeezed the springs, and the muskrat plopped onto the ice.

As I studied the carcass, I hoped that someday my own demise would be as quick, as painless, and as unsuspecting as this creature's death.

I trudged toward a channel where the water nearly crested my waders. Weatherbee tightened his life jacket and stared from the boat. I shuffled onward until something caught my foot. I tried to pry myself loose. A dead muskrat and a water-logged pack basket floated beside me.

"Oh, Lieutenant," I called, "I think I'm onto something — or something's onto me. Radio the boys would you?"

"What'd you find?"

"I don't know, but I'm up to my ass in quicksand."

I tapped my oar along the bottom. Something metallic clanked against it. "I've just discovered the wreck of the Titanic. Unfortunately, I'm tangled in it."

Cosette whined.

Eldridge fidgeted on the deck. "What am I supposed to do?"

"Hop in. Fast."

"Can't your dog do something?"

"She retrieves ducks, not humans. Now hurry!"

Weatherbee rolled his eyes, kicked off his shoes, sucked in his gut, and pulled up the waders. "I feel like I'm inside a giant condom," he said.

I couldn't help myself, "And you look like it, too. Hurry up, Trojan Man!"

Weatherbee splashed into the water and clung to the boat. He shuffled through the muck until he reached me.

I braced myself against Eldridge and flexed against a ponderous resistance — one tough leg raise. Turgid water heaved upward. I dislodged my foot. A mass appeared in the depths. We reached underwater, wet to our armpits, and hauled a huge chain with links the diameter of a fist.

Water churned as we lifted. The object grew large — a lower leg held fast in the jaws of a bear trap, which must have weighed a hundred pounds. No way could any man have wrestled his way out, much less an aged trapper. Muscle protruded from the end of the mottled extremity like the stuffing of a Polish sausage. Crayfish clung to the raw tissue. We released the chain, and the leg disappeared.

Weatherbee's jaw went slack. Just then, I noticed the alder branch with ripped duct tape and a laser-printed message, *Chew your leg out of this one!* The note confirmed Mr. Arbogast's hideous choice in the marsh the night before. A great blue heron squawked derisively overhead.

I caught the attention of the crew. Within minutes, the divers splashed into the shallows.

"You'll need at least four men and a torch to free the trap," I explained. "It's anchored to a mooring."

Weatherbee called out to Sergeant Pfleuger in one of the boats. He pointed into the swamp. "See that stick? It's wrapped with duct tape. And there's a note for Documents."

Pfleuger focused her binoculars. "Got it, Lieutenant."

I boosted Weatherbee into the bass boat and backed it into the main river while the rest of the state police task force splashed into the shallows.

The lieutenant stripped off his waders. He was sweating. "I should be cultivating Dill's Atlantic Giants and gorging on roast beef at the Hungry Duffer."

"You'd be bored in no time."

The lieutenant watched the divers hoist the waxen extremity onto a raft.

"I'd be better off bored. Now get me out of here."

Early that afternoon at the state police headquarters, we basked in the warmth of radiators which Weatherbee had cranked to full-blast. In addition to Arbogast's lower leg, the team had recovered a bow saw that had been taped to the alder pole and fibers adherent to the tape. Electron microscopy revealed Persian cat hair and tri-lobed synthetic scarlet carpet filaments that matched those found in Carlisle. The note had been printed with a Brother HL-1440 on cotton fiber Boise Cascade paper. The lieutenant ran a search of local computer stores and libraries.

"Imagine what Mr. Arbogast's night was like out there in the marsh," I said.

Weatherbee hunkered over his steaming coffee mug. "I'd rather not. One thing we know: our perp has tacky taste in carpet. Must be a child of the seventies."

"We ought to monitor the mall for *Brady Bunch* or

*Frampton Comes Alive* DVD rentals."

"Actually, Brant, that's not such a bad idea."

"Can we figure out where the bow saw was purchased?"

The lieutenant shrugged. "It could have been anywhere. In fact, I noticed one at the Real Value Hardware shop last week. But that model had no flesh on it."

"What do you make of the cat hair?"

"Maybe the perp works with animals or is a kitty fanatic."

My cell phone rang. It was Paige Sagoff. "Hello Brant. I'm disappointed that I haven't heard from you."

An uncomfortable pause followed.

"I'm still not sure why we've ended up so distant," Paige added.

"Me neither," I said, turning away from the lieutenant. I cupped my hands over the phone. "Sorry I left your party without a thank-you. That was poor form."

Shamelessly eavesdropping, Weatherbee leaned back in his chair, smiled, and folded his hands behind his head. Though my heart was pattering, I knew this would be a restrained conversation.

"What a pity our egos spoiled the evening," Paige continued. "Anyway, this is business. I need your help."

"Sure. What's up?"

"Somebody's stalking me, Brant."

I tried to suppress my anxiety. "Who's stalking you?"

"I'm not sure..."

"Has anybody been threatening Artemis Furs?"

"No."

"Not to pry, but do you have any unstable boyfriends?"

I cringed, awaiting her reply.

"Of course not."

"Have there been prowlers at the estate?"

"If there were, Kip Pearson would have made short work of them," she said. "But I've been hearing stirring at night. And last week at Taste of Tuscany, strangers kept staring at me."

"Can you describe them?"

"Not really. But I know I'm being stalked."

"It's not unusual that people notice you, is it, Paige?"

Weatherbee chuckled. I wished I could take back the comment. The "people" I was referring to meant men. I could picture Paige window-shopping in Concord Center, graying fathers whiplashing for a glimpse of her.

"Will you help me or not?"

"Of course," I said.

Her voice relaxed. "If you could stop by, it would mean a lot."

"Count on it. Meanwhile, let me run it by Lieutenant Weatherbee."

"Something evil has trailed you back to Concord, Brant. At least that's what the locals are saying."

"Is that a fact?"

"Yes. I was at a reception for the Concord Museum today. People claim that you're haunted."

"And what do you think?"

"I'm not superstitious," she said, "but I'm afraid."

"Until I get to the estate, stay with Malcolm Pearson."

My stomach churned, perhaps out of longing for Paige, jealousy, or true fear. But I decided to "play it cool" in front of the lieutenant.

After the phone call, Weatherbee smirked. "Mastered

your emotions, huh Brant? What's her business with you?"

"Someone's stalking her."

"Like you said, who wouldn't?"

"This is for real, Eldridge."

"Nobody's sleeping well these days. We don't have the resources to chase flimsy leads."

"I disagree. It takes a lot to scare Paige Sagoff."

"All women worry."

"Her business puts her at risk."

"A fur store seems far too obvious a target."

"Senator Stillwell was obvious, and now he's a wheezing squeezebox. And today I found a frozen amputee beneath my favorite bridge. I'm heading to the Sagoff estate."

Weatherbee held up his hand. "Whoa there, big boy. No, you're not. And that's an order."

"Why?"

"You don't need that socialite inside your head."

"I'm fine, Eldridge."

"You have other plans."

"What plans?"

"Rocky and I need you to scout veterinary hospitals."

"What about Paige? Don't I have a responsibility to protect her?"

"No. You're the one who made her paranoid in the first place." He tossed me a dossier. "Here's a list of every animal care clinic in a twenty-five mile radius and electron microscopy of every breed of cat fur. Start studying."

"But Eldridge..."

"I mean it, Brant, you're *not* going to the estate this afternoon, and that's final."

As I got up, my face was steaming. Weatherbee fired a candy bar at my chest, and I caught it one-handed.

"Bribery, Lieutenant?"

"No—combat pay, Deputy. Call me tomorrow after you're done. In the meantime, give your buddy Diana Loomis a call. I just learned that she debated none other than Mr. Warren Arbogast at the trapper's hearing. Made him look pretty bad."

"He looks even worse now."

"Ask her for a list of cat adoptions. Enjoy the ride, Brant. And stay away from purple M & M's."

All in the name of self-control, I'd missed a golden opportunity to become Paige's savior. Instead, as Eldridge Weatherbee had ordered, I phoned Diana Loomis, who had been remarkably tight-lipped about the crimes. I got right to the point.

"You've heard about Warren Arbogast?"

"Of course," Diana replied.

"Wasn't it you who was arguing with Mr. Arbogast at the trapper's hearing?"

"It wasn't much of an argument."

"You have to admit, the timing is uncanny."

"Look, I crushed those fools with words, not a bear trap. I've already told you that I don't deal in violence, but feel free to investigate me."

"You can't name a single suspect, Diana?"

"I'm sorry, but I'm far too busy to worry about your case. I have to coordinate my legions to thwart the Thanksgiving deer hunt on Plum Island."

"Did you say 'legions'?"

"It's a figure of speech. Don't associate me with those terrorists. Our donations are already down by half this year."

"We monitored the trapper's hearing the other night. Would you mind reviewing the footage?"

"I'd rather not."

"C'mon Diana, throw us a line."

"Fine, where shall I report?"

"Eldridge Weatherbee's office in the state police headquarters. We'll also need documentation of all cat adoptions within the past six months."

Diana Loomis let out an exasperated sigh. "Do you want to know a chilling statistic? One of our national polls actually showed a sixty-five percent approval rating for what happened to Dr. Fenwick. The public seems to be rooting for the Indians instead of you cowboys."

I gulped.

"Keep that in mind before you go risking your life, Deputy. Meanwhile, for friendship's sake, I'll do what I can."

# 16

The next morning, I wasn't the least bit motivated to investigate veterinary hospitals. I had a message from Dr. Fenwick to meet him at Massachusetts Medical Center. That's just what I decided to do. As I drove, I kept thinking about the public rooting for the Legion of St. Francis. The thought was sobering.

The elevator descended to the sub basement and I headed straight to Primate Lab. When I arrived, Dr. Fenwick and veterinarian Margaret Clouser, dressed in white coveralls and helmets, were injecting medication into a chimp through an IV port. When they'd finished, their "space monkey" bounded across the room and leapt atop the cages, hooting and stammering.

I could hear Fenwick's muffled voice through the vent. "Get down, Cheetah!"

I was astounded. Cheetah was now the embodiment of simian health!

Five minutes later, the vacuum door seal hissed open. In the holding chamber, Fenwick climbed out of his spacesuit. He had gained some weight, and his eyes gleamed with new intensity.

I cleared my throat. "That seems like one spunky monkey, Professor."

Dr. Fenwick didn't skip a beat. "I gave him a pharmacological makeover."

"Congratulations."

"Thanks Deputy. Nice of you to stop by. You've been a busy boy, so I've read."

"Busy, but unsuccessful in my quest."

"Maybe you haven't collared Nature Boy, but I believed you would," Dr. Fenwick said. "That belief inspired me. After our chat, I increased the potency of Reverse Transcriptocide and designed a new implantable drug delivery system."

"Which seems to be working."

"At least for the moment," he said. "Now that I've bought myself a little more time, we need to talk."

Today, there would be no elevator ride to a plush office. Instead, Dr. Fenwick escorted me into a small classroom adjoining the doggie lab. I turned my back to the OR and pulled up a seat.

"I must say, Doc, you're looking fit."

"Thanks. I've been hitting the weights. I'm sore as hell, but at least I'm trying." He leaned back in his chair. "You're wondering what I have to tell you, right?"

I nodded.

"Since we last spoke about my attacker, there's one image I can't seem to get out of my head."

"What image?"

"His eyes. Far stranger than yours. Glassy eyes like a mannequin's. Lifeless eyes that peer right through you."

A synapse connected, and my mind flashed to Walden Woods, the shoreline of Nashawtuc Lake. Through sheets of snow, yellow pupils glared. Yellow eyes, the color of bile. Yellow, the color of jaundice. An icy chill swept through me, and my ears began to ring.

"You still with me, Sherman?"

I snapped back to reality. The image disintegrated into flashes of color. I rested my head between my legs and shook off the cold.

Fenwick tossed me a bottle of grapefruit juice. "I guess I'm not the only one who zones out around here. Drink this. It'll boost your glucose."

I finished the juice. There wasn't much else to discuss with Dr. Fenwick. His description had certainly made my trip worth the effort. I thanked him, and then headed for the road.


That day, I covered a twelve-mile radius of the crime's epicenter, scrutinizing every alley and side street, every carwash, business, farmstead, and grocery store to no avail. I restrained myself from calling Paige Sagoff. Later, back at the cabin, I phoned Eldridge Weatherbee and told him about my visit to the medical center.

"So did you learn anything else?" he asked.

"More about the man we're chasing."

"You mean men?"

"It's one person."

"The Feds are thicker than flies on turds. How would one guy pull this off?"

"By knowing something about us. I can't tell you his name, but when Fenwick described the attack, I had a weird sensation."

"We can't arrest a sensation. Can you describe him?"

"Not exactly."

"When you can, let me know," Weatherbee said. "On another note, Diana Loomis stopped by the station to review the videos. She gave us a mailing list of pet adoptions and animal rights memberships."

"And what's going on with Paige Sagoff?"

"Nothing to speak of. She's got a macho safari-type guy looking out for her."

"You mean Malcolm Pearson."

"Right. Anybody stupid enough to trespasses on the estate will find a cavity as big as a pie plate blown out of his chest by an elephant load."

"What can I do to help?"

"Keep your distance. You're the one who whipped Miss Sagoff into this frenzy in the first place. I'm ordering cruisers to patrol the estate and an undercover cop to trail her downtown. More troopers volunteered for the night shift than I've seen in years."

My face heated up. "Did Paige mention me?"

"I told her that you were on another assignment. If it

makes you feel better, I could tell she was disappointed. By the way, where's Abby?"

The deliberate change of subject caught me off guard. "The ER would be a good guess."

"How long does she sleep after her shift?"

"About five or six hours. Why?"

"Abby sent that Carlisle blood sample off to a genetics professor, and I need the results. While we were at it, she checked my cholesterol. It turned out to be sky-high, so she put me on a lifesaving high-fiber diet that's killing me. The roughage is wreaking havoc with my bowels, so I've got to get going. Let's regroup in the morning."

"Okay, Eldridge. And good luck with your intestines."


Later that evening, I visited Dad in the hospice. Inside, the fragrance of narcissus dizzied me. Eugene Sherman sat up in bed and smiled when I entered the room. I handed him a paper bag.

"Excellent choice," my father said. "General Tso's and Crab Rangoon."

"The MSG ought to pump you up."

"My doctors told me that between relapses, I may have surges of energy. So tell me about the investigation."

"I just returned from a visit with Dr. Fenwick."

"Did you learn anything?"

"That I know Nature Boy, and he's part of the Legion."

"Are you sure?"

"I'm sure there's something you're not telling me."

My father kept smiling—a Chinese outpouring of

endorphins. "Why spoil a meal?"

"C'mon Dad, tell me."

"Sorry to disappoint you, son."

I'd never pry anything out of the old game warden tonight. I dished more food onto his plate.

"You look better. I was afraid I'd find you headed downhill."

"I *am* heading downhill, no doubt about it, but I had an incredible dream last night." Eugene Sherman chased the last crab Rangoon with a swallow of water, pushed his plate aside, and spoke in a hoarse whisper.

"I'm Canada goose hunting in a snow-covered cornfield during a nor'easter. My eyes water. The decoys are dark on the white backdrop. The wind is so fierce that no snow accumulates on their backs. Windsocks wag. The gale whistles through the bore of my flute call, making a doleful honk.

"I'm lying in our wooden coffin blind, with only my head and neck exposed. The sides are only a foot deep, so that I make a low profile in the cornfield. The white blind merges with the swirling snow. Invisible among the decoys, I'm head-to-toe in white camouflage.

"Enveloped by the coffin blind, I've become part of winter. To the birds, I'm just another patch of snow. I stare overhead into the silvery clouds. My eyes water in the sleet. I fold my arms across my chest, nestling into the comfort of my clothing and the shelter of my wooden coffin.

"In the distance, I see you and your brother skimming ice across the frozen river as snow wafts across its smooth surface. Suddenly, you and Timmy point to a flock of geese. You fellas hide in the snow and the retriever crouches alongside. There's something different about this flock...the metallic call of snow geese!

"My heart is pounding, because we rarely see snows in our flyway. The birds circle and parachute into the spread. Rising out of my white casket, I swing the bead ahead of the leader, focusing on its dark eye and pink bill. I flick off the safety and slap the trigger, but the gun won't fire. At first, the geese don't notice me, but soon they flare, gaining distance and altitude. The flock circles to gather its strays.

"All at once, I'm drawn out of the coffin blind, extracted from a shell, rising. I'm dizzy, carried into the gale, higher and higher. I'm drawn into a void, the vortex of the departing flock with you and Timmy in pursuit, shuffling through the snow between parallel rows of cornstalks. My gun tumbles into a drift, landing with a puff. The dog runs to the spot, sniffs, and peers upward. I cannot turn back. I squint against the stinging snow.

"I am with the birds then, so close that I can hear their honking and wind shearing through their pinions. Their chests rise and fall, pumping their wings. Serpentine rivers and a patchwork of farms pass beneath us.

"In a soft fluttering of wings, I bank into the clouds, bursting through, into sunlight so intense that I have to squint. Everything is smooth and featureless in the absolute light—beyond sensation, beyond gravity."

"Now *that's* a dream," I said. "You ought to send that one to your publishers."

"At least I know I'll be united with the flock when it's my time," he said.

I handed my father a fortune cookie. He cracked it open and cupped the message like a poker hand.

"C'mon Dad, pass along the Eastern wisdom."

"Okay. It says, *A lovely doctor looms in your son's future.*"

"What?"

"Abigail Reed dropped by to review my chart. She's as smart as Eldridge claimed."

I held my head.

"She understands you."

"What did she have to say?"

"That you're distracted."

"Anything else?"

My father nodded. "You should seek the poetry buried inside you."

"I've heard that somewhere before."

"Abigail Reed is one fine young lady. I'd gaff her before she gets away."

"I'm a jerk."

"And she's still around. That says a lot."

"I don't understand myself."

"By the end of this case, you will."

"What's that supposed to mean?"

"You'll have to figure it out for yourself, son."

I rolled my eyes. It was hard to get angry at a dying man, especially when he was your father. I began to wonder if tumor cells had metastasized to his brain. I changed the subject.

"Next Thursday's Thanksgiving. I'll bring you a turkey."

"A wild turkey?"

"This year it'll be from the Assabet Poultry Farm."

"I'll look forward to it. In the meantime, have a safe hunt."

Dad's energy surge cheered me up, but his cryptic messages frustrated me. He suspected something, but refused to share it, and I had no idea why. Dad and I had always differed in one major trait: patience. That's why I ended up chasing fugitives instead of investigating.

With so many federal agents now scouring the countryside after the Stillwell bombing, I hadn't a snowball's chance in hell of finding Nature Boy myself. Weary of the complex puzzle, I thought about quitting the team. Then, I considered those yellow eyes peering at me in Dr. Fenwick's lab and what the one-eyed veteran had told me about Nature Boy. Quality leads, by no means, but intriguing just the same.

I decided to give it one more week.

# 17

Other than a quiet Thanksgiving dinner with my father, the week was uneventful. It was the coldest November in years, never warmer than fifteen degrees. The good citizens of Concord struggled to rake leaves blown wild by biting northwest gales.

Cosette snored and slobbered in bed next to me where married men's wives would normally snore and slobber. The mattress sagged beneath her bulk, and she growled whenever I tried to reclaim the sheets.

I wasn't certain if it was Cosette's turkey-induced methane gas or the wind rattling the window panes that awakened me at four a.m., even before the phone jangled. It was Weatherbee again.

The infant son of Select Safari Society President-elect

Christian Evans had been kidnapped, snatched from his crib while his parents slept. The boldness of the deed made me shudder in the November predawn. The only reassuring fact was that unlike the past victims, I had no personal connection to Evans.

Because Evans was a political hotshot, the task force had mobilized in record time. Local and state police jammed Barrett's Mill Road and the driveway leading to his expansive colonial. Inside, Sergeant Pfleuger and the forensics crew dusted for fingerprints and vacuumed fibers. Agents scribbled testimony, photographed, and videotaped. From a corner of the living room, Lieutenant Weatherbee observed, reconstructing the crime scene.

A department psychologist kept trying to comfort the mother, Meredith Evans, a nice-looking woman at least fifteen years younger than her husband. Hefty diamonds glittered on her ring finger. I figured that Meredith had been his former secretary. Executives were always dumping their wives for newer models.

Similar to the other investigations, our efforts yielded small fragments, but no whole. A child's life was at stake this time, and Major Fallon kept darting from room to room. The shadows accentuated the Major's wrinkles as if he had suddenly dropped off the precipice of mid-life into the abyss of old age.

I stared through a picture window into the night. The wind stirred the pines. Cirrus clouds whisked past the stars. Sirens blared in the predawn and a Euro Star helicopter crisscrossed the sky, its spotlights glaring off frozen puddles. K-9 units fanned into the darkness and busloads of cadets began a grid search.

Rocky Fallon had called for a massive search and rescue.

All town borders had been closed. Local and state police were conducting house-to-house inspections, handing out leaflets, and stopping all outgoing vehicles.

Reports of Evans's international white collar poaching had always intrigued my game warden father. As a result, Dad and I knew a lot about the man.

I slipped past the other investigators and headed into the quieter recesses of the dwelling. The lower level housed massive gun safes. Farther beyond, an expansive trophy room stretched into the darkness.

One of the rarest trophies on earth, a Kara-Tau agali ram, the same ram pictured in a *New York Herald* anti-hunting editorial, hung on the wall. Its bulky horns curved a full thirty-six inches, with bases twice the circumference of a man's fist. Its ridged horns resembled the Sayan Khrebet Mountains from which the beast had been taken. The elements had blanched its face. I'd seen bighorns south of the Peace River in British Columbia and Dall sheep in the Yukon Basin, but this specimen topped them all.

Gaining permission to hunt the endangered beast had proven tougher than shooting it, the newspapers said. Evans had taken the ram from just north of the Mongolian border within the confines of a crumbling central Asian republic. At first, government officials had balked, but the *Herald* reported that well-placed donations had closed the deal. Since the argali was one of the rarest species on the planet, Christian Evans would probably be the last man to take one.

I glanced at the rows of animals he'd slain. Ivory tusks parenthesized his walls. Heads of the big five: a bull elephant, a lion, a leopard, a heavily-racked Cape buffalo, and a rhino stared down from the walls. Lesser species—kudu, impala, springbok, warthog, zebra, wildebeest, waterbuck, sable, gemsbok, and eland—filled in the gaps. Evans's trophy room held enough animals to populate the Franklin Park Zoo, if only they hadn't been stuffed.

In an alcove farther down the hall, silhouetted by a fresco of the savanna, a mounted leopard reclined with her cubs. Evans probably had no idea how the natives caught the cubs, and didn't want to know. Egotists grab whatever they can on their short, consumptive romp through life.

Call me a hypocrite, but hunting "dangerous game" had always bothered me—sort of like plugging the Cowardly Lion or Gentle Ben with a .458 magnum. Dad and I considered rich sports like Evans well-heeled collectors, with massive guns and diminutive weenies. Scattered about the world were other members of the Select Safari Society, an organization that Evans would soon chair, a club with a five-hundred thousand dollar initiation fee.

I hit the light switch. Flickering electric candlelight made the ram's eyeballs water and its ears twitch. I recalled the news account of the hunt:

*The ram bounded from its crag in an explosion of rippling muscle and a cascade of sliding rock three hundred meters away. At the crack of Evans's .270, the beast collapsed, rolling down the ravine until a gnarled stump snagged it. Everything fell silent, save the mournful howl of the wind.*

Back upstairs, agents escorted Evans outside for a news conference.

Christian Evans, youthful for a man in his fifties, presidential-looking, with a Grecian formula, blacker-than-black, thick head of hair, braved the dawn in his bathrobe and squinted into the bright lights of the news cameras. Haggard FBI profilers block-printed prompts. Evans spoke with polish derived from chairing board meetings.

"Tremendous effort, Mr. Evans," said the news director. "Next take will be live."

The camera focused on an investigative reporter.

"This is Daniel Diawa reporting live from Barrett's Mill Road, Concord, at the home of Christian Evans, whose son Cooper was abducted last night. The following is a public service announcement in an effort to facilitate the child's safe return." He stepped aside as the camera turned toward Christian Evans.

Evans stared into the camera, and began:

"To the person or persons who have abducted our son, our only son, Cooper Keating Evans, I am making this appeal: We want our son back.

"In spite of the controversy about my hunting, I'm a compassionate man. My wife and I know that the world has wounded you. We want to make things right." Evans's voice cracked. He swallowed back tears and straightened himself.

"Cooper is a sweet little boy, a miracle child who barely survived his birth. He spent six weeks in neonatal intensive care and lived to make the world a brighter place. He has a little sister who loves him. Notice how his eyes sparkle. You'll feel his love when he smiles. Cooper can bring joy into your life. Keep him safe. He's as lovable as a puppy. A cute little puppy."

The profilers had done their homework. Associating the toddler with an animal might soften Nature Boy's heart.

Evans continued. "Return our son, and I pledge that you'll have a chance to express your views to the world, a world that is waiting to hear your message. We have the means. We want to listen. I humbly offer my resources in return for Cooper's safe return."

"Start flashing the hotline number," the director whispered.

A biting wind tousled Evans's hair, but his eyes never deviated from the monitor.

The director made a motion to cut. "Fade on three."

Suddenly, Evans shook his fist at the camera. "If you hurt my boy, I'll gut you alive, you miserable bastard!"

Profilers wrestled Evans off camera.

Eldridge smirked. "Just great! What's the damage?"

"We cut the worst of it," an editor replied.

The police ushered Evans back into the house. Weatherbee and I headed upstairs to the children's bedroom where state police psychologists were questioning four year old Victoria.

The room was a replica of that depicted in Clement Hurd's *Goodnight Moon*. The carpet was scarlet, and the walls were green with yellow and green striped curtains. A toy red house with golden yellow windows stood in the corner next to a rocking chair and a braided rug. Paintings of three little bears sitting in chairs and the cow jumping over the moon hung on the walls. On a night table beside a blue lamp were a comb, and a brush, and even a fake bowl of mush. As pictured in the book, a real tiger skin rug (with a bullet hole in the middle) decorated the floor. A red balloon wafted overhead. Meredith Evans had overlooked no detail.

I nudged the lieutenant. "A green room, a red balloon, and a cow jumping over the moon? I'm regressing."

Weatherbee rolled his eyes. "When I was a kid, all I had was a ketchup-stained Howdy Doody poster."

The four year old was the only calm person in the house.

"Draw us a picture of the Fairy Man, Victoria," a psychologist urged.

Victoria plucked a black crayon from his hand and began to draw in an oversized notebook. I edged closer. The team hung on her every scribble.

"That's very good, Victoria. You write like a big girl. Now draw the man."

She gritted her straight Chiclet teeth. The psychologists gave her space.

I studied the room. Everything was in its place with no sign of forced entry or a struggle. But parents weren't responsible for this crime, not directly at least. The trophy hunter was now paying the price for his sport.

The little girl finished her sketch and revealed it to the psychologists. A few smiled. Most scratched their heads.

They displayed the portrait: a smiley-face head figure with dots for eyes. Spindly stick arms and legs extended from a circle body.

Weatherbee shook his head. "Fellas, issue an APB for Humpty Dumpty."

The girl yanked Weatherbee's shirtsleeve. "No goofy, not Humpty Dumpty. That's Fairy Man. Want to see me draw Tinky Winky?"

"Some other time, Victoria. Tell me more about Fairy Man. How big was he?"

She pointed to the lieutenant's abdomen. "Not that big."

"I can only handle my grandkids for an hour or two," Weatherbee whispered. "Afterwards, I need a four-hour nap." He turned back toward the little girl. "Did Mr. Fairy Man have a car?"

She nodded.

"What color was it?"

Victoria rolled her hands and fidgeted.

"C'mon, smartie pants, you remember."

"White," she said.

"Good. White."

Weatherbee motioned for his laptop and booted it up. He clicked on a screen full of vehicles. He pointed the cursor at one of the vehicles.

"Like this one?"

Victoria shook her head no. The query continued for a half hour, including over four hundred white automobiles, vans, pickup trucks, and SUVs of every model and make. The little girl began to yawn.

After another two dozen cars, the exasperated little girl stood up, placed her hands on her hips, and cast the lieutenant a sly grin. "You're one silly grampa!"

"Okay then, Victoria, maybe I am silly. I'm a Pee Wee wannabe. I'm fat Wiggle. I'm a geriatric Teletubby. I'm whatever you say I am. Just tell me about Fairy Man! Remember, I have chocolate."

*Chocolate.* That got her attention. Chocolate, the ultimate motivator, full of caffeine, sugar, antioxidants, and kiddie endorphins.

"Promise?"

"Sure," Weatherbee said, patting his pockets, genuinely concerned about making good on his bargain. He produced a fat Cadbury bar.

"How's this?" he asked, dangling it in front of her. Victoria reached, but the lieutenant yanked it away. "Not so fast, munchkin. First tell me about his car."

Victoria folded her arms and wrinkled her nose. "Okay. Not those cars," she said pointing to the laptop. She ran toward the window. *Those* cars!" she said, pointing toward the cruisers.

"You mean a police car?"

She grew impatient with these foolish adults. "No, a *funny* police car."

"You mean an ambulance?"

"No. Funny police *car*."

Eldridge displayed images of vans, rescue and transport vehicles, to no avail. After about an hour of questioning, the salmon glow of dawn illuminated the fields behind the estate.

In-laws dressed the girl in a red woolen Rothschild jacket with Tyrolean trim and snow boots. The lieutenant, the troopers, profilers and I escorted Victoria outdoors.

"Find us his car, Victoria."

We shuttled her over a stone wall onto the street. Barrett's Mill Road, usually a bustling rush-hour shortcut, was now nearly vacant. Fluttering yellow tape demarcated the crime scene.

Suddenly, Victoria tugged at my coat sleeve and pointed to a U.S. Postal Service delivery truck, yellow lights flashing.

Cruisers screeched forward and boxed in the truck. The driver poked his head out of the window to the greeting of two dozen frosty steel barrels.

"What the hell's going on?" the postman cried.

"Out!" ordered a trooper. "And let's see those hands."

A search of the vehicle yielded only mail.

"Are you sure this is the car you saw, Victoria?"

"Fairy Man's got no stripes and no birdie," she said, pointing to the eagle head insignia.

The troopers shook down the mailman and cross referenced his ID. I holstered my revolver.

"You guys nearly gave me a heart attack," said the postman. "Don't tell me those animal freaks are at it again."

"What time did you start your shift, sir?"

"Four-thirty."

"Have you noticed anything unusual?"

"No, other than you guys nearly blowing my head off." He thought for a moment. "If it's postal vehicles you're looking for, we've auctioned dozens over the past few years."

Weatherbee raised his eyebrows. "What kind of tires do you use on those things?"

"Standard-issue 13-inch Firestone Daytons."

The lieutenant turned to me. "Sounds familiar, doesn't it?"

The tire tracks in Carlisle.


The investigation continued through the morning. Victoria played downstairs, high on attention and chocolate. I discovered that the attic insulation over the children's bedroom had been agitated. No telling how long Nature Boy had been stalking the Evanses.

A tremulous Meredith Evans edged into the *Goodnight Moon* bedroom. A regal woman in her seventies guided her to a rocking chair alongside Eldridge and me.

Weatherbee murmured, "There's the old lady whispering 'hush.' Her name is Emily Keating. She's Victoria's grandmother, and none too thrilled with police."

Keating's face was wrinkle-free, the product of Valium, facelifts, Botox and chemical peels. The lieutenant offered his chair. She waved him off and raised her voice.

"My daughter's too upset to talk, so let me speak for her." She drew in a breath. "The most precious thing in our lives has been stolen from us. My family is angry—angry about the price we've paid for Christian's hunting, and outraged by the two of you."

"We'll do everything in our power to bring Cooper home to you," Weatherbee said.

"That doesn't reassure me, Lieutenant, not in the least. I know that you're famous for locating murderers, but years after the crimes." She deflected her voice away from Meredith Evans. "How many kidnapped toddlers have you ever recovered?"

The lieutenant stared at his feet.

"And how many have you ever recovered *alive*?"

Silence.

"No wonder you call them 'cold cases.' " Mrs. Evans's voice was a strained whisper. "We've lost our only grandson. And it was so unnecessary."

I had to rescue my partner. "I lost my own brother, and I know what you're feeling, ma'am."

Ms. Keating wagged her bony index finger within inches of my nose. "Don't patronize me, Deputy Sherman. I know who you are. You don't have half the character that your father did."

I stared at the ceiling. The red balloon had drifted toward the fan, ticking the blades.

Ms. Keating didn't let up. "You have untrustworthy eyes, Deputy. You knew this monster. You knew how dangerous he was, yet you did nothing to protect us. Nothing. And even more pathetic," she said, sagging into her chair, "everybody knows it's *you* that Nature Boy is after. I hold you responsible for our baby's life, Brant Sherman, if it still *is* a life."

Eldridge nudged his chin toward the door. I fled the room, wondering what would happen to the son of a trophy hunter in this new age of symmetrical violence.

I shivered on the back porch deck in the biting dawn. Snow tufted strawberry mounds in the fields. Mallards took flight from the misty Assabet River. The wind stung my face. Soon, a big hand slapped my back.

"You okay?"

It was Eldridge, with Major Fallon in tow.

"Take it in stride, Brant," the lieutenant said. "Desperation was doing the talking."

"You're not accountable for this," added Fallon.

I sighed. "Maybe the old bag is right."

"Be honest with yourself," Fallon said. "If what Ms. Keating said holds even a shred of truth, we need to find out about it right away. A child's life hangs in the balance."

Weatherbee nodded. "And we all know what happened to the animals Christian Evans shot."

After Fallon left, Eldridge said, "We need to talk. I know that you and Abby haven't been hitting it off lately, but the other day I asked her about those spells when you turn gray. Frankly, I'm concerned. She thinks that you're the connection to the Legion of St. Francis. That's why the events escalated ever since you hit the headlines. Rocky Fallon suspected it from the start."

"So that's why I was selected?"

Weatherbee nodded. "I had a little chat with my old buddy, Eugene Sherman. What he told me about you was eye-opening, to say the least. Up until this point, Brant, I've allowed you to suffer in silence, but now the stakes are higher.

"We're going to have a little pow wow with Demos Anastopoulos from the investigative support unit at Quantico. I need a better profile of this suspect, and to get one, we'll have to delve into your past."

"There's no time."

"We're going to make the time, Deputy. Something happened to you twenty years ago. You and your Dad know it. It's time to reach into that dark closet of yours."

I stared across the snow swept strawberry fields and thought about the little boy. For a moment, I pictured Timmy, his nose and lips, stung strawberry red in the chill of winter. Perhaps psychotherapy at the department's expense would save a child's life. Besides, the issue wasn't negotiable.

"Okay Eldridge," I said. "But there are limits."

"What limits?"

"Any free association about penis envy, and I'm out of there. Agreed?"

Weatherbee just shook his head.

# 18

As I said, I hadn't much faith in department psychiatrists, profilers, psychics or other flakes on investigations. Mired somewhere between my potty training and concrete operational stages, I'd cared little about abstract things that I couldn't shoot. After Timmy drowned, the adults forced me into therapy for about six months. The therapist ended the sessions after I said wanted to kill my father and marry my mother. Pretty childish, I have to admit, but old Oedipus did the trick.

Years later, while studying criminal justice at Northeastern, I realized that the shrinks might have helped me if I'd given them the chance. But that water was far over the dam.

Within an hour, I'd face an FBI profiler from Quantico,

Virginia who'd delve into my pathetic past while Nature Boy
practiced his taxidermy on a toddler. I wasn't exactly doing
handstands about it, but I had no choice.

Back at the cabin, I sat in an oversized armchair and
gazed at my sporting memorabilia: the fishing rods, the
photographs, the mounted fish and game birds on the
walls. Usually, outdoor lore relaxed me, but today, I couldn't
calm down.

I began to ponder the blinded senator, the kids who'd
swallowed fishhooks, the asphyxiated bug professor, and the
amputee trapper.

Cosette settled down at my feet, leaning into me, curling
herself into a ball.

I studied an outdoor calendar that contained Solunar
tables, the *Farmer's Almanac* of fish and game activity. Today,
the table predicted peak deer activity, a high-gear cycle for all
mammals—including humans—and an opportunity for reflection.

November's photograph was a ruffed grouse and
December's was a snowshoe hare. Suddenly, I visualized the
waxen images of Timmy, bland gashes on his forehead and
punctures in his hands. The wounds began to bleed, crimson
welling up like stigmata. Lids opened, and marble-white
eyeballs rolled. The ice child kept staring, and then disappeared
in a cloud of swirling mist, spicules of ice, and the stark white of
a silvery moon.

Something didn't add up. I knew I wasn't normal—
always looking over my shoulder, pissed off at the world, and
isolated. I could no longer deny it: something had rocked
my world, something now in my head, something that kept
haunting me.

I needed to speak with my father before the FBI profiler found out how truly screwed up I was.

I fired up my cripple of a Jeep and headed to the back to the hospice.

My father was waiting.

"You've heard about Cooper Evans?" I asked.

My father flicked off the television and nodded.

"His family blames me," I said.

"You're not responsible."

"Listen Dad, we're talking about a kid's life. I need to know what you're thinking. No bullshit this time."

"Fair enough."

"When you first encouraged me to join the task force, you said something about not knowing who I'd run into. Well, a few weeks ago, I ran into a grizzled veteran from the Rod and Gun Club who said that Timmy had been intentionally drowned."

"Sit down, Brant," my father said, his face gaunt. "I've dreaded the day I'd have to tell you, but for better or worse, that time has come."

"The police investigated Nashawtuc Lake, didn't they?"

My father nodded. "The most comprehensive investigation of its time. For my sake, they kept it from the public."

"What did they find?"

"The ice had been sawed in a semi-circle thirty feet from the collapse point and camouflaged before you got there. Someone set a trap for you, someone who knew your habits, someone who'd been watching."

"Why didn't you tell me? You'd have saved me one hell of a guilt trip."

"You were an impulsive teenager with a fiery temper. I was afraid I'd end up with both of my boys in body bags."

"You would have only had one. In case you've forgotten, they never recovered Timmy."

"Distancing you from the investigation was the right thing to do. The investigation lasted two years and produced no suspects or hard evidence. By the time it was over, you were on your way to Northeastern on a baseball scholarship."

"I never made it out of Pawtucket."

"It doesn't matter," my father said. "You have an innate sense of what's around you. You hit well because you anticipated pitches before the pitcher even knew what he was about to throw. You had an average arm for Division One, but you sensed when runners would steal and caught sixty-percent. Your perception, not your brawn, is what made you a baseball star, Brant. I hoped you'd use it for something other than killing."

"Well it didn't turn out that way for me, and I'm planning to kill again real soon. So who did it? A jealous redneck who wanted me out of his hunting spot? An animal rights activist?"

My father kept staring out the window.

"C'mon Dad. Let me nail this freak, so that I can get on with my life."

"Fine, son. I may be way off base, but lately I've had a strange notion. I warn you, it may sound ridiculous."

"Try me."

"Do you recall the date you shot your first deer?"

I didn't.

"December the sixth. This year it falls on a full moon, the Long Night's Moon."

I thought back to the calendar in my cabin, and the image the month of December triggered.

My father asked, "Does the name 'Baby Huey' mean anything to you?"

At that point, I was convinced that my father had lost it.

"Remember the day," he continued. "Sit back, close your eyes, and open your mind..."

Crazy as it seemed, I obeyed, and the memory crested like a wave.

*For most, crisp December mornings meant skiing or Christmas shopping, but for generations of Shermans, autumn mornings meant slaying deer. Today, deep in the woods, at age twelve, I prepared to enter their secretive world, a voyeur to the clandestine activity of the herd. For the moment, I was a predator — an assassin as deadly as a coyote, the harshest storm, or the cruelest famine.*

*A deer materialized from the shadows. Shivering atop my tree stand, I kept trying to focus my crosshairs on the fork-horn's shoulder. The yearling sniffed doe-in-heat urine on a tree trunk, his black nose drawing in the estrus scent. I clicked off my safety and squeezed. The recoil kicked me backwards, but I heard the impact of the sabot slug on tissue.*

*The shot rolled the deer. The animal thrashed on the forest floor, but managed to flip back onto its feet. I, too, regained my equilibrium, pumped another shell, and slapped the trigger. Tree bark behind the deer exploded, and the deer bounded away.*

*I emptied my chamber, lowered the gun to the ground by rope, and descended the tree stand.*

I looked for a blood trail. It didn't take long to find one. Crimson bubbles and clots spattered the leaves. I smeared the frothy liquid between my fingers, feeling for clues. Sticky bubbles meant a lung shot, a fatal hit that would produce quick but not immediate death.

I followed the trail into a thicket, over a stone wall, through a ravine, then lost it. The trail resumed on some oak leaves where the blood was thicker and more-copious. I trotted ahead and almost stumbled upon my deer.

Panting, the deer was lying down, head up, staring from a tangle. The buck looked younger than it had from the tree stand. We two adolescent mammals kept staring at one another. My reflection glistened in the pupils of my quarry's brown eyes.

Blood bubbled from its nostrils. I considered shooting the deer again, but I couldn't. Instead, I sat on the forest floor and held my head. Soon, my ears began to ring, and I grew nauseated.

It took Dad and his grizzled hunting buddy Addison Kroll less than ten minutes to arrive. I pointed to the deer.

The game warden put his hand on my shoulder, and jostled me. "Are you okay?"

"I dunno."

He pried the shotgun from my sweaty hands and whispered. "Try not to look into his eyes."

Old Addison drew a sheath knife and dispatched the animal. I shuddered as the last shivers of life left the carcass.

Addison wiped the knife on his pants and sheathed it. He held the deer by its antlers. A red slash smiled from the buck's white throat patch.

Suddenly, I felt the warm splash of blood on my forehead. "Now you're baptized," Kroll remarked.

Eugene Sherman forced a smile. Addison winked at my father.

*"I got a little subdued when I shot my first deer, too."*

*"And you haven't shut up since," Dad barbed.*

*Addison wiped his hands on some pine needles. "Young Brant has plenty more deer in his future. Not like us geezers."*

*I helped the men hoist my deer, its eyes now dull and lifeless. The meat swayed back and forth. A splotch of orange spray-paint on the hindquarter of the deer caught my eye. The two adults puzzled over the strange markings.*

*We reached the truck by nine o'clock. I waved away smoke from Addison's filterless Camels. Other hunters assembled to admire the buck.*

*Suddenly, a pimply stranger stumbled from the woods and stopped to catch his breath. The fellow was pudgy with scraggly hair, and his rear-end protruded when he waddled past me. He was in his twenties, but looked more like an overgrown child. He wore a forest-green unzipped sweatshirt, ripped and studded with burrs and underneath, a red river-driver's shirt. The young man darted about, twitching and mumbling.*

*"Who the hell have we here," Addison Kroll said, "Father Christmas?"*

*"I heard gunshots," the stranger said. "Are you poachers?"*

*Addison spoke up. "It's opening day of deer season, young man, and we're certainly not poachers. In fact, that handsome fella over there is the game warden."*

*"You didn't get anything, did you?" His voice elevated to a whine. "Did you?"*

*"Take it easy, young man," said Eugene Sherman. "What's the problem?"*

*"You're the problem. Leave my deer alone!"*

*Addison rolled his eyes. "Just what the world needs:*

another 'anti.' "

When the stranger noticed blood on the ground, he fell to his knees. "What have you done?"

He rubbed the blood between his fingers. Meanwhile, spectators gathered. Then the young man spied the deer carcass.

He shrieked, "You murdered Ralph!"

"Who the hell is Ralph?" asked Addison.

The stranger embraced the carcass and wept. "My pet. I bottle-fed and weaned him."

My heart sank.

Gene Sherman rested his hand on the stranger's shoulder. "Take it easy, young man. We feel terrible about shooting that deer. Really, we do. But we can't take back the shot. What's done is done."

The stranger shrugged my father off and glared at me. "I spray-painted Ralphie to protect him. I figured nobody would be cruel enough to shoot him. He'd have eaten out of your hand, but you killed him anyway." He pointed at me. "What's wrong with you, husky eyes? Did you enjoy watching Ralphie suffer?"

"Leave my son out of it!" my father said. "This is a hunting area, and there's a law against keeping deer as pets."

The young man shook his head. "You murdered my friend."

"Cut the crap!" Kroll grumbled. "The warden's trying to apologize."

"What makes you slaughter animals?" the young man mumbled as he began to lift the carcass from the tailgate.

Addison Kroll stepped in front of him. "What the hell are you doing?"

"You've got no right to this deer."

"That's where you're wrong, Baby Huey. Dead wrong," Kroll said. He pointed at the license pinned to his vest. "This entitles me to kill a buck and eat it whether it suits you or not."

"Eat Ralphie?"

"No way am I gonna bury good venison."

"You're not going to cut him up!"

"Wanna bet?"

"Take it easy Addison," the warden whispered. "He's just a kid, kind of..."

The stranger hunkered over the carcass. "I won't let you take him!"

"Easy now, big fella," Kroll said. "I don't know what sort of liberal horseshit folks have fed you, but hunting is harvesting. Like picking soybeans for tofu or oats for granola bars. You're the one who needs an attitude adjustment."

But the stranger kept pacing and stammering. The scene was so pathetic, that I began to pity the sissy.

"Look," said Eugene Sherman, "the buck is feeling no pain. None whatsoever."

The fellow wheeled around. "Pain? What would you know about pain?" Cords in his neck strained. I cringed. The overgrown child was cracking up right in front of us.

The stranger narrowed his eyes at me, and his voice seethed. "Hey kid, you should have listened to your heart. You've become a murderer, just like them. You knew it was wrong, but you killed for blood-sport."

Kroll elbowed the intruder in the midsection. "Shut up you cocky runt!" The stranger buckled onto the dead deer.

"I wish you hadn't done that, Addison," Dad said.

"Somebody needs to take control, Gene."

"Get into the truck, Brant!" the warden ordered.

I obeyed, but kept staring from the cab. The other hunters

*scattered. My father and Addison Kroll wrestled the carcass from the young man. It was pathetic to watch him fight; clawing, thrashing, and shaking like a pit bull. Finally, he crumpled onto the road, and the deer thudded onto the ground. The two men heaved the meat back onto the flatbed and shut the tailgate.*

*Dad and Addison climbed into the cab. Trembling, I slid into the middle between them. Addison Kroll rubbed scratches on his neck as we peeled out.*

*"Whew!" he said. "What a junkyard dog!"*

*"A certified bucking bronco," Dad added. "He may look like a fairy, but he fights like a beast."*

*The overgrown baby shrank in the rearview mirror. Addison Kroll lit up another filterless and Dad unrolled his window.*

*"Must be from the city," Kroll said. "Those crunchy Cantabrigians have been migrating here like lemmings."*

*"How are you holding up, Brant?" my father asked.*

*"I'm okay."*

*"If you want to hunt these days, you need to be tough. People who think nothing of ordering a tenderloin will crucify you for shooting your own meat."*

*As miles distanced us from the sorry character at Estabrook Woods, the heater made me drowsy. I glanced at the deer, its head bobbing on the flatbed.*

*Dad nudged me and pointed to the roadside.*

*"Look," he said. "In that spruce. Cardinals. Three of them."* *Blood red birds speckled the evergreens. "Cardinals bring sportsmen luck, and there's one for each of us. Let's hunt again this afternoon. We've got two more tags to fill."*

*"I'm with you, Gene," Addison replied.*

*Geese circled the cornfields. A full moon swung low on the*

*horizon. I'd almost fallen asleep when I heard Dad's voice above the*
*sound of the engine.*

*"Sometimes with memories, it's better to blot out the bad parts."*

*I sat up straighter. "When that flatlander started hugging the*
*deer, I didn't know what to think."*

*Addison sucked down the last millimeter of his cigarette.*
*"Don't worry, Brant, it'll eat as good as any other venison."*

I snapped back to the present and bolted upright. "Are
you suggesting some fat dork named Baby Huey killed Timmy
because of a deer?"

My father shrugged. "Maybe it's all payback. "

"Great. All I have to do is figure out who he is and find
him before it's too late for Cooper Evans ."

I was still shaking my head as I made my exit.

What a day! I tried to compose myself as I headed to the
state police barracks to face the profiler.

Ten minutes late, I bounded into headquarters where
Eldridge Weatherbee sat before a growing list of victims written
on the blackboard.

Special Agent Demos Anastopoulos, a profiler from the
FBI Investigational Support Team, sat next to him. Anastopoulos
was an athletic Greek in his forties with black curly hair, olive
skin, and an aquiline nose. A navy blue turtleneck emphasized
his tennis-player build.

After an introduction, Weatherbee said, "Demos was
kind enough to fly in this morning from Quantico. He hasn't

much time, so we'd better proceed."

For some reason, I was so edgy, I couldn't even manage an Aristotle Onassis joke. Just then, the station door opened and a breeze whooshed into the room. Notices tacked to Weatherbee's cork poster board flapped. It was Abigail Reed, still in her scrubs. After a brief introduction, Abigail and the agent checked each other out for an uncomfortable length of time. Anastopoulos wasn't wearing a wedding band. Abby didn't acknowledge me as she sat down.

Weatherbee picked up a clipboard and wrote UNSUB at the top with black marker.

"We received a call from someone who claims to be the kidnapper demanding that the governor cancel the deer hunting season," he said.

"Or what?" I asked.

"He'll kill Cooper Evans. The signal analysis unit localized the call to a pay phone at the Burlington Mall. That's the best they could do."

Relieved that the child was still alive, I asked, "How much time do we have?"

"The perp said 'by the Long Night's Moon,' which I'm told is the first full moon of December. This year it falls on the sixth."

I remembered what my father had told me about that date, but kept my mouth shut.

"The governor's meeting with the DEP and the Fish and Wildlife Service right now, which gives us a window to sort things out," Weatherbee said, turning toward the profiler. "What's your take on all this, Demos?"

"We don't know how many suspects comprise this Legion of St. Francis," Anastopoulos replied, "but the major

UNSUB is a Caucasian male in his late thirties or early forties. He is unmarried, with an occupation well below his intellectual ability. The man is large, but other than pockmarked skin, his looks aren't distinctive enough to draw attention to himself. The man works in the health care profession but isn't licensed. I'm guessing he's a medical assistant.

"What makes this case so difficult is the fact that Nature Boy doesn't actually kill his victims. Therefore, we have no funerals or gravesites to monitor. We've posted agents undercover as respiratory therapists in the rehab facility where Professor Spivack is now vegetating. Unfortunately, the perp hasn't made another appearance.

"Dr. Fenwick provided us with the best testimony. Judging from the mood swings and alliterative music, his attacker is a schizophrenic, raised by a single mother or an aunt. His early life was dominated by an aggressive male authority figure who coached him to use violence to get what he needed."

The profiler continued, "The subject eventually identified with the violence, embraced it, and resolved to overcome his abuser. Once he did, the violence gratified him. Empowered by the knowledge that others feared him, he sought new opportunities which are now headline news."

"This character identifies with animals, but despises humans," Anastopoulos said, squeaking out a list on the board with his marker. He turned toward Abby. "What about this HLA B-27 tissue marker?"

Abby smiled, pleased to add to the discussion. "The blood Brant found in Carlisle contains an antigen called HLA B-27 associated with arthritis, psoriasis, and inflammatory bowel disease."

Eldridge smirked. "Add me to the suspect list. I have

gastrointestinal distress from that oat bran you put me on."

Abby ignored the comment. "In plain English the suspect might present with a stiff spine, eye irritation, a scaly rash and spasmodic abdominal pain caused by colitis or gallstones."

"Sounds like an appealing guy," I couldn't help saying.

The profiler displayed his list of findings:


UNSUB


AKA "Nature Boy," "Legion of St. Francis of Assisi"

Sex — M

Race — W

Age — Early-forties

Hair — Red/brown

Height — Seventy-four inches

Weight — Two hundred and twenty pounds

Marital — Unmarried or divorced, may live with widowed mother or aunt

Military — None, or medical/dishonorable discharge

Occupation — Healthcare worker with no degree

IQ — Above average

Education — High School

Religion — Catholic

Personality — Loner, schizophrenic or other affective disorder

Vehicle — White postal delivery truck/red synthetic tri-lobed carpet fibers

Tires — Firestone Dayton 80s/ right front tire smooth surface facing out

Modus — Organized

DNA Marker — HLA B-27

<u>Blood</u> — ABO Serotype: B positive/Rh positive
<u>Physical characteristics</u> — Inflammatory bowel disease, arthritis,
                                visual problems, gallstones, psoriasis
<u>Quirks</u> — Affinity for 1970s rock and roll songs

"We know a fair amount about this man," the lieutenant said. "The question is, what's his name, and how do we find him fast?"

Demos Anastopoulos turned toward me. "That's where *you* fit in, Deputy."

"With all due respect, Nature Boy is about to stuff a toddler, and you want me to sit through a Freudian psychotherapy session?"

"Enough, Brant," Weatherbee said. "There's something you know. We need to hear about it right here and right now." He sat back in his chair, crossed his feet on his desk, and clicked off his computer screen. "Start talking."

I was reluctant to reopen old wounds so I kept my mouth shut for an eternal five minutes while everyone in the room kept staring at me. The ticking clock reminded me of little Cooper's plight. I swallowed my pride, cleared my throat, and turned toward the profiler.

"All right," I said. "I hope my tale of woe doesn't make you miss your flight."

"We've got ten minutes. Not enough time for the Odyssey, but plenty of time for a good short story," Anastopoulos answered.

I stared back at Abby, Weatherbee, and Anastopoulos. There was no room for negotiation.

The profiler chose his words carefully. "How did your brother's drowning affect you, Brant?"

"I felt guilty about it."

"Abigail tells me that you have unpredictable spells, like absence seizures. What happens to you?"

"My ears ring and I break into cold sweats. I see and hear things."

"Like what?"

"My brother struggling beneath the ice."

Abby shivered. Anastopoulos took a long, reflective swallow of coffee.

"Before the drowning, did you ever hallucinate?"

"No. Believe it or not, I was nearly normal."

"You said things were better for you in Boston."

"Until I ended up in the ICU with a gunshot wound."

Abby interrupted. "Brant had a nightmare while he was in the ICU. His heart nearly stopped."

Anastopoulos lowered his voice. "You know who murdered your brother, don't you?"

Abby looked at me.

I hesitated. "Today was the first time I heard anything about it being murder." Wind rattled the windows and the radiators hissed. "But my father reminded me of something that happened a long time ago — before my brother died."

"Enlighten us."

"When I was twelve and a half, on opening day of hunting season in Concord, I killed my first buck. All of a sudden, this pathetic kid — an overgrown 'Baby Huey' as my father called him — stumbled out of the forest claiming that I murdered his pet deer. At first, he kept bawling. Then, his mood changed. He said I could hear the voices of stricken animals and that I was wrong to ignore them. The porker didn't get me to stop hunting, but he was right about the voices."

"Can you describe him?"

"All I recall is a loser whose butt protruded when he walked. At first, I felt lousy about shooting that deer. But at the time, Concord was evolving into a suburb, and I got used to defending our sport. Anti-hunting groups began to annoy me. I forgot about the episode and kept on hunting. I'm from a sporting lineage. My father was game warden and an outdoor writer. Hunting did a lot for me. It gave me the confidence indoor kids don't have."

"Until you were sixteen."

"Right."

Anastopoulos wrote *December the Sixth* on his clipboard and circled it three times.

Weatherbee furrowed his forehead. "What's that supposed to mean?"

"As Dr. Reed suspected, all of these events are connected, and Brant is the precipitating factor. He killed a deer on December sixth a quarter century ago, and as trivial as it sounds, Nature Boy has never gotten over it. The initial attacks — including Fenwick's — were sporadic. Now that we have Brant Sherman on our team, this perp has something to prove. Extensive news coverage has made his deeds even more gratifying."

Anastopoulos picked up a calendar, flipped a page forward, and tapped a smiling full moon with his marker. "December sixth is the Long Night's Moon. On that dark night, Deputy, you'll be hearing from Nature Boy. Demon or saint, he has a read on you. And watch yourself—there are others."

Anastopoulos was a profiler with a credible record. I listened and tried not to tremble.

"You'll find Nature Boy or he'll find you by December sixth. Meanwhile, the team has an abundance of physical evidence: paint, blood, cat fur, and carpet fibers. You have an unusual gift of vision, Brant. Trust your intuition, don't fear it."

Eldridge and I looked at each other.

Anastopoulos checked his watch, "I ought to get going. Call if you need me." He paused. "You too, Abby."

Demos Anastopoulos handed Abigail his card and she smiled. Instant jealousy.

The profiler gathered his coat, stood up, and paused at the door. "One more thing, Eldridge. Protect those who are near and dear to Brant. You'll be glad you did."

Abigail gulped.

"Don't worry, Dr. Reed," Weatherbee said, "we've been monitoring your carriage house for over a month."

Abigail shot me an accusatory look.

Eldridge jingled his keys. "It's been fun, kids, but I've got to whisk Demos to Hanscom before he misses his flight."

The profiler shouldered a duffel bag and held the door for Abby. She never looked back.

The door slammed, leaving me alone in Weatherbee's office. As the cruiser's engine trailed off, I glanced at the pewter bulldog poised on the desk, and then to the names of Nature Boy's victims on the chalkboard.

It was quiet, save for the sputtering radiators.

# 19

The following morning, I unrolled a topographical map on my kitchen table. I anchored each corner with mugs and ran my index finger across the concentric brown rings of the hills, green blotches of forests, and meandering blues of rivers. I marked the crime scenes in Lincoln, Concord, Bolton, and Carlisle, connected the dots, and circled the "hot point" at its epicenter. Nature Boy was nearby, no doubt about it.

The kidnapper had made no further contact. News of the governor's imminent cancellation of the hunting season had leaked to the public. I flicked on the TV and awaited the announcement.

Lieutenant Weatherbee was conducting a trace of postal truck sales in Massachusetts and an extensive medical record review. The state police and federal agents were canvassing the suburbs door-to-door. Local police organized roadblocks and random car searches while officers on trail bikes pedaled through the conservation land.

What could I offer?

Abigail had suggested that a volatile anesthetic agent might have detonated the explosion at Bolton Flats. I'd done nothing with the lead. With the Long Night's Moon approaching, I decided to consult the analysis laboratory before embarking on another futile search.

I called the lab for the results. A few minutes later, my FAX machine awakened and I scanned the data: *Nitrates: positive.* Black gunpowder. *Micrometallic fragments: steel and lead.* That was also easy to explain: steel jacketing around the mine and lead residue from buckshot. *Hydrocarbons: trace Exxon unleaded with MTBE additive.* I remembered fiery entrails bursting through the scarecrow's sternum, pluming into the October sky and a smoking crater where the scarecrow once stood. Something more powerful than a little "tiger in the tank" had detonated that blast.

I phoned analysis laboratory scientist, Dr. Vivek Patel. Vivek and I used to play racquetball at the YMCA. He'd been an anesthesiologist in India, but fools on the Board of Medical Examiners declared him ineligible to practice in the US. Like everybody from India, Vivek was brilliant and hard-working. I referred him to our forensics department, which turned out to be a boon for the U.S. Marshal Service.

"Vivek, your chromatography analysis of the bomb residue confuses me."

"Allow me to unconfuse you," he replied.

Vivek sounded so smart with his twinge of a British accent, that I'd have believed anything that came out of his mouth.

"I've been told that a gas was the catalyst for the bomb, yet you found only a trace of hydrocarbon residue," I said. "Could an anesthetics gas have detonated the black powder?"

"We've already assayed for halogenated hydrocarbons and ethers."

"Have you ever heard of cyclopropane?"

"Yes."

"Could a terrorist get his hands on the stuff?"

"Not likely, Brant. Cyclopropane is explosive. I wouldn't risk it on my dog."

"What did you say?"

"I wouldn't risk it on my dog. It was just a figure of speech."

"Okay Vivek, tell me. If the residue had been present, would you have picked it up?"

"It may be too volatile to pick up on SPME. Why didn't you mention it before?"

I remembered my phone conversation with Abigail Reed following the explosion. Her advice wasn't the only thing I'd neglected...

"We still have tissue samples and clothing in the materials unit," Vivek continued. "I'll head-space what I can and run it through the chromatography."

I thanked him. It was a cold, gray day. Ice had locked up the river. In a newsflash, the governor announced the moratorium on the Massachusetts deer season. The camera shifted to Major Fallon and an FBI spokesmen.

The program flashed to the Massachusetts State House

where a mob of outdoorsmen clad in fluorescent orange vests and camouflage jeered the legislators. These sportsmen had taken the week off for the annual deer hunt. It was a tough looking crowd. A Disney vacation would never satisfy these dyed-in-the-wool hunters. Animal rights advocates were notably absent.

A depleted Christian Evans appealed to the public, announcing a multi-million dollar reward for evidence leading to Cooper's safe return.

The broadcast concluded with a photo of Cooper Evans, as cute in his one-piece pajamas as the stuffed Tigger doll he was hugging. Considering the leopards in his father's trophy room, it seemed ironic that the little boy was cuddling a stuffed animal. The camera panned in on Cooper's sparkling eyes while the hotline number flashed below.

Vivek Patel called back thirty minutes later. "I ran MR spectroscopy on the Bolton Flats samples."

"What'd you find? Curry?"

"Not quite. Evidence of detonated cyclopropane or a similar compound. Homerun, Brant. Now catch the maniac."

Armed with the lab results, I hit the road with new enthusiasm, my eyes peeled for dumpy fannies. Expansive butts abounded in the suburbs. Unfortunately, none of those asses belonged to Baby Huey.

After visiting small animal hospitals and a feline ophthalmology practice, I had one last veterinary practice to investigate. My stomach kept growling, so I bought one of those low-fat subs that melts your waistline away in under a month. As

I ate, I kept picturing Cooper Evans whimpering, and suddenly lost my appetite.

"Eat Fresh" my foot. I trashed what was left of the sub and fired up my sad old Jeep.

The Assabet Animal Hospital was an unassuming gray ranch with three long rows of indoor boarding kennels extending from the back. A sagging garage containing animal feed, bedding, and medical supplies adjoined the clinic. It was an old-time practice, more homey than the "Doc in the Box" fast-food medical clinics. Aged owners streamed into the building with cats in carriers and assorted mongrels.

The clinic looked innocent enough, but for some reason, my ears began to ring, faint at first, louder as I approached. Inside, I cut to the front of a long waiting line. It seemed implausible that a crowded clinic could hide a terrorist, but I had nothing else to investigate.

Posters on the wall illustrating blighted cells of feline leukemia and the life cycle of the West Nile encephalitis mosquito made my skin crawl. As I read, a veterinarian tapped me on the shoulder and introduced himself.

Dr. Raskind, who'd eaten a few too many knishes in his time, had thinning curly hair. I had trouble deciding if he was a *schlemiel* (the klutz who spills the soup) or a *schlimazel* (the guy who gets the soup spilled on him). Perspiration moistened the underarms of his scrub shirt. Blood-stained gauze encircled a wound on his wrist.

I almost wished him Happy Hanukkah, but instead I said, "Looks like things are hopping around here."

"We run a down-to-earth practice—short on profit, but big on compassion," he said, with a trace of a Brooklyn accent. "Actually, I'm tickled that you're here, Deputy Sherman. I'm a bit of a crime buff."

Raskind motioned me into an examination room and closed the door. An antiseptic odor permeated the air. Instruments soaked in disinfectant solutions. Fur balls had accumulated in corners like tumbleweeds.

"I'd like to ask you a few questions, Doc, then have a look around."

"By all means. You're aware that state police and federal agents scoured the place back in August?"

I nodded.

A bisected dog heart, its chambers packed with a Gordian knot of stringy white parasites, bathed in a jar of yellowing formaldehyde. A jar of mineral oil held ticks in suspended animation. Some of the arthropods, even in death, clutched tufts of flesh in their mouth parts.

"Looks like a banner year for parasites, Doc."

"I hold the Guinness World Record for tick removal."

"Who treats patients around here?"

"You're looking at him."

I noticed a box of purple examination gloves on the counter. "Interesting color, Doc."

"They're Nitrile."

"Don't you use rubber gloves?"

"I can't. My assistant has a latex allergy."

"Do you have any other assistants?"

"Just part-timers."

"Are any male?"

"No."

"What anesthesia gas do you use around here?"

"Isofluorane or halothane."

"How about cyclopropane?"

"No way. I'm surprised that you've heard of that stuff."

"Do you store anything flammable here?"

"The fire department removed rusty tanks of God knows what from the garage after I bought the practice. That was years ago."

"How'd you cut yourself, Dr. Raskind?"

"A Doberman cross chose my forearm for an appetizer. Lucky thing Emmet saved my butt."

"Emmet?"

"My aide."

"Tell me about him."

"There's not much to tell. He's a quiet fellow — boring if you ask me."

"But you reported no male veterinary assistants."

"He's an unlicensed aid, not an assistant."

"How long has he worked here?"

"Fifteen or twenty years. I invited him to stay on when I bought the practice. He has a way with animals."

"The task force never mentioned him."

"He was out with back spasms in August."

"Does this Emmet have intestinal problems?"

"How'd you know? I referred him to a gastroenterologist, but he never kept his appointment. One thing for sure," Raskind continued, "the man's got the gift."

"What gift?"

"The Presence. Animals connect with certain people,

and tolerate the rest of us mortals with indifference. You can't acquire the Presence just by spending four years in veterinary school. A person either has it or he doesn't. Those with the Presence are savants — gifted, but unable to function in society. One girl I knew in vet school had it."

"What became of her?"

"She hung herself."

I stiffened. The insight rushed over me: the ringing in my ears and the visions...

"What's even weirder," the vet continued, "Emmet has a degree in electrical engineering from U Lowell, but works here for minimum wage."

*The tripwire at Bolton Flats...*

"Does Emmet perform procedures?" I asked.

Raskind fidgeted.

"Please, Doc. I'm running out of time."

"Okay, Deputy Sherman, I'll level with you. He assists me in the OR. In Massachusetts, it's illegal for technicians to operate, but I couldn't manage otherwise. It's tough to keep a practice afloat that offers *pro bono* work."

"Is that why you didn't tip off the team?"

The veterinarian stared at the floor.

"Forget about it, Dr. Raskind. Now tell me, is Emmet under psychiatric care?"

"Not that I'm aware of."

"Where does he live?"

"With his mom in Maynard."

"What kind of vehicle does he drive?"

"He walks the tracks."

"Does he have any allergies?"

"Just a contact rash from the scrub solution."

"I haven't earned my dermatology degree, Doc, but could it be psoriasis?"

"I suppose."

"One last question: What color are his eyes?"

"I can't say, " Raskind answered, "but one thing's for sure, he has the kind of stare that gets your attention. Harbinger's an odd duck, but he has a strange sort of wisdom about him."

My hand crept toward my revolver. Raskind noticed.

"You're wasting your time, Deputy. Emmet wouldn't hurt a flea."

"I'm not worried about fleas, Dr. Raskind. Where is he?"

"Out the back with the post-ops."

"Is he alone?"

"I believe so."

"Good. Point me in the right direction, and then stand off to the side."

Raskind stared at the handgun. "Don't hurt the poor guy."

My voice was a firm whisper. "I mean it, Doc. Act casual and give me room. That way *nobody* will get hurt."

I notified headquarters. The .357's grip was the handshake of an old friend. The air bristled with energy as I followed Raskind into the hall.

The signals from the far end of the animal clinic grew stronger. The buzzing in my ears became shrill ringing. I stared into the kennel. This was too easy...

Raskind's OR clogs click-clacked down the corridor. He swung open the recovery room door, revealing rows of bleary-eyed dogs and cats. I motioned him toward an alcove out of my line-of-fire and whispered, "Okay, Doc. Call him."

Raskind trembled. "I don't like guns."

"Call him!"

The veterinarian cupped his hands around his mouth. His voice trickled out. "Emmet?"

No answer.

"Emmet, I need you."

Creaking hinges replied.

"Shit!" I shouted, sprinting ahead. I barged through a series of swinging doors and burst through the emergency exit. Branches quivered at the edge of a thicket eighty yards away. I fired a warning shot, but Harbinger was long gone.

I thundered into the thicket and sprinted for at least a quarter mile, barreling through thorns until the scrub became too thick to continue. I caught my breath, then lurched through a brushy draw until I reached the Fitchburg Line train tracks. Stumbling up a crushed-stone trestle fording the Assabet River, I peered up and down the rails.

The ringing in my ears trailed off. Harbinger had vanished.

Seconds later, sirens screamed and cruisers screeched to a halt along the train crossing. I sprinted down the tracks, motioned the ground units in, and then dialed Weatherbee from the kennels behind the clinic.

"What the hell's going on?"

"I had a close encounter."

"How close?"

"I nearly had the son-of-a-bitch."

"Did you see him?"

"Barely. He's a loner, a mama's boy who fits our profile, complete with medical problems and a sixth sense about animals."

"How did he escape?"

"He must have heard me through the intercom."

"Who fired the shot?"

"I did—a mere fart in the wind..."

"Listen, Brant, keep your head in this."

"You don't think I agitated him enough to kill the kid, do you, Eldridge?"

Silence. Clouds swirled, and the sky grew darker.

"C'mon, answer me!"

The lieutenant said nothing.

I kicked the ground. A pair of cardinals, bright as blood, flitted in a spruce. Had I acted thirty seconds sooner, an eighty-yard snap-shot would have slammed the door on decades of pain.

The K-9 Unit stumbled out of the thicket first. The handler cursed the absence of scent and his dogs' unusual lack of motivation.

Moments later, an angry Dr. Raskind trotted into the backyard in his scrubs and mud-caked surgical clogs. "This show of force is far too aggressive, Deputy."

"It's time to get past your denial," I said. "You'd better look over your shoulder next time you drown a tick."

The Eurostar police helicopter rumbled overhead and blaring sirens multiplied.

The veterinarian shivered. "You think I've been mentoring a psychopath?"

I nodded. "Of the most deadly variety. Lucky thing you were nice to the doggies."

Raskind stared at the SWAT Team and turned ashen.

An hour later, the team reassembled. Weatherbee's hair was mussed, and in spite of the cold, his glasses steamed.

"I don't get it, Brant. We've got this radius sealed tighter than a super-glued anus and there's still no sign of the man. We can't find a Maynard address, next-of-kin, social security number, or utility bill under the name of Emmet Harbinger. His prints don't match anything in A.F.I.S. How does a guy just vanish?"

*These predators know the woods and the shadows. They disappear like ghosts. They know how to stalk men...*

"Okay," Weatherbee said to his detectives, "issue a standard tape-and-trace on the clinic phones. Monitor Harbinger's PO box and scour Concord, Acton, and Maynard door-to-door. We'll track down class photos from Harbinger's elementary school and broadcast his image to the world. No one can hide forever—not even a recluse."

That night, a black-and-white sixth grade photo of pre-adolescent Emmet Harbinger smiled at America from the evening news. On televised interviews, Emmet's classmates, now in their forties, described an awkward lad who skipped a lot of school and spent recesses alone in the playground feeding his peanut butter sandwiches to pigeons.

Emmet's sixth grade teacher had Alzheimer disease. When queried about Harbinger, he yelled, "Howitzer!" and dove under the bed.

A blue-haired teller at the Nashoba Saving's Bank remembered Emmet Harbinger as a polite customer who should have invested his paycheck on a haircut and a good dermatologist. Emmet's only crime had been hoarding complementary tootsie pops after each transaction.

The legend of Nature Boy continued to intrigue and shock the world. Talk shows buzzed with animal rights controversy. News vans constipated local thoroughfares as the chill of winter descended on New England.

After a week-long manhunt, there was no sign of the kidnapper. Some speculated that Harbinger might have committed suicide. More likely, I had frightened the suspect into hiding, the profilers said.

It was already December first, and the Long Night's Moon would not tarry.

I remembered Ms. Keating's judgmental stare. Her words kept gnawing at me.

I returned from a morning jog with a sidearm in my sweatshirt. The exertion dispelled some of my guilt. The impending holidays made me feel more isolated and lonely than ever.

I thought about Paige Sagoff; her outdoorsiness, her achingly-beautiful face, and her blonde hair. The possibilities were intriguing. But this was no time to rekindle flickering flames.

Suddenly, my cell phone rang. It was Diana Loomis. "We've received a donation that you'll find rather interesting," she said.

Diana was waiting outside the shelter, her graying ponytail bound in a Christmas bow. She led me to her desk and pointed to an envelope.

I gloved and examined the letter which contained a new one hundred dollar bill and an unsigned note scrawled on spiral notebook paper.

> *Sustain hungry creatures through the bitterness of winter and the chill of the human heart.*
> — *God's Merciful Legions*

I must have reread the message ten times before Diana Loomis said, "I thought you'd be impressed."

"Please leave everything as it is. I'll have the analysis team pick it up."

"Including the donation?"

"I'm afraid so. The Department will reimburse you."

"I feel like a traitor," Diana said. "This so-called maniac has managed to close deer hunting season and shut down the Select Safari Society."

"He's nothing more than a monster."

"Let me ask you something, Brant. Don't you find it curious that in all the years I've worked for animal rights causes, in spite of the many organizations I represent, I've never encountered this character?"

"What are you saying?"

"That Harbinger isn't your man, at least not the only one."

"What about the donation?"

"It's a bad prank."

"I'll leave that to the documents unit."

"And in case you've been wondering, Brant, Big Papi's still up for adoption."

"I don't want to deprive the big fella of the attention he deserves."

"Remember, I helped you."

"Is this blackmail, Ms. Loomis?"

She smiled. "Whatever it takes for a creature in need."

# 20

The team left me in the dust to "follow my instincts" as the profiler had suggested.

That night, tossing and turning in bed, I kept replaying my close call with Nature Boy and agonizing over the cost of my failure. The waxing moon glared at me through the frosted cabin windows.

At two a.m. I got a call that made my blood run cold. Someone had attacked Paige Sagoff. Lieutenant Weatherbee tried to spare me the details, but it sounded bad. Very bad. Dreading what I'd find and shaking like mad, I sped to Monument Street.

A corridor of flashing blue and red illuminated the long driveway. State police had already secured the perimeter and the advanced life support team had assembled on the patio.

The orange cascade of trumpet vines was now brown and withered, and the porch hammock hung deathly still. I followed the medical team inside and barreled up the stairs.

Eldridge Weatherbee acknowledged me with a sheepish wave. I followed him upstairs and into the palatial bathroom adjoining Paige's bedroom. Bare heels rested upon a wooden trauma board. A gold ankle bracelet glimmered as manicured toes began to wriggle. Paige groaned.

My skin crawled. Blood spattered everything, stark against the white tiles. Droplets on the mirror left vertical snail-like trails. The room reeked of rubbing alcohol and nail polish remover.

Paige had been scalped. Beefy-red muscle contrasted with exposed white skull. She kept moaning. The fumes and the specter of her wounds dizzied me. A trooper opened the window, and brisk air rushed in.

A shrine had been desecrated. I began to tremble. I should have been her bodyguard. Instead, I was forced to ignore her. Paige was a magnificent woman who had begged for protection, and I'd let Nature Boy tear her apart. What a hideous price to pay for concealing a crush.

*Protect those who are near and dear to Brant.*

One of the paramedics was having trouble trying to start an IV. "She's as dry as a bone," he said. Finally, he managed to snake a line into the vein. He withdrew the metal stilette and blood dribbled from the hub.

"What's her BP?"

"Seventy-four over palp. Her heart rate's one-twenty and thready."

"Get her into Trendelenburg position and run the

ringers wide open."

Something as matted as road-kill floated in the sink. It was Paige's scalp.

"The freak threw it into a chemical soup," Weatherbee explained, pointing to empty bottles of rubbing alcohol, hydrogen peroxide, and fingernail polish remover scattered over the marble countertop.

A medic grimaced as he lifted the mass out by its strands. Sopping scalp dangled beneath. He held the hair at arm's length, rinsed it with saline, and plopped it into a plastic bag and a Playmate cooler of chipped ice.

We followed the team downstairs. The IV infusion had began to revive Paige, but she was now an even "whiter shade of pale." Even her port wine stain had blanched.

Her eyes flickered open, and she caught sight of me. I touched her cheek as they opened the ambulance doors.

"I'm sorry Paige," I whispered into her ear. "So very, very sorry..."

She smiled faintly and closed her eyes. A massive lump welled up in my throat as the doors closed and gravel crunched beneath tires.

Wailing sirens trailed off into the predawn. A somber hush enveloped the house. Sergeant Pfleuger and forensics dusted fingerprints, collected blood samples, and vacuumed fibers. The melancholy team went through its motions slowly, reminiscent of a wake.

We went back upstairs. In the hallway outside Paige's bedroom Eldridge Weatherbee focused his flashlight over our heads where insulation protruded from the open attic access. Paige was right: someone had been stalking her, lurking overhead for days, perhaps weeks—the same *modus* as the Evans kidnapping.

I was an idiot. Nature Boy had always been in my head. Had I listened to the Presence, I could have saved Paige. My father was right about my gift, and I should have believed him.

The sights and smells made me queasy. I punched the wall and glared at Weatherbee. "I had no faith in your men, none whatsoever. I'm the one who should have been here."

"I'm sorry," he said.

I pointed to the insulation. "How in hell did they miss *that?*"

He shrugged.

"Everyone around me is getting decimated," I said, "and there's not a damned thing you let me do about it. I acted indifferent toward Paige. Now look at her."

"I won't stand in your way next time."

"Unless the next time is within forty-eight hours, Cooper Evans will wind up on exhibit at the Smithsonian."

I stomped down the stairs. Malcolm "Kip" Pearson hovered in the foyer in his khaki safari attire with a magnum pistol gleaming in his holster. I tried to ignore him, but Pearson stopped me.

"A pisser of a night, wouldn't you say?"

I stared at the floor.

Pearson's voice softened. "You're not alone. I failed her, too. Things might have been different if you'd been here."

Pearson sighed. "Paige enjoyed her privacy. Her room was so isolated that nobody heard a thing. Yet, for some reason, I couldn't sleep. I sensed danger in the air, the urgency of safari. The moment I smelled rubbing alcohol, I ran upstairs." He shook his head sadly. "Over the years, I've witnessed sports gored by wounded beasts, but the sight of Paige brought me to my knees."

We stood silently for awhile.

"For what it's worth, Deputy, you made quite a run at Paige."

"What do you mean?"

"She could have been yours."

"Mine?"

"I've never seen Miss Paige as taken with anybody as she was with you."

I began to sweat.

"That's right," Pearson said, "all you had to do was protect her, and you two would have ridden off into a golden sunset." He gritted his teeth. "If you do catch the bloody savage, make sure you finish him off."

I kept staring.

"Even so, old chap, considering what he's done to our lovely Paige, even that will be too little, far too late."


I paced outside the all-too-familiar Hawthorne Hospital trauma room. Weatherbee and his sergeants skulked at the far end of the corridor.

Suddenly, a team of nurses wheeled Paige into the room. Her eyelids flickered. Scarlet rings saturated gauze wrapped about her head. Several IVs including two units of blood dripped rapidly. I couldn't bear the sight, so I fled to the empty waiting room.

I collapsed into a chair and closed my eyes, trying to erase the image of Paige's glistening head. In the same way Paige had exsanguinated, part of my self bled out that evening, the part of me that saw colors, the part of me that had nearly apprehended beauty. My world was no longer stark, but a muted gray. There was no love left, only guilt and a profound urge to kill, an urge I could barely contain.

Just then, footsteps approached. It was Abigail Reed.

"We have to stop meeting like this, Brant."

I held my head.

"Maybe we should walk away," she said.

"I tried to once. It doesn't work."

To my surprise Abby sat down next to me and rubbed my shoulders. "You're cold again."

"Her face is so pale, so incredibly pale, Abby. And it's my fault."

"It's no secret that you like her."

I looked at her in surprise.

"The medical staff talks," she continued. "Apparently, you were quite a sensation at the party. In any case, when I got the call this morning, I knew right away that Paige Sagoff was the victim." Abby sighed. "Her face is perfect, even in this condition. I can understand why any man would fall for her. I should feel betrayed, but instead, I feel sorry for both of you."

"You're a bigger person than I am, Abby."

"I'm learning to grow through tragedy. Perhaps someday you will, too."

Just then, a nurse returned with lab results.

"Her crit's twenty-one, Dr. Reed."

"Hang two more units of packed cells, please."

"Did she feel anything?" I asked.

Abby studied the laboratory sheet. "Her ETOH level is nearly normal, but her benzo's are off the wall. Someone sedated her."

"We found a wine glass at the bedside."

"Laced with Ativan, no doubt."

"Thank God she wasn't conscious," I said.

Abigail Reed and the nurse looked at one another, and the nurse left the room.

"Benzodiazepines aren't analgesics."

"Meaning?"

"She felt *everything*."

I owned Paige's unspeakable suffering and took a moment to swallow the bitter reality.

"Will she survive, Abby?"

"Yes."

"And her hair?"

"The scalp is denatured — pickled, so to speak. There's no hope of saving it. Plastic surgeons can cover the defect with tissue flaps and skin grafts. At least she'll live."

"Which is more than I can say for Nature Boy," I said, patting my .357.


My yearning for Paige had disintegrated into pain, and my pain into anger. The urge for vengeance began to well up inside me again, stronger still. I trembled, not with fear, but with the anticipation of a chase and a killing shot.

I couldn't get out of that hospital fast enough. I kissed Abby on the forehead and ran for the Jeep.

# 21

It was now two in the afternoon, December sixth, a day and a half since the assault on Paige Sagoff. In less than three hours, the sun would set, and the Long Night's Moon would loom over New England.

It was a somber first Saturday in December, unseasonably warm and drizzly, courtesy of global warming. The first snow had already melted, with no white Christmas in sight. I hadn't heard from Abigail Reed, and I can't say that I blamed her. Even I was sick of hanging around with myself.

With only seventeen shopping days before their Savior's birthday, credit card-waving consumers searching for the true meaning of the holiday invaded Concord center. I thought about fleeing to northern Maine to fish and trap for a living. I'd have left in a heartbeat if my father wasn't dying.

     The team had pulled an all-nighter in a last-ditch effort to save Cooper Evans. Bleary eyed, I kept driving the back roads of Lincoln, past stately federal and Georgian-style homes. I studied each site as my father used to, seeking any irregularity that didn't blend with the barns, the silos, the trees, the pastures, and stone walls. So far, there were no new danger signals.

     On Codman Hill Road, a cardinal darted in front of my Jeep and glanced off the front bumper — not exactly the most auspicious start to my afternoon. I pulled over and held the terrified bird in my hand. Its crimson plumage shone stark against the dreary backdrop. I smoothed its feathers. Killing a cardinal in New England would have been like shooting the proverbial Albatross with a crossbow. Call me superstitious, but no way could I let that bird die. Even Cosette knew enough not to harass cardinals. I told that bird that he was too good-looking to croak with all the old codgers in Lincoln. Thankfully, the bird listened to me. In time he recovered, and flitted away.

     *Bad Moon Rising* by CCR blared on my Jeep radio. I changed the station as Cosette's tongue flapped in the breeze.

     Just then, the mother of all sport utility vehicles nearly rear-ended me. I accelerated to avoid the collision. The driver continued to tailgate, but recognizing my marshal windbreaker, dropped back. I motioned the vehicle ahead. A *Support Your State Police* sticker decorated the rear window, and a radar detector adorned the dashboard. The driver was a blonde whose head barely cleared the dashboard. She gave me a cute little wave, certain to get her off the hook. Unfazed, she inched by, still yapping on her cell phone.

One thing I'd learned in Concord: never get in the way of a mother on a mission. In suburbia, little women in Amazon-sized SUVs posed a constant threat to one's life and well-being, more intimidating than any beast I'd encountered in the wild or any pistol-wielding felon.

DeCordova Road wound between pumpkin patches and a cornfield speckled with starlings. Farther beyond, a white church with a tall steeple nestled in a pine grove. I steered into the empty parking lot behind the church and let Cosette out to relieve herself. Bells in the steeple pealed *Joy to the World.*

Just then, my cell began to jangle, clashing with the chimes. It was Dr. Vivek Patel, speaking quickly.

"I have caught you a fish, Brant. A big one I think!" he said. "Where are you now?"

"In Lincoln. Why?"

"Because I'm about to decipher Nature Boy's address."

"How?"

"Remember the letter from the animal shelter? I couldn't get the little boy off of my mind, so I worked on it all night in the DA Unit. About an hour ago, I ran the paper through a device which detects writing imprints from notebook pages on top of it."

"What'd you find?"

"A return address. I need your help."

"Shoot."

"I'm in a dark room right now with the letter on a
scanning microscope."

I listened from the Jeep while Cosette terrorized squirrels
at the edge of the parking lot.

"There's a capital C preceded by a five or a two," Patel
continued. "A small *e* and *a* appear in the middle of a long word.
Does it mean anything to you?"

Words scrambled in my mind. Suddenly, an old address
materialized. "Commonwealth Avenue. It's next to the prison in
West Concord!"

"Now, save that child."

I dialed Weatherbee.

"Eldridge, Vivek Patel just traced imprints on that
Buddy Dog letter to a return address."

"What address?"

"Commonwealth Avenue, Concord."

"That's within a quarter mile of the barracks."

"I know."

"Do you have the street number?"

"Not exactly, but it's one of those row houses. My ETA is
five minutes, and I'm going in."

"Whoa, partner; the case belongs to the tactical unit
and HIT."

"But I need to nail this guy."

"That's just the point. You're too emotionally tied to this
case. Somehow, this freak has a read on you. You've already
given us what we needed."

"That's unfair, and you know it."

"Look," Weatherbee said, "the concept may disappoint
you, but my cases don't end in high drama."

I refused to believe him. I boosted Cosette into the passenger seat and swung open the rear hatch. Then, I wriggled into my black U.S. Marshal Special Operations Group coverall, secured my .357 Korth/Beeman magnum revolver in its holster, and Velcroed a semiautomatic sidearm, a Sig-Sauer P-230 4-inch automatic 9 mm, into the carrier beneath my pectoral muscle. Like I said, I care enough to send the *very* best.

I flicked my Zumbo elk knife from its black ballistic cloth sheath and turned the six-inch stainless steel blade over and over. On the reverse side, a heavy duty bone saw and gut hook glistened. I sheathed the knife, strapped on the leg scabbard, then fired up the Jeep.

I screeched down the road, cracking through ice puddles en route to West Concord. Were we too late for Cooper Evans?

*What goes around comes around, what we do to animals, we do to ourselves.*

Even if the team captured Harbinger alive, he'd languish in prison somewhere, with access to psychiatric consultations, attorneys, and free education.

Any psychopath could wave the white flag and walk away from his crimes, gloating with newfound fame. Fiends enjoyed protection in liberal states like Massachusetts. After years in court listening to silver-tongued defense lawyers, I knew there was nothing I could do about it.

Worse, if Harbinger were schizophrenic, defense lawyers could raise an insanity plea. Even if convicted, the maggot would be eligible for parole! My stomach began to knot.

I thought about my brother crashing through the ice and his waxen face staring up, imploring me to avenge an unspeakable wrong. I recalled the cyanotic face of an asphyxiated

Harvard professor, fluid oozing from a politician's eyeballs, children gagging on fish hooks, a surgeon — instead of basking in the glory of a panacea — melting away with each rigor that ravaged his body, and the bleeding stump of a frostbitten trapper.

And last of all, I remembered Paige Sagoff, her face translucent as frosted glass, blue eyes staring into space.

If only I had caught Nature Boy...

As I drove, my mind drifted back to Nashawtuc Lake. The hole that had consumed my brother seethed.

A dark figure stared from the wooded shore. He reached up and tore off his ski mask, revealing a harrowing image: my own face! But the eyes were no longer blue and brown, they were dead eyes of a mannequin. Shrill buzzing, and soon, the distressed voices of victims resounded in my head: *You hurt us, Brant. Because of you, we suffer.*

I skidded onto the shoulder. Cosette slid off the front seat into the dashboard. I slammed the Jeep into park and rested my head on the steering wheel. My life in Concord had been far from deliberate. I had not sucked the marrow from life as Thoreau had professed — I had just sucked.

In reality, I knew that I'd never end up living in Maine or anyplace that pristine. I'd retreat to what I knew, to what I'd become — The Worst of Boston. I'd return to the courtrooms, the pawnshops, the flophouses, back to vans transporting the dregs of humanity from court to jail and from jail back to court in a futile effort to sequester them from the gentle world. I'd leave my father, Abigail Reed, and my twisted past.

A bleak future loomed ahead. My brother had drowned,

and Dad was fading fast. Soon, I'd be alone. My future? Chasing low-life fugitives. I punched the dashboard. No worse for the wear, Cosette cocked her head and wagged her tail.

Without explanation, a tantalizing vision of justice began to take shape, and I tensed with the urgency of a sapling about to snap. In my imagination, I observed Emmet Harbinger's capture:

*Major Fallon leads Harbinger from the dilapidated house. The SWAT team covers him from the rooftops. German shepherds strain on their leashes. Hostage negotiators, row upon row of state troopers, marksmen, FBI agents, paramedics, and news teams crane their necks for a peek at the suspect.*

*I stand off to the side with my back toward the prisoner. Fat-assed Harbinger keeps grinning as cameras flash, spotlights glare, and videotape rolls. My trigger finger twitches. Nobody notices my deadly intention.*

*My extremities surge with adrenaline. Suddenly, I whirl around and aim between Harbinger's eyes. The muzzle kicks in slow motion and the 110 grain jacketed hollow-point mushrooms through the fiend's forehead, spewing hunks of bone and pluming blood into the air. The head absorbs the impact, the back of the cranium falls away, and the body twists upon itself. The muzzles of one hundred weapons are trained on me as I stand over the lifeless heap.*

*Smoke that, Baby Huey...*

I snapped out of the daydream and pulled back onto the road. No doubt about it, justice demanded a calculated blast from my .357.

The more I pondered the deed, the more it made sense.

Manslaughter meant a ten to twenty-year jail term. But there was no other option. I accelerated across the Assabet River Bridge toward Commonwealth Avenue.

The ringing of my cell startled me.

"Deputy Sherman?"

My voice was raspy. "Speaking."

"This is George Kazanjian. Remember me?"

"I remember you, George, but you've picked a bad time to talk."

"This is payback for that trout dinner a few months ago."

"I don't have time to chat."

"Make time, Deputy. How close are you to catching Harbinger?"

"Very close."

"Not close enough," said the veteran.

"Our team has the situation in hand," I said.

"They may think they do, but you're the one who'll nail Nature Boy."

"Not likely, George."

"It's more than likely, Deputy—it's inevitable. You're different from most cops—and I'm about to make you famous."

"Believe me, the state police are taking care of business."

"That's what they think. The Staties are storming a house on Commonwealth Avenue, and you're feeling left out. They're planning to steal your credit, but I know better."

"How'd you know that?"

"I used to work in Intelligence. These days, I have buddies—garbage men, DPW employees, prison guards, and friends in mighty low places—who have CB radios and don't miss a trick."

"Why are you calling me?"

"Come to the concert for preservation of Walden Woods in West Concord. The John Haverly Band is playing. I've found something. See for yourself."

I fidgeted. "That's behind Nashawtuc Lake, right?"

"You're good, Deputy Sherman. Damned good."

"It's a bit late in the year for a concert, don't you think?"

"Haverly needs to raise enough money to save Walden Woods by New Year's Eve, or developers will pave paradise. His roadies have set up tents and heaters. C'mon down."

I hesitated. Nashawtuc Lake. The first big freeze of winter. Jagged ice could peel off scabs. I could hear electric guitars wailing in the background.

"Are you coming or not?"

"Call the Concord police, George."

"I don't want the police, I'm giving him to you. Now get down here before it's too late."

I hung up and phoned Eldridge Weatherbee. "I just received a tip from one of my informants."

"Who?"

"A veteran named George Kazanjian. He's got a suspect at the Haverly Concert."

"Oh, I'm sure he has," Eldridge said. "You're not going to miss our moment of glory for some LSD flashback, are you?"

"It's a state police moment."

"If you hustle down here, Brant, there's a Skybar in it for you. This time, you can have the whole thing."

"I don't know..."

"Look buddy, we've already amassed enough firepower on this street to blow away a small nation. If we take Harbinger alive, I'll arrange a little quality time for you two in a holding cell."

I visualized a fat hollow-point shattering my enemy's forehead. Kazanjian would have to wait.

Any hope of taking Harbinger alone evaporated when I arrived on scene. The manpower astonished me. Rows of marksmen on rooftops trained their 6 mms on a dilapidated white house on Commonwealth Avenue. Outside of the buffer-zone, cruisers, ambulances, and armored vehicles clogged the street. Meanwhile, K-9 Units swept the waist-high reeds along the shoreline of Warner's Pond. Troopers herded news vans a safe distance away while the tactical surveillance team set up audio monitors. Major Fallon and Lieutenant Weatherbee approached the special OP commander.

"Any sign of the child, Zebco?" Fallon asked.

"We hear something, sir, but it doesn't sound human."

The lieutenant and the major inspected the backyard. Weatherbee stiffened and shielded us from a branch. The bushes bore three-inch spikes.

"Hawthorn and flowering quince. This yard is a veritable crown of thorns."

"Our boy seems rather inhospitable, but we're going to invite ourselves in anyway," Fallon said.

The emergency services unit surrounded a barn behind the house. I joined them. Agents battered the door down and stormed in. The place was packed with animal feed, hay, and pine shavings. A trooper yanked a green tarp, and in a swirl of dust, revealed a white Postal truck.

Fallon peered inside. "Complete with the tacky carpeting. Get Sergeant Pfleuger in here."

Soon afterward, I discovered a low-profile duckboat camouflaged with reeds. "A Barneget Bay Sneakbox," I explained.

"That's how our boy ferried his explosives into Bolton Flats," said Weatherbee.

"And his bear trap into the marsh," Major Fallon added.

The team cleared the rest of the barn. In a rebirth of enthusiasm, forensics collected hand-cut carpeting from the floor of the Jeep and chips from the keel of the Sneakbox.

Fallon barked orders into his radio. The hostage intervention team surrounded the old house. Agents focused their audio surveillance equiptment. The SWAT team steadied their weapons.

Commander Zebco gestured toward his men. "Ready when you are, Major."

Spotters using infrared goggles, four men with shotguns, and another four with MP-5 9 mm machine guns flattened themselves along the foundation. In a guard tower across the street, snipers trained their crosshairs on the living room.

Sergeant Pfleuger emerged from the barn, out of breath, waving a bagged sample over her head. "These scarlet carpet fibers have the same tri-lobed weave we found in Carlisle, Major. And the left front Firestone is reversed with the black wall facing out."

Major Fallon scanned the endless array of sniper barrels. His face relaxed for the first time in months. "This time, we get to win..."

Commander Zebco jogged toward Fallon.

"Sir, the place sounds like it's swarming with vermin,

but there's nothing to indicate our subject or the Evans kid."

Fallon wrinkled his brow. "You sure?"

"I'm sure."

"Are your men out?"

"All present and accounted for."

Fallon pointed to the glow of the full moon rising, and signaled to the rescue team.

"Hammer time, boys."

The hostage intervention team crept along the foundation. Using glass cutters and suction cups, they extracted sections of window from each quadrant of the house. The agents glanced at their watches and in unison, tossed in explosives.

In seamless choreography, four explosions blew out panes of glass. The officers stormed in. Birds spiraled from the windows. Screeching cats leapt from the upper floors. Animal mayhem at its best.

At the commander's signal, the team and I burst through the doors. Donning a Kevlar vest several sizes too small, Weatherbee followed. Inside, the odor of cat urine made me gag. I tore down a window shade, and light streamed into the dander-filled living room. Urine-soaked newspapers blanketed the floor, including a headline of me at Bolton Flats with a pee stain smeared across my face. A sea of mangy felines rippled around us. Disgusting.

Weatherbee leaped onto a couch for higher ground. His foot plunged through the stuffing, skinning his shin on a spring, and he uttered an impressive string of expletives.

A trooper trotted toward Weatherbee. His voice was solemn, without urgency. "We've found the kid, Lieutenant. He's in the basement."

Weatherbee and I creaked across warped floors slick with droppings and paused at the cellar doorway. The troopers motioned us down the cinderblock stairs into a fieldstone basement. In the dim light of a naked bulb, I saw a running space heater and an empty playpen littered with sippy cups and soiled blankets. We clawed our way through cobwebs toward a cluster of flashlight beams dancing in the gloom.

The men had formed a semicircle around something at the far corner of the cellar. Spotlights swept up to the rafters, where the body of a little boy was bound to a shaggy fir beam. The child's head hung limply. My heart sank.

A dozen troopers stared at the curious specter of a toddler-sized body clad in stained blue Eeyore pajamas. The skin had a pasty, inhuman texture. Cameras flashed, and a camcorder panned across the room, then focused on the body.

Fallon burst into the cellar and cleaved his way through the crowd. He looked up, and his jaw dropped.

"I don't believe it," a trooper whispered, "the freak actually taxidermied the kid!"

I nudged Weatherbee. "Is it possible to stuff a human?"

The lieutenant's eyes never shifted from the grim figure lashed above him. "I don't know. Just cut him down."

The troopers stared at one another.

"Don't just stand there — cut him down!"

The men boosted a trooper to the rafter. "There's a noose around his neck, sir. It looks like parachute cord."

The trooper nudged the corpse. The body slipped from its perch, dead weight falling, until the rope jerked it back up. The men recoiled from the swinging child, who creaked in the half-light of the cellar. Gloved men supported the body. One loosened the noose and felt for the carotid pulse.

"Hey wait a minute... this is a CPR dummy!"

He tore the one piece outfit from the body, exposing flesh-colored rubber pectorals.

"We've been had, fellas," Weatherbee said. "But those are Cooper's pajamas, so keep looking."

Inspired, I searched with rest of the team. Spotlights penetrated the gloom as we filtered through the basement. Weatherbee ripped cobwebs from his face and radioed the agents upstairs. "Any sign of the suspect?"

"No, Lieutenant. Just rodents. Rats the size of beagles. And rabbits. Shitloads of rabbits."

Suddenly, I heard muffled crying. My eyes jumped to the dummy, but the sound was more distant. I sprinted toward the rear of the cellar. Light gashed into the basement as the team axed through the bulkhead. The crying grew louder.

A specialist with headphones had already pinpointed the sound behind the padlocked steel door of what seemed to be a meat locker.

A beefcake of a trooper stepped forward with bolt cutters. It took all of his strength to sever the bolt and several sledgehammer blows to dislodge the lock. The door swung open to deafening crying. Naked and soiled, Cooper Evans sat amongst pacifiers, sippy cups, and puddles of curdled milk under the very dim light of a single bulb. Mercifully there was no hum of a refrigeration unit.

The toddler stopped crying and gazed us, snot streaming across his face. At the touch of Weatherbee's hand on his forehead, he resumed his ear-splitting shrieking.

"Get this kid into an ambulance," the lieutenant said.

"He's as cold as a fish."

A department psychologist gathered the toddler in a blanket.

Weatherbee radioed the rest of the hostage intervention team, "We're exiting via the rear cellar stairway with the child. Have you found anything yet?"

"Negative, Lieutenant."

Inside the meat locker, we ducked several dessicated carcasses of pigs and one cow swinging by their hocks.

Gun drawn, I squinted through the gloom and trained my flashlight on a figure sitting in a chair against the back wall. It was a woman with a mummified face as dried-up as an apple doll's, lips retracted in a permanent sneer, hair wild and scraggly beneath her bonnet. She wore a flowing dress, with pine tree car deodorizers pinned to her chest like cameos. Her eye sockets were empty, yet she'd been positioned as if she were about to sit for tea. The ambiance hinted of mothballs, air freshener, and dead old lady mixed with the stench of curdled milk and dirty diapers.

"Greetings, Mrs. Harbinger," Eldridge said.

He motioned the others forward. Major Fallon bristled at the sight of the corpse.

"Emmet didn't bother letting anybody know that his mother had died," Weatherbee explained. "The utility bills are still in her name, but about seventeen months ago, the handwriting on the checks changed. Harbinger attacked Dr. Fenwick on the anniversary of her death." He pointed to the stairwell. "Harbinger had an alcoholic common-law stepfather the size of a Sumo wrestler who supposedly tripped down those stairs and died of a brain hemorrhage."

I raised my eyebrows. "Tripped?"

"I suspect that Emmet made the assist."

We climbed the bulkhead stairs. It was cloudy outside, but bright compared to the basement.

Weatherbee squinted. "Imagine spending a week in a meat locker with a pruned old lady?"

"A far throw from Cooper's *Goodnight Moon* room," I said.

Commander Zebco approached Weatherbee and Fallon in the backyard while the troopers dismantled the house. Cats bolted out of the domicile in singles and in small groups. Weatherbee shook his head as white rats scurried along the foundation.

"Time to pay the Piper," he said.

Fallon turned toward the commander. "Any sign of Harbinger?"

"The bedroom looks like a Taliban warehouse, but he's gone."

"Have you checked the crawlspaces and the attic?"

"We've looked *everywhere*."

That's when I sprinted for the Jeep and sped to the Haverly Concert.


Kazanjian, clad in his Army parka and black eye patch, was waiting at the gate as I pulled into the muddy parking lot. A traffic officer motioned me to a VIP parking space next to a limousine and the band's custom bus. I greeted the veteran with Cosette at heel. Five thousand fans crowded beneath tents in a sixty-acre fairground.

Years before, this area had been a broccoli farm. Farther beyond, Nashoba Brook snaked through swamps, cornfields, and finally, Walden Woods. Out of sight, but less than a mile away, was Nashawtuc Lake. I turned up my collar.

The snow had melted, leaving small white mounds at the perimeter of the fields. The southeast wind strengthened.

John Haverly was singing numbers from his country rock hit album. The crowd drew in close. Graying baby boomers swayed to the music alongside teenagers mouthing the words. Green balloons with the blue earth logos swirled in the gusts.

Kazanjian's thinning salt-and-pepper hair was gathered back in a small ponytail. His one eye gleamed. "What took you so long, Deputy?"

We jogged across a soccer field and sat on the highest bleachers while Cosette sniffed for meadow mice. Kazanjian handed me a spotting scope. I focused on the spectators eighty yards away.

"Check out the fourth row on the right," he said.

Months before, Kazanjian had been a poacher. Now he'd become my unlikely guide. I had my doubts, but went through the motions. The heat blowers muffled Haverly's voice, but his groupies kept swaying to the beat.

I scanned the sea of faces, but saw nothing unusual. "George, I should be on my way."

"You *are* on your way."

"This is like finding a needle in a haystack."

"Let me show you the needle," said Kazanjian, redirecting the scope. "See the loser in the green snorkel jacket?"

I found the man.

"That's the same guy I followed down Monument Street."

"You're not jerking me around, are you, George?"

"Deputy, who other than social rejects and Eskimos wears snorkel jackets? Besides, my AA sponsor, Perch Taggart, runs an organic farm on Monument Street south of Punkatassett Hill. He noticed that creep poking around the Sagoff estate. We followed him for a few days. Me and Perch had no idea what the creep was up to until we got the news about Paige Sagoff."

"Why didn't you call the police?"

"The place was already crawling with cops. Besides, who'd have listened to the likes of me?"

"When did you notice this?"

"A week before Paige was attacked. I don't sleep too good, so I drive around at night. The guy took off when he caught sight of me."

"That's one hell of a story, George."

"It's not just a story," Kazanjian said. "Like the saying goes, 'Always hire a vet.' "

I focused the spotting scope. The man in the snorkel jacket was facing away. "By the way," I asked Kazanjian, "what kind of vehicle was he driving?"

"You already know the answer. A white Postal truck. Perch noticed the vehicle driving in and out of the estate the night before Paige was attacked. It had a do-it-yourself paint job. I thought about making a citizen's arrest, but I've had a little domestic trouble and lost my license to carry. Like I told you, I don't care for cops. But you're one of the good guys, Sherman. That's why me and my brothers decided to give him to you. All you have to do is snap on the cuffs."

I tossed Kazanjian a leash. "Walk Cosette back to the vehicle, George. Contact Major Fallon and tell him that I'm bringing in a suspect."

Kazanjian smiled. "Have yourself a merry little Christmas, Deputy Sherman."

The stranger was standing in the center of the audience close to the performers. A furry hood concealed his face. Ambushing him from backstage would draw too much attention. Waiting meant losing him in the crowd. I decided to stalk him, using the spectators as camouflage.

Haverly began to sing a top-forties hit, and I was hoping for the long version. I jostled my way through the crowd. Spectators threw me looks, then noticing my SOG combat attire, gave way. Fifteen rows closer, I crouched. It was tougher going than I'd expected.

The stranger swayed to the music. I leap-frogged five rows ahead and ducked. Without warning, he whirled around. The man was about six foot-two, good-sized, but tackle-able. I still couldn't see his face. When he turned away, I tiptoed ahead. The song ended, and John Haverly began to speak.

"Henry David Thoreau once wrote about the tranquility of the place he loved. Are we willing to allow corporate America to steal Walden Woods?"

"No," the crowd replied.

"With your support, Walden will remain a place where a man can stroll deliberately."

The audience, including the figure in the snorkel jacket, clapped. I slipped forward as the next tune began. The man suddenly turned and canted his head. He knew. Recognition sparked across the seventy yards that still separated us. The spectators cringed as feedback reverberated through the air and the wind played across the staging and taut guy lines of the canopy. That's when he stiffened, turned, and ran.

It took me awhile to break free of the crowd. Behind the stage, footprints veered around the base of a knoll, across a muddy field, into the wetland that cradled Nashawtuc Lake, a body of water I had managed to avoid for over two decades.

Revolver drawn, I sprinted ahead, my boots slipping on the half-frozen surface. The music faded. The trail led into a swamp. I high-legged through the calf-deep water. In the middle of the swamp, the ice was barely thick enough to support my weight, buckling as I slid across the surface. Every so often, I'd break through, and frigid water would gush into my boots.

But the same obstacle impeded the fugitive. His blood flecked the sharp edges of the ice. I smashed my way through the muck, tripping on thorny vines. Fifty yards ahead, I made it to dry ground and trotted into the trees. Before I knew it, I was deep in Walden Woods.

I entered the pine grove on the western shore of the lake, the same bank from which somebody had watched my brother drown. Here, the evergreens grew thicker and taller than I remembered.

I peered at the lake, entombed by black ice. Gulls dotted the surface. I slunk closer. In the center, the spring hole rippled as in my frequent nightmares. Just north of the opening, I visualized the teenage version of myself kneeling on the ice, gun in hand, coaxing Timmy forward. The memory dazed me for a moment. But I gritted my teeth and forged onward.

Agitated pine needles, blood droplets, and broken twigs showed me the way. Fortunately, the trail led away from the water.

The woods became gloomier now, the underbrush thicker. Most of the snow had melted, but small mounds persisted in the northerly shadows of the tree trunks. Mist wafted into the air. Wispy snow insects fluttered in the breeze. Winter had temporarily lost its foothold, but it wouldn't be long before arctic blasts would again immobilize the forests of New England.

Farther ahead, I noticed a tool locker with its lid flung open. I reached into the corner of the wooden box, amongst saws and axes, and pulled out a still warm, balled-up snorkel jacket.

Anvil-like nimbus clouds obscured the sun. The woods darkened. Trees creaked, and wind rushed through their boughs. It had been a long time since I'd roamed these woods, and I was disoriented. As in the tunnel, I had no landmark to use as a reference point — no John Hancock Tower, Prudential Building, or CITGO sign.

I ran my hand along a broad maple trunk. Expanded and distorted by time, were the carved initials of two lovers from 1978. The far side of the tree was damp and mossy, indicating north.

I drew in a deep breath, and took the next tentative steps, pivoting through the woods, scanning each tree trunk and beyond.

For the next fifteen minutes, I dared only two or three paces at a time. I soft-stepped across the pine needles and kept watching for the glimmer of eyeballs. My index finger kept twitching, but there was nothing to shoot at. Nuthatches and chickadees flitted in the branches overhead, and a red squirrel scolded from its perch.

Considering the blood and broken ice, I reasoned that an out-of-shape suspect hadn't time to escape. I glanced at my watch. Twenty minutes had elapsed.

Dry brown cattail reeds rustled in a hollow. Something clattered through the underbrush. I tiptoed forward, pistol ready. A brown blur emerged. It was a doe. She peered back into the cover. Her yearling fawn trotted out. More annoyed than frightened, both deer stared. They ambled off then, abruptly, white tails flagging, bounded away. Bedded deer meant that no other human had passed this way.

I could scarcely feel my frozen wet toes. *What if the dork in the snorkel jacket were just a dope-head hiding an ounce of pot?*

Yet soon, my ears began to ring, faint at first, but then increasing in volume. I had the feeling that I was being watched, that *I* was being stalked. This time, there was no turning back.

I headed toward the vague glow of the sun, low in the southwest sky. A stand of hardwoods with trunks broader than a man's body surrounded me. The wind strengthened, and the skies grew darker with thickening cloud cover. I patted my carrier. My sidearm was secure, and in spite of the ice, the sheath knife was still seated in the leg scabbard. Flattening my back against the smooth trunk of an ancient beech, I held the pistol in ready position.

Faster than I could react, something hissed toward me. The revolver flew from my grasp. I saw black and faltered, but my searing right shoulder jolted me back onto my feet. An arrow's fletching scraped my cheek. I was pinned to the tree trunk.

I grasped the carbon shaft. Hemorrhage expanded toward my chest and armpit. The pressure sensation made me queasy. The broadhead had impaled me through muscle and tendon, and every time I buckled, pain radiated through my marrow.

I couldn't pry myself from the hardwood. I reached for my leg scabbard, and as I bent down, the landscape began to shift. Barely discernible from the dead vegetation, a mound of leaves fifteen yards away came to life. The leaf pile became a recumbent human form in 3-D camouflage who rose to his feet and shuffled forward holding a nocked compound bow.

Yellow eyes glared from holes in the face mask. As I nearly lost consciousness, his image blurred into the background of the forest as if he were an apparition. I kept blinking my eyes, but he didn't disappear.

The stranger drew the bowstring back. I stared along the shaft of a glistening broadhead, and hugged the tree.

"Well, well, well... Let's see what I've brought to bag," the stranger said. I slouched to avoid the broadhead aimed at my heart. Razor-thin blades two inches in diameter extended from the arrow tip like the fins of a Cruise missile. This bowhunter had done his homework. Those blades could part human flesh like paper. I glanced at the magnum Korth/Beeman resting beyond my reach on the forest floor.

The figure lowered the bow, relaxed the string, and began to sing Queen's *Bohemian Rhapsody* in a crazy baritone. Using the bow as an electric guitar, he strutted like Freddy Mercury, and shook his index finger at me.

*"I see a little silhouetto of a man."*

There would be no reasoning with this twisted lunatic. I struggled like a gaffed fish. The arrow creaked, but refused to yield.

*"Mama mia, mama mia, mama mia, let me go?*
*No, no, no, no, no, no, no."*

The stranger trotted closer. His voice grated. "Your pissing me off, Sherman! Animals endure their wounds, so must you."

The suspect drew the arrow to the corner of his cheek and snapped off a shot. The arrow thwapped into the trunk within millimeters of my neck, shaft quivering with terrible energy. He nocked another arrow, studied my crucified shoulder, and nodded with approval.

"Your heart is pumping now! Pitter-patter, pitter-patter. How does it feel to be hunted?

"Amazing these weapons of destruction, aren't they Sherman?" The stranger ran his gloved hand across the compound bow. "This overdraw and eighty percent let-off has exceeded my expectations. How efficient your murder machines have become. What a piece of work is man. How noble in reason. So much effort invested in killing, so little spent on salvation."

The assailant modeled his camouflage suit. Not that I cared at this point, but his butt didn't protrude in Baby Huey fashion. One thing for sure, he was weirder than any lunatic I'd ever encountered.

"This 3-D Scent-lock Leafy Tree fooled even the likes of you, Sherman. No wonder the deer haven't a chance. Your instruments of death are too effective. I've become adept at using them myself, as you'll soon find out."

"Are you Emmet Harbinger?"

"That's a human name."

"Then who the hell are you?"

"The voice inside your head, the one you chose to ignore, your conscience."

I tried to pry myself from the tree and nearly blacked out. The man trotted close, and kicked me in the stomach.

"Pay attention!"

I gasped for breath. The arrow's torque vibrated through my core.

"You knew that killing was wrong," the stranger said. "You heard the creatures screaming, yet you wasted your gift. We tried to save you years ago—so long ago—when you murdered my fawn, and now it's payback time."

I hurled myself at the madman, but the arrow's grip was relentless.

"You have always known me," said the stranger, reaching up to his mask. "I live in your nightmares. Behold the face of your death."

He removed the camo hood, and said, "I know you, you know me. One thing I can tell you is you've got to be free."

A husky, pockmarked Caucasian with sparse rust hair held a broadhead at arm's length and pointed it at my heart. Vacant, amber pupils rolled back into the man's skull. It was a grim, unfeeling face, bearing no semblance of the doughy, bawling teenager in Estabrook woods.

"I warned you to change, Sherman. I knew you'd be foolish enough to venture onto the lake. *You* actually killed your brother, Sherman. I only assisted. What goes around comes around. The ducks on Nashawtuc Lake rejoiced that season, and every season since. You forced me to cull your brother from the human herd. Poor Tiny Tim, tiptoeing through the ice where it's too dark for tulips. Tiny Tim. So cold and blue. Pity, pity."

"You murdered a child over a freaking deer?"

"It wasn't just a deer!"

Wind howled through the trees. Harbinger stared overhead and began to whisper: "I hear their voices, so many voices. And make no mistake, little Timmy's still screaming, too."

I lunged, but still the arrow held fast.

"Many have atoned for your sins," Harbinger continued. "The rich bitch who skins animals, the needle-and-the-damage-done doctor, the bug impaler, the blowhard politician with *joo-joo* eyeballs, stumpy the trapper who sawed off his own leg, and others the Legion taught about suffering. You, too, must learn.

"You have animal eyes, Sherman. You see what others cannot, and feel what others can't feel. You hear their voices. You have the Presence. It radiates throughout the forest. That's why you're so easy to stalk, so easy to torment.

"Living creatures impart beauty to the world. It's a sin to efface beauty. And the gravest sin of all is to render an animal — once warm, once feeling, once animated — still forever."

Harbinger hefted his bow. Razor-edged blades gleamed. Vapor wafted from his mouth. He aimed full-draw at my gut. I imagined paper-thin broadhead blades cleaving through my intestines.

"Yes, Sherman, you will share their agony. And a final thought — you've led me to your father. After I kill you, I'll make him suffer long and slow before he dies. And as he writhes, he'll learn that I've bagged *both* of his boys."

Suddenly, crackling branches startled Harbinger and he lowered his bow. The ground rumbled. As Harbinger whirled toward the sound, my left fingers crept millimeter by millimeter toward the automatic Velcroed within the carrier.

The shrill ringing in my ears grew louder. I slipped my

hand inside the carrier and released the Velcro a few fibers at a time, just below the threshold of hearing. The sidearm tumbled loose inside the compartment. I located the pistol, wrapped my hand around the grip, and flicked off the safety. The forest began to swirl.

Harbinger focused on the approaching sound. A big furry animal bounded toward us through the trees and burst into the clearing — Cosette dragging her leash behind her! Harbinger held up his hand. At his command, the retriever braked and nearly upended. The dog growled and her fur bristled.

Harbinger turned to face the retriever. "Even your dog obeys the Presence, Sherman."

Abruptly, Cosette's fur flattened. She trembled and crouched. I eased the 9 mm from the carrier.

The muzzle's glimmer caught Cosette's attention. She canted her head. Harbinger spun around. Cosette surged, knocking him a step backwards.

I flicked the pistol up and focused with my brown eye. Harbinger's image blurred, then sharpened. I squeezed off five shots. Lead walloped through soft tissue. When the gun smoke cleared, Harbinger was gone. Tail wagging, delirious to hunt, the retriever bounded toward me.

"Atta girl, Cosette!"

A helicopter droned in the distance. I lifted my leg, reached across and flicked the elk knife from the leg scabbard, and began to saw the arrow's shaft until it cracked. I slid my shoulder from the shaft, and a clot welled up. I snatched the .357 from the ground, holstered the still-warm 9 mm, then staggered toward the spot where Harbinger had been standing.

Frothy blood on the ground confirmed a lung hit.

Cosette followed the scent trail through Walden Woods. Lightheaded but inspired, I jogged ahead, my right arm dangling.

The deciduous trees gave way to the pine grove at the edge of the lake where blood had dribbled thicker and darker. I forged onward to discover blood-soaked camouflage on the ground and farther ahead, pants, boots, and socks.

At the edge of the lake, gulls swirled. Offshore on the black ice, Harbinger was staggering in circles, sloshing through puddles. Clad in only his undershorts, he kept coughing up clots. A quarter-sized hole bubbled beneath his right collar bone, and a fist-sized exit wound cored-out his back. My retriever bolted after him.

"No, Cosette. Heel!"

I stamped the thin ice. The surface buckled, and rainbow cracks plumed beneath me. Harbinger kept wheezing and gurgling fifty yards away. His eyes narrowed.

From a standing position, I fired six shots with my left hand. A bullet exploded Harbinger's knee cap, which flapped by its tendon. He buckled.

Mergansers took flight from the unfrozen center of the lake.

Harbinger hobbled farther, nearly reaching the spring hole. I ventured another ten yards until a pressure crack boomed. I dove onto my abdomen, ribs throbbing and shoulder searing.

But Harbinger was in worse shape, gasping, his complexion grayer than the clouds.

I emptied my brass, struggled to load six more rounds one-handed, and snapped the action closed. I aimed from a prone position and slapped the trigger. The bullet skittered across the ice and sent Harbinger reeling. He struggled back onto his feet and tried to limp away. By then he was ashen, ghostlike in the swirling mist. Crimson swatches congealed in the puddles.

Harbinger wavered, steadied himself, and then stood still as a statue. He raised an arm and pointed right at me. His icy stare transfixed me.

Suddenly, the ice rumbled, sagged, and Harbinger crashed through. He clawed onto the unbroken precipice. Blood bubbled from his nostrils and oozed from the corners of his mouth. All at once, he heaved an agonal breath. His eyes rolled back, and he slid underwater. Hands grasped at the air, then disappeared like the masts of a sinking ship. Slush rippled, then calmed.

A helicopter rumbled through the cloud cover and the waning light. By the time the dog and I made it ashore, the helicopter had trailed off. Then silence, save for cardinals flitting overhead.

I folded a handkerchief over my shoulder, leaned back against an ancient white pine, and began to shiver.

A pair of red-tailed hawks spiraled over the new defect in the ice. The gulls reassembled, attracting legions of white compatriots, swirling like confetti.

Sirens began to whine on the shore road. Ambulances, cruisers, and fire engines screeched to a halt.

I reclined on a bed of pine needles and stared into a cloud billowing overhead. The ringing in my ears trailed off, and the yellow eyes began to fade. Blood loss made me thirsty. Cosette kept pacing and whining.

"Thanks, girl, I never knew you were so intimidating."

ATVs approached. I gazed back at the lake, its surface calm and gulls gliding overhead in the pre-darkness.

My brother's high-pitched voice began to whisper through the forest, *You heard us, Brant.*

It began to rain, softly at first, then harder. I rested the warm pistol against my chest, closed my eyes, and drifted off.

# 22

As soon as I was discharged from the hospital, I decided to visit my dad. I should mention that Abigail Reed drove. My shoulder ached like hell, and I was in no shape to shift my decrepit Jeep. Abby had little to say as we headed toward the hospice. At least she hadn't eloped with the FBI profiler.

A wet snow spilled from the heavens. Big moist flakes stuck to the branches and ran down the windowpanes. All television sets in the hospice were tuned to the national news. We paused in the waiting room to watch.

Christian Evans displayed Cooper before a dazzling array of microphones. The governor shook Rocky Fallon's hand. A photo of pimply-faced Emmet Harbinger sporting a wide brown tie and a bushy seventies hairstyle followed. Lieutenant Weatherbee accepting his Bulldog Award flashed up on the screen. And finally, my photo.

Abigail nudged me. "Lucky thing it's a black and white."

"Enough about the eyes, Abby."

The next newsflash pictured Cosette, and I chuckled. "Now *that's* a hero. Or I should say, 'heroine.' "

Eugene Sherman was sleeping when we arrived. Outside, the heliport's red light pulsed on and off, a weakening systole obscured by sheets of horizontal snow.

"Dad," I whispered, "it's me."

Eugene Sherman managed a smile. The whites of his eyes were now a deeper shade of yellow, and his cheeks sunken.

"So was Harbinger human?"

"He sure died like one."

"How do you feel?"

"Pretty good. You were right about vengeance, Dad."

"And you, Abby?"

"Don't worry about me, Mr. Sherman. Things should settle down now."

"Will you stay in Concord?"

"For awhile."

Eugene Sherman began to fade. His breathing slowed. I knelt and rested my head on his failing chest. The old man's heart was thumping a labored rhythm, a long dash up Heartbreak Hill. Abigail wiped her eyes and retreated to the far corner of the room.

"It's okay to go if you need to, Dad," I whispered.

The old man nodded. "It's just about time."

"I'm going to miss you."

"And I'll miss you. Just promise me something?"

"Name it."

"Let someone take care of you, son. It's not such a cold world out there." His eyes flickered toward Abigail's corner of the room.

"I hear you, Dad."

The ticking clock slowed. Wind rattled the windows. Twenty minutes later, Eugene Sherman began to drift off. Saliva ticked off the roof of his mouth.

"It's snowing outside," I whispered. "The flakes are big, the way you like 'em."

The blizzard swirled against the window. I felt Dad's hand tighten. His voice was a hoarse whisper.

"The geese are hovering over the field now, Brant, and it's not just a dream. You and Timmy are with me, all white, invisible in the snow. The coffin blind shelters me from the storm. The birds are above me now, calling, and I am rising with them. They are sweeping me up. I can feel it. I'm lifting into the wind.

"The sky is white with geese. The heavens echo with their voices. We are now beyond the dark water, Brant. The answer is not beneath the ice, or in the ice, or on the ice. It is over our heads, in the clouds, soft clouds white with geese."

The old man drew in a deep breath and closed his eyes. Tension ebbed from his face.

"There is only light here, Brant. Always choose the light..."

Warden Eugene Sherman relinquished his grip on my hand, and exhaled for the last time.

Later, Abby and I stood in the long hospice corridor. I turned back toward my father's room. The hall became a wintry tidal channel in the Newburyport estuary. In my mind, I was sitting piggyback on his strong shoulders high above the spartina grass and phragmites rustling in the northwest wind. Dad's room became a grassed duck blind at Northeast Point, decoys bobbing in the whitecaps beyond.

It was hard to imagine a world without Eugene Sherman in it. As I glanced back at his white shrouded body, I thought about the coffin blind, a betrayer of birds, and the final resting place for a man.

Major Rocky Fallon consoled me in the lobby. "We never told you how much your father guided us through this investigation. He lived to see you make things right."

Fallon winked at Abigail Reed. "You've got a knack for criminal psychology, Doctor."

"I'm glad that I could help."

Fallon turned toward me. "I've spoken with the governor and the attorney general on your behalf."

"The attorney general?"

"Yes. It's time to start moving up the ranks, Brant. Your days with the Federal Marshal Service are numbered. Move ahead and give the rookies a chance."

"Thanks, Major. I'll give it some thought."

Back at headquarters along the bank of the Sudbury River, snow hissed into the water. Birches and alders swayed in the gale. Abigail and I sat cross-legged on a shaggy rug, sipping tea in front of a hardwood fire. Cosette leaned into us, chewing a rawhide toy she'd macerated beyond recognition. The scene was as intimate as I had imagined. Yet I didn't dare touch Abby.

"I can't believe Dad's gone."

"I've never witnessed such a lovely death," Abigail whispered, "...if there is such a thing."

"Dad was a poet. He wanted me to load his ashes into my shot shells so that I can fire them across the marsh next hunting season."

There was a knock at the door. It was Eldridge Weatherbee carrying an over-stuffed plastic garbage bag.

"Merry Christmas, old boy! How are you holding up?"

"Not bad, Eldridge, considering."

"I'm sure there are mixed emotions for you right now. At least my department didn't steal your thunder. With you in the picture, the mortality rate for criminals has been rather high this year."

"Speaking of mortality, did the team ever find Harbinger?"

"Not yet. We're wary of ranging the divers that far beneath the ice. Nashawtuc Lake's over eighty feet deep."

I stared back.

"Don't worry, my friend. He'll rise soon enough. Believe me, you don't want to lay eyes on a floater, especially one that bled out the way he did."

Abby motioned to an armchair. "How about some tea, Eldridge?"

"I'd love to stay, guys, but I've only got a few minutes. I've got an interview with the newspaper, and since this is my swan song, I have to make sure those clowns get my story right," Weatherbee said. "You know, every time I take on a case, all I can think about is ending it. When it's finally over, I'm happy, but at the same time, there's a void inside of me. Anyway, I brought you each a token of my appreciation."

He opened the bag and reached inside. "Santa's early this year. Brant, this is for you." Weatherbee produced a case of Skybars. "You've earned both halves now, buddy. I only bestow Skybars on the bravest."

The lieutenant produced a rawhide chewy bigger than a human femur for Cosette.

"And here's a little something for our medical consultant, Dr. Abigail Reed," he said, removing a small package.

"You shouldn't have," she said, unwrapping the present. It was a gift pack of tea.

"I was afraid that after all those sleepless nights, you'd leave Concord. I won't let that happen. Try this St. John's Wort blend. My wife tells me that it calms her down. Believe me, anything that can mellow out my old lady has to be potent."

"You're a thoughtful shopper, Eldridge. I'm impressed."

The lieutenant tapped me on the shoulder. "So what are *your* plans?"

"My injuries entitle me to retire with three-fourths salary plus full benefits," I said. "Not bad for my age."

"You're a U.S. marshal. You can't just walk away from it, can you?"

"We've put the terrorism behind us, haven't we?"

"I wouldn't be so sure," Eldridge said. "Copy-cat animal

rights crimes are spreading like wildfire. The human mind is a dangerous thing when it's twisted," Weatherbee continued. "And there will never be a shortage of warped minds. You now have the dubious honor of being *the* authority on animal rights terrorism, Brant. You've got a national reputation to uphold."

"I need a break," I said.

"Then consider a different angle."

"Like what?"

"Tracking cold cases. You may find it rewarding."

"I could never replace the Bulldog."

"Somebody has to, Brant. If you use that antenna inside your head to hear voices, you'll elevate forensics to a new level. Besides, cold case investigation is a safer lifestyle for an aspiring family man. I'm proud to say that I've never been shot. Even though I whined every so often, I've loved my life as an investigator. I've grown with every case I've handled."

"You're right," I said. "I've learned from this case. They say that life isn't a dress rehearsal, but after listening to my father and the sad reflections of Dr. Fenwick, I'm not so sure about that. What if life *is* a test?

"My mother disapproved of us hunting crows because she believed that crows were the spirits of Indians. We used to laugh her off, but what if she was right? What if everything I've hunted had a voice, and I chose to ignore it?" I motioned out the window. A wedge of mallards fought the snowfall, banking into the river. "Then again, there's the irrepressible call of the wild."

Abby nodded. "You are a predator, Brant. You can't help yourself."

"Once my shoulder heals, I may sneak down

to the old duck blind," I said. Cosette's ears perked, and her tail began to wag.

"What about the nightmares?" Weatherbee asked.

"They're gone. I've been sleeping through the night." I gazed at the river. "I've had a taste of what it's like to be the quarry. When I hunt from now on, I'll be bagging memories, not my limit."

"You can have your outdoors," Weatherbee quipped. "I'll be putting in the clubhouse with a stack of pastrami sandwiches at my side."

"At the Hungry Duffer, right?"

"You bet. No more thrashing through swamps for this guy."

Abby smiled. "On a lighter note, no pun intended, how's your low-fat diet going, Eldridge?"

"No offense, but there's more to life than explosive diarrhea. I'd be better off having the big one."

"Give it a chance. This world needs you."

"So what have you decided, Abby?" Weatherbee asked. "Are you staying or not?"

"That depends," she said, casting me a sidelong glance. She retreated to the whistling teapot.

I shrugged.

The lieutenant changed the subject. "Have you heard from your pal, Dr. Fenwick?"

"As a matter-of-fact, I have," I said, pointing to an e-mail on my computer screen.

*"You did it! Candace and I thank you. Does your workout offer still stand? Regards, Charles Fenwick."*

"You gave the guy one heck of a boost," Eldridge said.

"By the way, Brant, I got an update on Paige Sagoff. She's in stable condition at Shriner's. She can't have visitors for a few weeks."

For a few minutes, we absorbed the magnitude of our tragedy and triumph.

Just then, a brown UPS delivery truck rumbled down the driveway and skidded to a halt in front of the cabin. The driver emerged with a large box, trudged through the deepening snow, and knocked on my door. "Deputy Marshal Brant Sherman?"

"That's me."

"I just saw you on the news. This delivery is for you."

"In an unmarked box?"

Abigail and Eldridge laughed. "Relax, Brant," said the lieutenant. "We've fluoroscoped it already. No explosives or anthrax."

The driver stamped snow from his treads.

"Where would you like it?"

"In the living room, please."

"You don't need to sign anything," the UPS man said, placing the carton on the rug. "Enjoy."

"Go ahead, check it out," Weatherbee said.

I tore the flaps open. Inside was an animal cage. The lieutenant grabbed the handle, lifted, and set the cage on the coffee table. A burly tomcat stared from the corner.

"It's Big Papi!"

"He's the size of a lynx," Abby said.

I read a note attached to the cage:

*Congratulations and condolences, Brant. I thought you could use the company.*
*Merry Christmas! — Diana Loomis.*

I smiled. "Let it be known, sports fans, I'm the guy who kept Big Papi out of free agency."

"Diana will put Evans's bounty money to good use," Weatherbee said. "Harbinger's letter turned out to be worth a lot more than his donation."

Abby said, "Instead of jail time for importing endangered species, Christian Evans chose five-hundred hours of community service at the Buddy Dog Animal Shelter. Evans gets his son back and avoids jail because of Diana, the anti-hunter. Meanwhile, his cash reward will save her animals. Ironic, don't you think?"

Eldridge nodded. "No matter where we stand, sooner or later, we depend on each other."

"Well I'm sick of all of this irony," I said. I reached into the crate and lifted the big tomcat who nestled in my arms. Cosette wagged her tail. "This beast likes me. I don't expect that he'll mind Cosette after living in the kennel." The cat began to purr and I set him down.

"I've had enough of cats for ten lifetimes," Weatherbee said, "but this seems like the start of a healthy relationship." He winked and reached for his coat. "I must say, things happen here along the Sudbury River if you let them. I don't expect that you two will mind getting snowed in, but I've got to hit the road."

The lieutenant shook my uninjured left hand. "It's been a pleasure."

"You've ended your career with a bang, Eldridge."

"Thanks to you, buddy."

The lieutenant's eyes watered as he lumbered toward the door. "You kids take care now," he said. "And stay away from purple M & M's."

We watched the Bulldog trudge to his cruiser. Weatherbee cleared his windshield, fired up the engine, and wound down the snowy road. I closed the door. "There he goes, Lieutenant Eldridge Weatherbee, the Bulldog, riding into the sunset."

Abby sat on the couch and reached for a blanket. "*I'm* a cold case right now. It's freezing in here." To my surprise, she kept motioning me closer. I obliged.

Abby leaned against me. "That's better," she said. "At least I know there's a little warmth left on this planet."

I stared into the fire and then at Abigail Reed. She snuggled nearer and drew the blanket over us. The fire crackled with reassuring warmth. Big Papi balanced atop the couch and began to purr.

"My apartment in Cambridge doesn't allow cats," I said.

"Concord landlords are more lenient. It's a fact."

"What are you saying, Abby? Should I stay or not? I wouldn't blame you if you've had enough."

"So that's what you're wondering?"

"I need to know where we stand. The connection you made with my father meant a lot to me."

Firelight sparkled in her eyes. She leaned closer and wound her arms around my neck. Her hair smelled fresh and her body felt lithe. We kissed tentatively at first, then harder. Suddenly, she pulled away.

"C'mon Abby, are you with me or not? I need to know."

She smirked and drew me closer. "You're so male, Brant,

it's pathetic. But I can't fake it. The second I saw you on that stretcher, I knew I'd wind up with you."

Serenaded by the purring cat, whispering flames, and Cosette's thumping tail, we held one another in the shadows of the snowy afternoon. For the first time, I kissed her with my eyes closed.

An hour later, my shoulder began to throb and I downed two Percocets. Abby had fallen asleep, cocooned in an afghan that my grandmother had knitted.

Big Papi's novelty had worn off. Exhausted by trailing the feline through the cabin, Cosette had curled-up in front of the fireplace. The intimacy of this new little family pleased me.

As the sun set, flames flickered. The sweet scent of hardwood filled the air. Embers whistled softly, lulling me to sleep.

*Carrying no gun, I was back on Nashawtuc Lake in the middle of the night. A thin layer of ice had just sealed the center of the pond in a hush of falling snow and silence of inert water.*

*Skim ice began to quiver, and water began to tremble, oozing up through the little cracks and holes, seeping onto the snow. Crystals at the perimeter tinkled, quickening with subtle energy.*

*All at once, a pair of arms punched through the ice. I recoiled. Water churned. Blue fingers crept onto the edge, groping, flexing, nails digging in. Forearm sinews strained and knuckles blanched. The arms trembled.*

*A head and shoulders burst through the surface. The ashen, naked figure of a man braced against the edge and vaulted onto the ice. Coughing and gagging, spewing water, the man lay on his side. Peering back-and-forth, he climbed to his feet and shook himself. Vapor rushed from his mouth. The stranger glanced at me, and did a double-take. I shuddered in the penumbra of his cruel stare.*

*A hideously-pale but grinning Emmet Harbinger lifted his head and raised his arms toward the heavens. An aura glowed about him. Dark birds began to descend from the gloom, trickling down one or two at a time, then in numbers. Revolving stiffly as if on an axis, Harbinger cleared his lungs with an inhuman bellow.*

*And bold laughter echoed through the night.*

# Acknowledgments

The author would like to thank the following individuals:

U.S. Deputy Marshal Mark Lewis for his expertise and guidance in the law enforcement details of this story.

Bob Oberlander and the memory of his father Henry, in appreciation for sharing their passion and knowledge of the New England coastline and the sea ducks that visit it each winter.

Boston University educator Larry DeLamarter for his humorous and unique insight into local human behavior.

William G. Tapply, famed author and outdoorsman, who through the years has been a generous and caring writing mentor.

Kelly Skillen for her confidence in my writing and assistance in editing the manuscript.

Annette Chaudet for sharing the vision and message of *The Coffin Blind*.

## About the Author

Mark Robbins is a MRI radiologist, a former emergency physician and general surgery resident who has always longed to be a writer. His medical short stories and his sporting tales have appeared in national publications including *Gray's Sporting Journal*.

Mark lives in Massachusetts, a stone's throw from Walden Pond. He enjoys fishing, bird hunting, running, weight training, baseball, and rock and roll guitar with his children, Tom and Hillary and crazy but enthusiastic English setters, Molly and Scout.

Printed in the United States
104300LV00002B/4-21/P